THE PERFECT BLEND

LOST CREEK, TEXAS HILL COUNTRY
BOOK ONE

ALEXA ASTON

OLIVERHEBERBOOKS

Cover art by Dar Albert at Wicked Smart Designs

Published by Oliver-Heber Books

0 9 8 7 6 5 4 3 2 1

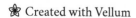 Created with Vellum

PROLOGUE

AUSTIN—FEBRUARY

Harper Hart finished touching up her makeup, digging in the drawer for a tube of lipstick to complete her look. She found one she had borrowed from Cynthia Fox, her sorority sister at the University of Texas, who had become her best friend and roommate for the past six years since their college graduation. Cynthia, known as the Realtor to the Rich, had moved out last week, telling Harper it was time she invested some of her hard-earned income and buy a place of her own. Harper could not wait to see what her best friend had purchased and how it would be decorated. Cynthia also had a side business, staging homes which were for sale, and her taste was impeccable. She planned to organize a housewarming for Cynthia, but that would have to wait until Harper and Ath returned from their honeymoon to Bali.

Just the thought of her handsome fiancé brought a

smile to her lips. It still surprised her that she had landed a man such as Atherton Armistead, son of the Lieutenant Governor of Texas. She had met Ath at an event she had planned for the UT School of Law, which he had attended. Ath was an attorney at Armistead & Watson, his father's firm, where he was a partner and trial lawyer, and she had yet to speak to him today, knowing he was trying to put the finishing touches on a case that would come to trial soon after they returned from their honeymoon.

Picking up her cell, Harper texted a quick message to him.

> Love you. Can't wait to see you at the rehearsal dinner.

She hit send and placed the phone down, combing her long, auburn locks. She hoped Ath would be able to let go of work so he could enjoy their wedding and honeymoon. He had seemed distant for the last week or so, and she knew he had been consumed by work. She had tried to back off and give him the space he needed. As a partner in the firm, he had many responsibilities, especially since his father had moved into politics full-time.

Harper went to her bedroom and slipped into a pair of Christian Louboutins. She earned a decent salary as an event planner in Austin, but the Louboutins had been a splurge. She wore them frequently, though, knowing those clients she worked with seemed to trust her more because of small details such as that. It was the same with her wardrobe. She bought expensive, classic pieces which were timeless and would last throughout her lifetime, but her closet was sparse when compared to Cynthia's.

Ivy should be here soon. Her sister was driving them to the rehearsal dinner, which was being held at an exclusive Austin steakhouse. Frowning, Harper hoped everything would go well this evening. Her parents were still unhappy with the arrangements regarding the wedding, and if she had to be honest, so was she. Instead of her parents hosting the wedding in Lost Creek, where she had grown up and where her family's winery was located, the wedding was being held in Austin, planned entire by Bethany Armistead, Ath's mother. Bethany had convinced Harper to hold the wedding in Austin since so many of their portion of the guest list was in the government there. Because the guest list was so large and lopsided, Ath's parents had insisted they must pay for the wedding, allowing Bill and Cecily Hart to handle the expenses for the rehearsal dinner instead.

Bethany had also taken over organizing every last detail of the wedding, explaining to Harper that she shouldn't have to do that for her own wedding, just like it would be wrong to host a shower for herself. She would like to say she had been busy and willingly turned things over to Bethany, but the truth of the matter was, the woman simply bulldozed her way into getting whatever she wanted. It had been simpler to step back and let Bethany take control instead of arguing with her. Harper had an idea that Bethany was the true power behind the political rise of Army Armistead. Her gut told her that

Bethany intended to see them in the governor's mansion at the end of the next election.

Harper wasn't sure how she felt about marrying into a political family. Though Ath had no political ambition, she knew, as an extension of Army and Bethany, they would be thrust into the spotlight if and when Army ran for governor. Since her political leanings were the exact opposite of her in-laws' opinions, Harper wasn't certain how much she would want to get involved in the campaign, even if she and Ath were only window dressing at a few events. That would be a bridge to cross in the future. For now, she would merely enjoy marriage to her attorney husband and put off worrying as long as she could.

A knock sounded at the door, and she grabbed her purse from the kitchen counter. She opened the door. Seeing her sister made Harper suddenly tear up. She hugged Ivy tightly. They had been so close growing up, but both had busy jobs in different cities, and they didn't see one another as much as Harper would have liked.

"Are you ready to get this show on the road?" Ivy asked. "I still think it's bizarre not having a rehearsal before the rehearsal dinner."

She locked the door to the apartment and fell into step with Ivy.

"I thought so, too, but Bethany said that all of us had been in enough weddings, and that we should know what to do. She's right, I suppose."

Ivy sniffed. "Bethany Armistead thinks she's always right. About everything. Honestly, Harper, I don't know how you're going to do it. Being around her. I only saw her in action at your engagement party, and that was enough for me. I can't imagine her being in your life, much less as grandmother to your children."

"It will be fine," she assured her sister as they reached Ivy's car and got in, ignoring the little voice warning her that her future mother-in-law would be the kind to use her grandchildren as props during an election.

She had been surprised when Bethany canceled the rehearsal at the church two days ago. Yes, all of them had been in weddings before—but this was *her* wedding rehearsal. Harper would have liked to have walked through the ceremony, watching the wedding party practice going down the aisle, and standing with Ath at the altar, where they would exchange their vows. Bethany had said not only had everyone been in a wedding and knew what to do but that the lieutenant governor had a full slate and wouldn't have been able to attend. Bethany also had mentioned how Ath, too, was swamped at work and could use the extra couple of hours to finish up things at the law firm and be prepared to bring his case to trial the day after they returned from Bali.

"Tell me how the gallery is going," Harper urged. "And your painting. I haven't heard you talk about painting for quite a while."

She watched Ivy's nose crinkle.

"What I have learned is that the assistant gallery manager is actually the gallery manager, at a discounted salary," Ivy declared. "My boss shows up sporadically and never seems to know what pieces we have on hand. I'm his personal Spark Notes when he does show up, giving him all the highlights of what is on display and what openings are coming up—which I've completely planned —along with what is selling."

"What about your personal painting?" she pressed.

Ivy glanced over as they pulled up to a stoplight. "What painting? I haven't had time for my own work in months."

"No wonder you seem a little frayed around the edges," Harper said. "I know your art is your outlet. You have always used painting not only to express your creativity, but as a kind of therapy."

"I'm thinking of quitting the gallery," Ivy shared.

"What would you do?" she asked, surprised by the announcement.

The light turned green, and her sister shrugged. "I'm not sure. Maybe go back to Lost Creek."

"What would you do there?"

"Maybe work for Mom and Dad. I just don't know, Harper. Don't push me now, all right?" Annoyance sounded in Ivy's tone.

"I'll back off for now. Once I return from our honeymoon, though, we're going to have a long conversation about all of this, okay?"

She glanced to her sister, who nodded, focusing on the road ahead.

They reached the steakhouse, and Ivy handed her keys to the valet. As they entered the restaurant, Ivy said, "Swanky place."

"Bethany wanted to have it at their country club, but I put my foot down about that. Tonight will already be expensive enough for Mom and Dad, but the country club would've been out of sight."

"I still don't see why you have to be married in Austin," Ivy complained. "Oh, I know it's all because of the politics and appearance, but it's *your* wedding, Harper. You should be getting married where you want."

She took Ivy's hand and squeezed it. "It doesn't really matter where we get married. Just that we are. Oh, I can't wait to begin my life with Ath."

"I'm surprised you didn't live together first," Ivy said. "I thought everyone did that these days."

"We practically did. I spent more nights at his place than mine and Cynthia's apartment. We've already established our joint bank account. We'll move the rest of my things to his apartment after we get back. I've got another month on my lease. Then we'll take our time and go house-hunting."

"What are you looking for? Seems like you should've found something before the wedding."

Harper sighed. "He wants a forever house, but I want a right-now one. One we could be comfortable in, and then we could move to something larger down the line. Ath thinks we should just go big now and find something we could grow into."

Ivy shrugged. "I guess that makes sense. But could you afford something big? I know Austin has gotten pretty expensive in the past few years."

"Exactly," she agreed. "That's why I want to wait. Get something now. Build equity. Then as our family grows and hopefully our salaries, as well, find a more permanent home." She frowned. "Bethany has assured me that financing won't be a problem. That she and Army can loan us the money."

"But you don't want to do that, do you?" Ivy asked.

"Nope. I want this to be all us. She's already had enough say in this wedding. I want my marriage to be mine and Ath's, with no more boundary crossing from his mom."

They stepped up to the hostess stand, and the woman on duty recognized Harper.

"Miss Hart," she said, smiling.

But the smile didn't quite reach her eyes. She seemed troubled. It gave Harper an uneasy feeling.

"Here for the rehearsal dinner," Ivy said happily.

"Yes, I know," the hostess said. "Are you the maid of honor?"

Ivy beamed. "I'm Ivy. Harper's sister."

"If you don't mind, Ivy, I'd like to borrow you for a few minutes."

Harper decided Ath had been up to some surprise, and the hostess would fill Ivy in on it, recruiting her for whatever her designated role would be.

"I know where the room is," she said to the hostess. "I'll make my way there now."

It was only five-thirty, and the rehearsal dinner was schedule to begin at six o'clock. She had wanted to be here early, just to see the room decorated and take everything in before all their guests arrived. When she opened the door, however, Harper froze.

Nothing had been done to the room.

She glanced about, taking in the bare tables. No table-cloths. No plates, glassware, or silverware. She did spy several floral arrangements sitting on the floor next to the door, recognizing them as the ones she and her mom had picked out for tonight.

Her stomach lurched, and Harper knew something was terribly wrong.

Then she spied Trey Watson rising from a chair in the corner, coming to meet her. Trey was Ath's best friend from their days at an exclusive Montessori preschool. They had gone to school together. Played on sports teams with one another. Roomed together at UT as fraternity brothers. Trey had opened his own successful architectural firm two years ago, and she and Ath had talked about him being the one to design their home.

The look on Trey's face was enough to let Harper know the best friend—and best man—had been tapped to deliver the worst news she would ever hear.

With sympathy written in his deep brown eyes, Trey said, "I'm so sorry, Harper."

Numbness filled her, but it was quickly replaced with anger.

"Are you sorry you are the one stuck telling me that things are off? Or are you sorry that Ath was such a coward and wouldn't do it himself?"

"The latter." He touched her shoulder, and Harper flinched, pulling away.

"How long?" she demanded. "How long have you known? He tells you everything."

Guilt caused Trey's cheeks to flush. "A while. Actually,

longer in my gut. I knew something was off with Ath, but I couldn't put my finger on it. And then he told me two weeks ago."

"*Two weeks* ago?" she said through gritted teeth. "You let me go on for two weeks, blithely thinking I would be getting married tomorrow?" Disgust filled her. "You are no better than he is, Trey."

Her mind whirling, she said, "Well, I guess I have a lot to do. People to call. My family. My friends. I need to tell them not to show up at the church tomorrow night. Tell Bethany she can call her side of the guest list. Of course, it'll take her the rest of the night and into tomorrow since she invited half the government of Texas and half the people who live in Austin." She shook her head. "Maybe the local news anchors can make it their lead story at six and ten tonight. That might save some time."

She turned to go, but Trey caught her elbow, turning her. "I need to tell you something, Harper. I don't think Ath treated you right. At all. In fact, I've ended our friendship because of this whole mess."

"You have?" Respect for this man grew within her. Standing up to Ath—and his parents—wouldn't have been easy, especially because Trey's dad was the Watson of Atherton & Watson. "But you've been friends forever."

"I can't be friends with Ath anymore, Harper. Not after this. I've already chosen. I'm on Team Harper all the way."

She mustered a smile. "Then I guess we'll have T-shirts made up. Be sure to text me your size and color preference."

He took her hand and squeezed it. Suddenly, Harper

knew it was going to be much worse than what she had already learned.

"There's someone else, isn't there?" she asked dully. "Ath isn't just backing out because he doesn't want to marry me. He's found someone else, hasn't he?"

New anger boiled within her as Trey nodded. "I'm afraid so." He swallowed. "This is so hard, Harper."

She jerked her hand from his. "Let's not make this all about you, Trey. Yes, you've been designated the messenger—and I'd like nothing more than to kill you myself. Just spit it out and be done with it."

"It's... Cynthia."

It was as if he had slammed his fist into her in the gut. Harper physically recoiled, wrapping her arms protectively around herself.

Not Cynthia.

Not her best friend.

And yet she couldn't help but look back and see flashes in her mind. Ath and Cynthia laughing together, seeming so cozy. She had merely thought she was blessed that her fiancé and best friend got along so well with one another. But it had been more than that. They had been sneaking around behind her back. The thought sickened her. Bile rose in her throat, and she swallowed it, shivering.

Her gaze met and held Trey's. "How long?"

He shrugged. "I'm not sure. I honestly don't know, Harper. I wouldn't have known if I hadn't caught them together. That's when I found out about them. Ath confessed everything. He swore me to secrecy. Cynthia blubbered all over the place. They swore they were going to tell you. I assumed they did, but I cut off contact with him after that. I planned to call you, but I wanted to give you some time to lick your wounds first."

Trey shook his head. "Ath showed up today at my office. He was panicking. Said he still hadn't manned up. That Bethany had called off the rehearsal at the church tonight." Sympathy filled his eyes. "If I would've known what was going on, I never would have left you hanging, Harper. I just thought Ath had already told you."

She made a sound, something that came from her throat. She refused to cry. Not now. Not when she had to walk through the restaurant.

"He begged me to meet you here and break the news to you. I agreed because I was afraid if I didn't, you would show up tonight—and still not know. Ath did say your parents are off the hook. Army wrote a check for tonight's dinner."

"Of course, he did," Harper said, resentment pouring through her. "That's the Armistead way, isn't it? Pay people off."

Trey swallowed painfully. "There's more, Harper." He raked a hand through his hair in frustration. "The wedding is still on for tomorrow night. All that's been changed is the bride and her family."

Harper froze, like a rabbit sighted by a wolf. She couldn't move. Couldn't breathe. Couldn't think. Panic rushed through her.

Ath was still getting married tomorrow.

And she wasn't the bride.

"I let Ath know exactly what I thought of him, Harper.

Even though he begged for my forgiveness, I won't be at his wedding. I refused to stand beside him while he betrays you."

Trey pulled out an envelope from inside his jacket pocket and thrust it at her. She looked at it suspiciously.

"What's this?" she asked, surprised she could even find her voice.

He took her hand and wrapped it around the envelope. "It's the tickets to Bali. Somehow, Ath pulled strings. You know how he can do that. Or rather Mommy and Daddy can. The name on one ticket is blank. He told me to encourage you to take whoever you wanted. Maybe Ivy?" he suggested.

"So, he wants me to get out of town while he celebrates marrying my best friend," she said bitterly. "Who *does* that?"

Harper stuffed the envelope in her purse. "Maybe I will do just that. Travel half a world away and either kick up my heels or drown my sorrows."

"He's not worth it, Harper. He's not worth you. He never was," Trey said sadly.

She gave him a weak smile. "I'm sorry I took out my anger on you, Trey. You didn't deserve it. It took guts to come here and tell me all this. If you really have broken off your friendship with Ath, then good for you. You can do better, too."

He enveloped her in his arms, kissing the top of her head, then pulling away. "Can I drive you home?"

"No. Ivy drove me here."

His arms fell away. "I'm sorry, Harper. I really am. For

my part in this. I should've have come to you sooner. I get that now. I just thought Ath would handle things and not leave you hanging. Instead, he is a world-class jerk."

She shook her head sadly. "Don't beat yourself up over it, Trey. As you said, Ath is not worth it." She stared up at him. "Thanks for being a gentleman."

Turning, she left the room, feeling like a zombie as she walked through the steakhouse. She spotted Ivy, who quickly ended her call and came toward her.

"I've got you," her sister said, wrapping an arm about Harper's shoulders and leading her from the restaurant.

They walked in silence to the valet stand. Neither said a word until after Ivy handed over her ticket and the valet left.

"Was that Mom on the phone?" she asked quietly.

"Yes. She's going to call our side and explain that the wedding is off. Finley is going to help with the calls. I haven't been able to reach Cynthia yet, but Mom said she and Finley can divide up the guest list and handle things."

Harper burst out laughing, hearing the hysteria in her voice, tears finally running down her cheeks. She knew Ivy must be wondering if she had gone temporarily insane, but her sister merely sat quietly, her hand rubbing Harper's back.

Finally, she composed herself. "You can't reach Cynthia—because she's the bride."

Ivy frowned. "What? I don't get it. Harper, you're not making any sense."

Suddenly, she felt deflated. The laughter died. "Let me spell it out for you. Ath has been cheating on me. With

Cynthia. And the wedding is still on. Same time. Same place. Different bride."

Ivy gasped. And then she cursed. A very un-Ivy-like thing to do.

"It's okay," she assured her sister. "I'm going to be okay. Better to know Ath is a cheating asshole now than to marry him and divorce down the line, right?" she asked, her body quivering.

Fury lit Ivy's eyes. "This is wrong on so many different levels, Harper. Like nuclear, seismically wrong. But you're right. If Ath cheated before the wedding, he was going to do so after it. And Cynthia. Of all people. You've been close for years now. Why would she *do* something like this?"

"Lust? Love? Or wanting to move up the social ladder?" she guessed. "It doesn't really matter. It's over. Done." Taking a deep breath, she slowly exhaled. "Ath did give me a parting gift. The honeymoon tickets. Would… would you like to go to Bali with me? Charge all the room service and spa treatments and drinks to his bill? I just can't be here tomorrow when they speak their vows."

Hot tears poured down Harper's face now. Ivy leaned over and hugged her tightly.

"I would be delighted to go to Bali with you."

"What about work?"

"What about it? I'm due time off. I'll take it. If they fire me, then my boss will actually have to do some work until they can find a replacement for me."

Ivy whipped out her cell and tapped a few buttons. "How long is the Bali trip?"

"We were going to be gone ten days."

"Yes, this is Ivy," her sister said crisply. "I will be taking off the next ten days, using my accrued vacation days. I have a family crisis."

Harper watched as Ivy frowned. "I know that reception is coming up. I planned the entire thing. No, I cannot be there for it. You heard me. I'm taking the time off. Oh, really? Then I quit."

Ivy ended the connection. Her phone rang almost immediately. She smiled, looking at the call coming in, letting it go to voice mail. A few more taps and she said, "Blocked the gallery. Blocked my boss. Let him figure it out on his own."

"What about a reference?" she asked, worried about Ivy's career imploding when her own was most likely going to do the same. "You've worked so hard. I hate to see all that go down the drain."

Her sister gazed at Harper a long moment. "You have always been there for me. It's time I was here for you. Besides, I told you I was thinking about quitting. This just spurred me on—and I get a free trip to Bali."

She couldn't help it. She started laughing—and Ivy joined in.

"You'll need your passport. We were going to fly to Houston early Sunday morning and take the direct connection from there to Bali," Harper said.

"I think you should see Mom and Dad now," suggested Ivy. "Then grab your suitcase, and we'll drive to Houston tonight. We can stop at Sonic for fries and slushes. It'll be like the old days."

Ivy's words brought back fond memories of family road trips.

And Todd.

"Okay," she agreed, wiping the tears from her cheeks.

As Ivy's car arrived, they looked at one another and, in unison, said, "Bali—here we come!"

1

AUSTIN

Braden Clark removed the sticky destination tag the baggage handler had attached to his suitcase's handle yesterday in California. He tossed it in the trash and sat on the unmade bed of the cheap motel where he'd spent the night.

If he didn't land this job at Lost Creek Vineyards today, he wasn't sure what he was going to do.

He had spent his last money on the plane ticket to Austin. Out of work for more than two years now, he was like a car whose gas tank was running on fumes. Bitterness swept through him, his anger still raw and real after all this time, directed at Peter Clark.

His father had been arrested three years ago on a litany of federal embezzlement charges, including fraud, money laundering, and racketeering. He had been escorted off their winery's land, and Braden had done all he could to save the label.

It had proved impossible.

Having never had anything to do with the books, he'd had no idea of the dire state the family business was in, especially because they had several bumper crops in a row, and their wines had sold like hotcakes. The FBI had cleared him, all members of his family, and the workers at the winery, but the Clark Vineyards label was tainted by all the news stories regarding the scandal. Longtime customers canceled contracts. Merchants and restaurants refused to carry Clark Vineyards wines. Since the government had confiscated almost everything regarding physical production in the winery—and then the land itself— he was left with no way to continue producing the wines his family had done for four generations. From the land to the vats, everything was gone in the blink of an eye.

Though he had hoped to get a bank loan in order to buy some more land, workers deserted left and right when he couldn't make payroll, leaving him with no one. His father was convicted and sentenced to twenty-two years in prison, along with hefty fines which totally wiped out the Clark family's funds. No bank wanted to take a chance on the Clark name, especially since no collateral existed.

His mother had quickly divorced her husband, even before his case came to trial and rapidly landed on her feet, marrying their neighbor, an aging film star who had been popular in his twenties and thirties. Miles Miller had invested his box office earnings in the vineyard next door to them and was the name and face of what had turned out to be a productive label. Margery Miller told her three sons they were on their own and turned her back on them.

His older brother Stan simply disappeared. One day, Braden woke up to find Stan gone. He hadn't heard from him since, even though he'd tried calling him several times. Each time, his call had gone to voicemail. After several attempts, he finally left a message, telling Stan to call if he ever wanted to talk. As for Beau, his younger brother, he had been the dreamer of the family, becoming a lost soul with all the legal problems and resulting scandal. Beau had committed suicide eighteen months later, leaving no note.

Braden still blamed himself for not realizing how bad things had gotten with Beau. Then again, his own life was falling apart at the time. Not only did he wind up losing Clark Vineyards and everything connected with it, Freya Gallagher had ended their engagement. His fiancée had said she couldn't be dragged down into the mire of his family's infamy and disgrace and wanted nothing further to do with him. Of course, she'd kept the two-carat diamond engagement ring, something Braden could have sold and used to keep himself afloat a bit longer.

He was on his own now. Didn't even have the two proverbial nickels to rub together. He'd spent the past two years trying to find a job in the industry. The winemaking world in the U.S. was a small one, though, highly competitive and prone to gossip. Though he was a talented enologist, no one wanted to hire someone whose reputation had been sullied with the horrific scandal which touched him. Braden applied to work at vineyards all across California and Oregon, to no avail.

Now, he'd turned to Texas as his last hope. He was headed today to Lost Creek, about two hours outside of Austin, in the Hill Country which was famous for its many wineries. The town of Lost Creek was located in the Guadalupe Valley, near the Guadalupe River. It was to the north of Boerne and Bandera, located on Lost Creek, which was more of a river than a creek, and a tributary of the Guadalupe. Lost Creek fed into Lost Creek Lake, a good-sized lake on the outskirts of the town.

Braden had studied maps of the area on the internet and the Lost Creek Vineyards website, while he'd holed up in the shabby motel which rented rooms by the day and week. He had sold his clunker of a truck in order to purchase the one-way plane ticket to Austin. Returning home to California was not an option—because he had no home. Everything he owned had been packed into the lone suitcase which had made the trip with him, along with his backpack.

If the viticulturist job didn't pan out at Lost Creek Vineyards, he would return his rental car to the airport and hitchhike to Fredericksburg, which was located about ninety minutes from Austin. That area was the epicenter of the Texas wine business. He had visited Fredericksburg about five years ago, attending a wine conference. He wouldn't apply for a professional position because every winery in and around Fredericksburg had shot him down. Instead, he would try to be hired on as a vineyard worker and hope the distance from California would be enough to help him find a job on the lowest rung of the vineyard ladder.

Lost Creek Vineyards was his last hope at trying to win a job he was qualified for in an industry he loved. They were beginning to expand, and he had seen the open position for a viticulturist on a professional job site and applied. It had surprised him when Bill Hart, the owner and founder of Lost Creek Vineyards, had contacted him, saying he wished to interview Braden in person. He couldn't help but wonder why Hart was doing so since the rest of the industry had seemingly blackballed him because of his family ties. Guilt by association was his only crime.

He put his suitcase and backpack into the rental's trunk and returned his key to the motel's office. Thankful the car had come with a full tank of gas, he set out for Lost Creek, Texas, already familiar with the route after Googling it. The drive was pleasant. He found the Texas Hill Country serene, a place that seemed to soothe his soul.

A little under two hours later, Braden arrived in the town of Lost Creek itself. Since he was early, he drove around town to become familiar with the place. This area of Texas was picturesque, a place he knew he could enjoy living. A place where he could put his experience to work.

A place that might offer him a second chance...

He passed a high school and a couple of churches. Drove around the town square and down its main street, seeing the typical shops located in a small town, along with a few restaurants and a bookstore. Several shops would cater to the tourists who flocked to the Hill Country, including boutiques, galleries, and antique stores.

Leaving town, he drove by a couple of chain motels for tourists who came to visit the area, as well as a few bed-and-breakfasts.

Ten minutes later, he spied the sign for Lost Creek Winery and turned in. The vineyards stretched as far as his eye could see. He had studied the website and gleaned as much as he could about the operation. Bill Hart had started the winery with a friend of his over twenty-five years ago. They produced both reds and whites and were also gaining a reputation with their blends.

Braden continued along the road, spying a long ranch house, and assumed it was where the Hart family lived. Further down, he came across where the tasting room and business office were located. Pulling into a parking spot in front of the building, he exited the car, his heart pounding in anticipation, his mouth dry. Where once he had been a confident man, the events of the past three years had beaten him down. He knew he was still a great enologist and could be the viticulturist Lost Creek Vineyards was looking for. He had to sell himself in the coming minutes, however, in order to be able to remain in a profession he loved. If he couldn't nail down this job, his ability to remain in a leadership position in the wine industry would dry up.

Signage pointed to the tasting rooms on the left. He entered the office on the right and saw there was no reception desk, only a few chairs and a coffee table with a few magazines atop it. Instead, he noticed a woman sitting inside a glassed-in office. She looked up and smiled, rising and coming to greet him. She was tall and thin, with blue eyes and auburn hair pulled into a messy bun, probably in her mid-fifties.

"You must be Braden Clark," she said, offering her hand. "I'm Cecily Hart. I keep the books around here."

"And she keeps everyone in line," a voice said.

As he shook Cecily's hand, Braden glanced to his right, seeing a man approaching. He looked a few years older than Cecily and was lean, about six feet in height, with salt-and-pepper hair. Braden assumed this was the owner of Lost Creek Vineyards.

"Mr. Hart?"

"Make it Bill," the man said, thrusting out a hand and shaking Braden's. "I'm the owner and founder of Lost Creek Vineyards, but my better half here is the one who really runs the show."

Cecily laughed. "Well, someone has to keep this guy in line. I'll let you two have at it. Nice to meet you, Braden. And Bill, don't forget to offer Braden something to drink."

Cecily returned to her office, and Bill motioned Braden to follow him.

"Want a bottled water or Dr. Pepper?" the older man asked, stopping at a small kitchenette.

"I tried Dr. Pepper on my only trip to Texas a few years ago. It's pretty addictive."

"That it is."

Bill entered the room and snagged two cans of the beverage from the fridge. Handing one to Braden, he led them to a conference room, where a model of Lost Creek

Winery sat in the center of the large table dominating the room. Bill left the door open, and Braden couldn't decide if that was a good or bad thing.

He came to stand by the table, studying the model. Since Bill didn't say anything, Braden walked slowly around the conference table, taking in the model from all sides.

When he had done so, Bill indicated a map on the wall. "Here's an idea of what the acreage looks like and where things are located."

Bill pointed out the vineyards themselves, showing Braden an area where they would soon be planting new vines, as well as the building where the actual winemaking took place.

"Have a seat," Bill offered.

Taking one on the side of the table, he waited until Bill took his own at the head of the table, just to Braden's right. His mom had been from South Carolina and had drilled good manners into her three sons. Where he had once scoffed at them, simply because his California peers were not nearly so aware of such polite moves, he saw Bill Hart nod appreciatively at the gesture.

The vineyard owner set the manila folder he had held on the table and opened it. Braden could see that it was the résumé he had emailed.

"You have a gap in your employment history," Bill noted. "I know why."

A sick feeling washed over him. "Then why did you bother to have me come all the way to Texas to interview?" he asked, a bit too abrasively.

Bill closed the folder and pushed it aside, his gaze meeting Braden's. "Because you come from a great tradition. Clark Vineyards had a stellar reputation for producing classic wines—and you were a big part of that for several years."

The older man leaned back in his chair. "Tell me about yourself and what you did at Clark Vineyards."

Talking about the professional side of things was easy for him.

"I have my WSET certifications, Levels One through Four, which you know is the premier, internationally recognized program for wine certification. Holding that certification sets me apart from my peers in regard to knowledge and expertise. That is in addition to my practical experience—and my nose and taste for wines."

Bill studied him a moment. "Walk me through these. As if I have no idea what you're talking about."

The vineyard owner was testing him—and Braden was determined to shine.

"The courses are comprehensive in nature," he began. "The curriculum covers wine production and styles, tasting techniques, service, and pairings."

When Bill continued to sit in silence, he went into a brief explanation of each level, wanting this vineyard founder to understand the depth of his knowledge.

"Level One explores wine through sight, smell, and taste. It gave me the basic skills to learn the principles involved in storing and serving wines. How to accurately describe them. How to taste and identify them. How to pair the correct foods with them."

"Go on."

"Level Two teaches you to decode a label's information to understand a wine's style and quality. You learn to identify the principal grape varieties from around the world, both fortified and sparkling. It also includes guided tastings which elevate your tasting skills."

Without being promoted, Braden continued. "By Level Three, you become familiar with eighty benchmark wines. You gain a deep understanding of the key factors in wine production."

"Such as?"

"The effects of location. The actual growing of the grapes. The winemaking process, based upon the fruit's maturation. Even bottling. A key component is numerous blind tastings, where you must describe wine accurately based upon its style, quality, and potential for ageing."

"And Level Four?" Bill asked, amusement in his eyes.

"The final level is, by far, the most difficult," Braden explained. "Two full years of study. Five exams. One independent research assignment. You delve into wine production and the actual business. You become an expert at the factors which influence a wine's style, quality, and price. You hone your tasting skills. On top of my WSET certification, I also took specialty courses throughout the years, while I was employed fulltime at Clark Vineyards. I specialized in US climate, geography, and wine regions and also took classes in grape varieties, wine laws, and industry trends."

Braden paused. "I know my stuff, Bill. If it's wine, I have an innate affinity for it. I live it. Breathe it. Know it."

"And after you earned all your certification?" Bill asked. "Résumé aside, what did you actual *do* at Clark Vineyards?"

"You have to realize, Bill, that I grew up in my family's business. I was picking grapes by the time I could walk. I worked in the vineyards from the time I was six years old. Yes, not doing nearly as much as the adult workers, but I listened—and I learned. I continued working on the land and in production after school and summers until I graduated from high school. I've done the backbreaking work of caring for the grapevines. Pruning them. Fertilizing fields and tilling the soil. Harvesting and sorting the grapes.

"Not only did I work in the fields, I learned other sides of the business. I shadowed our viticulturist. I had already, since middle school, been tasting wines, so I already had a sophisticated palate. Both our enologist and viticulturist trained me in the finer points of wine creation and tastings before I ever had any formal training. The official training I sought was merely icing on the cake, which had been my practical experience. I started at twenty as a viticulturist and soon became an assistant winemaker and then the chief winemaker for Clark Vineyards."

Bill stroked his chin thoughtfully. "What were some of your favorites—and what years?"

Braden was so comfortable with this line of questions, he mentioned various varieties of wines and the years they had been produced, going back two decades. How he had babied the grapes and worked on various blends. He spotlighted the four varieties Clark Vineyards had focused on—Chardonnay, Cabernet Sauvignon, Zinfandel, and Merlot.

"I stand behind the work I did at Clark Vineyards, sir."

Bill nodded thoughtfully. "Let me tell you a bit about Lost Creek Vineyard."

For the next ten minutes, Bill Hart walked him through the beginnings of the winery and the different wines which had been created and produced.

"As you know, climate has everything to do with the direction taken at a winery."

"Yes, climate is the chief factor influencing production in Texas."

"I'm about to lose my viticulturist. I know it's not the winemaker position you previously held at your family's business, but I can tell you that it could lead to that in the near future. I've taken on that role of chief winemaker for many years, but I'm two years shy of sixty, Braden. I see myself stepping away from the dual role I've held and having someone else in charge of development and production, while I represent the brand itself and focus solely on the business aspects.

"Tell me why Lost Creek Winery should hire you."

Placing his proverbial cards on the table, Braden said, "I won't give you a song-and-dance about why I'm the best candidate. I've already proven that by sharing my experience and expertise with you. The position is a step back for me professionally, but it's a job I've held and know. I can do it better than anyone else you interview and help bring your winery to the next level."

He gazed at his potential employer steadily. "I need

this job—and I'm willing to fight for it. Because it's my last chance in the industry, Bill. The gap on my resumé isn't my doing. The wine community is a small one. I'm sure you've heard gossip regarding the nitty-gritty details of why my father was sent to prison. Although the FBI cleared me of any charges, no one has been willing to take the risk and hire me. I'm down to the last few dollars in my bank account. I bought a one-way ticket to Austin because that's all I could afford. If you don't hire me for this position, my plan is to hitchhike to Fredericksburg and try to get on as a vineyard worker."

He took a long breath and expelled it. "I'm hungry as hell, Bill. I'm eager to get back into the game and share my knowledge. Use my creativity. Make my mark. I can be a true asset to Lost Creek Vineyards, especially with your ideas regarding expansion of your operation and your desire to step away from a day-to-day, active role as far as production goes. I'm dependable. Loyal. And as I mentioned, broke."

Bill studied him thoughtfully. "You could go the route of a sommelier," he suggested. "You obviously have the knowledge to do so successfully."

"I could. But that's not me. I need to be out in the vine-yards. Walking the land. Touching and tasting the grapes. I have a lot of knowledge and experience and am eager to put both to good use once more. I've never needed to beg for anything, Mr. Hart, but I need this job in order to stay in the wine industry. You're my last hope. I just wish you'll be open-minded enough to give me a chance to show you what I can do."

The older man gazed at him steadily. "I would be a fool to pass up the opportunity to hire you, Braden. You've got all the bona fides. You have vision into wine. I'm looking to expand Lost Creek Vineyards. I think you are the exact man to help me do so successfully."

Hart rose and offered Braden his hand. He sprang to his feet. The two men shook as the owner said, "We have ourselves a deal. As long as you'll promise to call me Bill."

He couldn't help but grin shamelessly. "Bill, it is. From now on."

"Then let's go see the vineyards and the production building," his new boss said. "Give you an idea about our operation. Then we can talk salary and any other particulars."

Relief swept through him. He would have a job where he could use everything he had learned in the past, with a chance to advance to winemaker more quickly than he would have hoped. He would need to demonstrate his capabilities to this man.

"Thank you for taking a chance on me, Bill," Braden said. "I promise you, you won't regret it."

---

s Austin receded in Harper's rearview mirror, the burden eased from her shoulders. She was headed to Lost Creek.

Home...

The last two weeks had been ones of soul searching. Thankfully, she'd had Ivy with her for the ten days in Bali. The sisters had talked over every decision Harper needed to make, and she couldn't imagine having gone through this ordeal without Ivy's support.

One thing had been clear to her from the start. She had to break all ties with her life in Austin. The city had been home to her for the past ten years. Four of those had been spent as a student at the University of Texas, while the next six had encompassed her work as an event planner.

For all the growth in the city's population, however, Austin was still very much a small town, ruled by a tight-knit group of movers and shakers. They had been the clients she had worked with. Harper had planned their parties and receptions. Organized celebrations for graduations, engagements, anniversaries, and retirements. Spearheaded corporate events and planned entire conferences. Set up high school and college reunions.

Because it was at heart a small place, she knew she would constantly run into people who were business associates, colleagues, friends, or acquaintances with Ath and Cynthia, not to mention Army and Bethany. She did not want their looks of pity or curiosity, nor did she wish to watch them whispering about her.

What Harper needed was a clean start in a new place.

Once she had reached that decision, she had emailed her resignation letter to her boss in Austin. The two had worked well together over the years, with Sandra Bellows praising Harper's organizational skills and creativity in planning and running events. She had received a text from Sandra, saying she understood why Harper was resigning and if she changed her mind down the line, there would always be a spot waiting for her. Sandra had also emailed a wonderful recommendation letter and told Harper to use her as a reference when she was searching for a new position.

Where the next stage in her life and career would lead her was up in the air. She had always enjoyed San Antonio and thought that city might be a possibility. Plenty of opportunities would also be available in larger cities such as Dallas and Houston. She couldn't see herself leaving Texas, though. Her family had been here for several generations, and it was in her blood. She wouldn't let a cheating fiancé and a former best friend's betrayal chase her from the state.

Since her apartment's lease had run out and not been renewed, Harper had rented a storage space and placed the bulk of her clothes and personal items in the unit for the time being. She would move her things once she had a permanent place to live. Fortunately, money would not be an issue. When she had gone to the bank two days ago to remove the funds she had placed in the joint account she and Ath had established and asked the clerk for her name to be removed from that account, the teller obviously recognized her name and asked her to wait a moment.

Soon, she was ushered into the office of the bank's president. He explained to her that Mr. Armistead had already taken care of removing his name from their joint account and had emphasized she was to keep both the account and the funds in it.

Surprisingly, the president had reached into his desk drawer and handed her a note. Steeling herself to read it, the note consisted of only two lines. Ath told her all the money in the account was hers. And that he was sorry. She had refrained from balling up the note and tossing it into the trash. Instead, she calmly folded it and slipped it into her purse and asked to see how much was currently in the account.

The banker had turned to his computer screen and pulled up her account, motioning for Harper to come view the record. When she did, she gasped inwardly. She herself had placed almost fifteen thousand dollars the account, all she had in checking and savings, and she recalled Ath had put in thirty thousand himself. The number reflected on the screen had been more than twenty times that, slightly over nine hundred thousand dollars. Her gut told her it was a bribe, something to have her keep quiet. To take the money and not cause waves.

Harper's first instinct was to reject it. To pull out what she had put in and walk away. Yet if she had sued Ath for breach of contract, she very well could have gotten such an amount, if the lawsuit had also included emotional distress suffered. She had made a split decision to keep the money. It would allow her to take her time in deciding what her next step would be. She might even use it to start her own event planning company. The money would be an investment in her—and her future.

She kept the radio off as she drove through the Hill Country, relaxing more and more as the towns became fewer and farther between. She was a country girl at heart and had missed being in wide, open spaces. She wanted to take time to breathe in the fresh air. Spend some time in nature and atop a horse. Maybe even work in the dirt at the vineyard some. Just a pause in order to renew and recharge herself.

Deciding to call Ivy, she tapped in her sister's number. Ivy answered on the second ring.

"Are you on your way?" her sister asked anxiously.

"I am. I'm also in a good frame of mind," she confided. "I know we rehashed this many times, but I'm grateful that I learned about Ath's character before the ring was placed on my finger. If he was going to cheat on me before, while we were engaged, he certainly would've have done so after we were married. This way, I don't have to worry about dissolving a marriage. No kids are involved. Yes, my heart is bruised, but I will get over it in time. I already feel lighter, just leaving Austin behind."

"I'm glad to hear this, Harper. I've been so worried about you."

"Enough about me. How about you? Have you settled in this past week?"

"Yes, I really have. I talked to Mom and Dad for a long time, and I'm now working as the manager in the tasting room."

"Ivy, that's fantastic!" Harper exclaimed. "Of the two of us, you've always had the better nose for wine."

Her sister chuckled. "Well, I've had a little brushing up to do, but I'm comfortable in the position. I have two other employees, so I can trade off shifts I work with them. Harper, it's going to give me time to pursue my art again. That's what I've wanted more than anything. And you know, there are plenty of galleries in the Hill Country, even in Lost Creek itself. I hope to build a personal relationship with a few of them so that they'll agree to display my work."

"I can hear it in your voice," she said. "You're happier already."

"I really am," Ivy said softly. "I didn't realize how much I'd missed Lost Creek until I got here a few days ago." She paused. "Gotta go. Have some tasters who just walked in. See you soon."

Harper ended the call and began thinking. Ivy had sounded different than she had for several years. Once they had reached Bali, Ivy had confided in Harper just how stressed and overworked she was. Her sister's passion and pleasure had always been found in her art. Now she had time to pursue it, and Harper couldn't be more grateful.

As she drove along the highway, soaking up the beauty of the landscape, a thought began forming in her mind. Something that would be challenging and exciting. She would have to run it by her parents once she got home. It would not only involve her—but her family's winery.

She focused on the idea the next hour, firming things up in her mind, ready to make the pitch to her parents. Then she reached the town of Lost Creek, which held so many wonderful memories for her. A few bittersweet ones, too. She passed an elementary school, where her friend Finley Farrow taught fifth grade. Finley had been one of her bridesmaids from the called-off wedding, and she had left a voicemail for Harper, telling her she would support her in any way she could.

She would definitely be in touch with Finley soon. She knew her friend lived with a fellow teacher and former college roommate. Emerson Frost had been an elementary education major, and Finley had met Emerson when they'd been potluck roommates their freshman year. While Harper knew Emerson only as an acquaintance, maybe they might become friends while she was here in Lost Creek. She had eaten cupcakes and cookies baked by Emerson on different occasions and thought her an extremely talented baker. She recalled how Finley had shared that Emerson was working weekends and summers at The Bake House on the square. Harper would stop in when she had more time and pick up goodies for the family and their vineyard workers.

She made the familiar turn into Lost Creek Winery, gazing out at the vineyard. Mustard, a cover crop, blanketed the ground between the rows of vines. It prevented soil erosion and prevented pests in the soil, giving off a beautiful color this time of year. A few workers pruned the vines. She caught sight of a tall man, not recognizing him from a distance. Then again, she hadn't been involved in the day-to-day operations of the winery for many years. She, Ivy, and Todd had worked summers for their parents, but once Harper hit college, she either did summer school or worked internships in Austin.

Driving her SUV directly to the house, she stopped to take the time to bring in the two suitcases she'd brought with her. Harper headed to her old room and unpacked, filling a few drawers and hanging clothes in the closet.

Returning to her car, she drove another mile to the offices, which were attached to the tasting room. A couple of vehicles were parked in front, and she figured they must belong to tasters occupying Ivy's time since anyone working here usually parked in the back. She headed inside the office instead.

Her mother must have been keeping an eye out for her daughter because she leaped to her feet the moment Harper walked through the door. It felt good to have her mother's arms about her.

"It's so good to see you, honey," Mom said. "Did you have a good trip from Austin?"

Harper looked at her mother, thinking this is what she would look like in thirty years. She had inherited Cecily Hart's auburn hair, deep blue eyes, and thin frame.

"All is good, Mom. I stopped at the house and unpacked. Is Dad around?"

"He's meeting with a new client in the conference room. They should be done soon."

The two men appeared moments later, and she saw her dad's face light up when he caught sight of her. Dad introduced her to the client, a restaurateur from San Antonio who would be carrying Lost Creek Vineyard wines in his three restaurants within the next week. They chitchatted for a moment before the client took his leave, and then her dad wrapped her in a tight bear hug. Harper felt as if she were truly home, safe and loved.

"How's my girl?"

"Your girl is thirsty," she declared. "Can I get into your stash of Dr. Peppers?"

Bill Hart was known for consuming the unofficial state drink of Texas throughout the day.

"Let's go grab a few and talk."

"Actually, I'd like Mom to come with us. I have something I'd like to run by both of you."

Dad cocked an eyebrow. "Is that so? Come on, Cecily. Join us."

She and her mother went to the conference room, while her dad stopped and picked up cans of DP for the three of them. He handed one to each of them and took a seat, asking, "What's on your mind, Sweetheart?"

"I appreciate you hearing me out, simply because this

is something I hit upon while I was driving home today. Normally, I would have a professional presentation planned, with beautiful PowerPoint slides and be able to answer any conceivable question you came up with. I just want you to understand I'm talking off the top of my head and would have to work a lot of the logistics out. I'm apologizing upfront for my lack of preparation."

Mom smiled encouragingly at her. "You must be excited if you want to share something with us that's in the early stages of planning."

Taking a deep breath, Harper nodded. "I am. Because it involves the winery."

"*Our* winery?" Dad asked, frowning slightly. "What do you have up your sleeve, Harper?"

"I want to become the event manager for Lost Creek Winery," she said, feeling good about hearing that spoken aloud. "I want to organize and coordinate events held on the grounds."

She could tell her dad was taken aback, but the look on her mother's face was one of intrigue.

"Go on, Harper," Mom encouraged.

"We grow the grapes on site. Make the wines and bottle them. Ship them out to individuals and businesses. I know on a few occasions, you've let a Scouting or civic group come in to take a tour and see the process, but other than that, we don't have contact with the public, other than through the tasting room."

"Are you suggesting organized tours?" Dad asked. "I know some wineries do that. Frankly, I wouldn't want to deal with the hazard insurance, much less have strangers traipsing through the winery, distracting everyone."

She tried to slow the swirl of ideas in her head. "No, I'm not really thinking about tours, but that is food for thought down the line. What I'm wanting to do is far beyond that. I'm basing it on wineries I've used in the past, places where I've held events. The biggest thing would be to hold weddings here. Both indoor and outdoor ones."

Mom grew thoughtful. "Hmm. We could set aside an area for an outdoor wedding. Put out benches and cover it. But we have no facility for an indoor wedding, Harper, much less a place to hold a reception. You know we've always been all about the wine and nothing else It took me yanking your dad's arm to even have us put in a tasting room."

"We would need to build a facility. Not a chapel. Too many couples today are staying away from overtly religious ceremonies. I would want a large space where half could be where the ceremony would take place, while the other half would be designated for the reception. I'm thinking large, like a barn in structure, but way prettier. Go with concrete floors for ease. Neutral colors inside, so weddings could use that as a palette or bring in decorations. Or I could even style the events with things I've accumulated."

"That would involve catering," Dad pointed out. "You'd need a kitchen. And restroom facilities."

"Yes, I agree. I'm not saying Lost Creek would do the actual catering, though. We have several places nearby that could manage that. Blackwood BBQ comes to mind.

A Hill Country wedding, complete with barbeque and all the trimmings. We could serve our own wines. Have The Bake House do the bride and groom's cakes."

She paused. "That's just the start. I would like to be the event manager for weddings, but I can see us doing so much more. Bridal luncheons. All kinds of parties—for graduations, anniversaries, and retirements. Family reunions or other private gatherings. Eventually, we might pull in a few corporate events. The event center could host whatever we desired."

"Not to rain on your parade, but you're talking an expensive venture," Dad said. "At a time when we're expanding the vineyards again. While the banks would most likely give us a loan if we requested it, I don't want to be spread too thin financially. Maybe in the future, Harper."

"I wouldn't be asking you to fund this project, Dad. I have a good chunk of money," she revealed. "A parting... gift from Ath. At first, I was reluctant to take it and then I thought, why not? It could help me start a new life. It's pocket change to his family, but it would give me the chance to stretch myself professionally, against the back-drop of Lost Creek Winery, and start my own business."

Thinking a moment, she said, "It could start as Weddings by Hart, a play on my last name. In fact, I could set up the business as an LLC, all in my name. You wouldn't be responsible for anything. I would focus on weddings first and then possibly expand down the line. I —and the bank—would provide the funding to build this event center and could even pay you a rental fee for the land it sits on."

Her excitement grew. "I've planned my fair share of weddings, even if I had nothing to do with organizing my own. I could contract with merchants in town to provide catering and floral arrangements. Why, Finley could be my photographer!" she declared.

"Oh, Finley is building quite a nice little side business for herself," Mom shared. "She's been taking senior portraits for a few years now, taking students out for photo shoots in picturesque places. She's also done some engagement photos. Baby's first photo shoot with their family, too. I've told her she's going to eventually make more money with her photography than she does teaching."

"She would be perfect," Harper agreed. "Okay, I know this is all rough and I have a thousand and one details to iron out—but is this doable? Is this something the two of you would be interested in? And don't answer as my parents," she warned. "Think with your business caps on. In fact, I don't even want to be here when you discuss it. Talk it over. Let me flesh out more ideas and the details. We can meet again in a few days."

Harper saw the look her parents exchanged. It was one married couples who had been together many years gave one another. Wordlessly, she realized they had already come to some agreement.

"No need to talk about it, honey," her dad said. "The winery would be a great backdrop for a wedding, especially with the type of structure you're talking about. It would help add business to the town, with you contracting the services of various nearby merchants. I just worry that people won't want to drive this far out for a wedding."

"Dad, we're only about forty-five minutes from San Antonio," she told him. "That's not far at all. Especially if we're giving the bride her dream wedding. And with Lost Creek being only ten minutes away, there's plenty of places guests could stay."

"I agree with Harper," Mom said. "A bride would have a very unique wedding if it were held against the background of a Hill Country winery." She smiled warmly. "I'd say we're all in."

Leaping to her feet, she hugged both her parents. "I have so much to do," she told them. "Ideas to get down. Meeting with a bank. Hiring an architect. Contacting merchants in town." She thought a moment. "I'll need some office space."

"You can have Jerry's old office," Dad volunteered, referring to the business partner that started the winery with him years ago. "It's turned into mostly storage space, but we can work around it."

"Thanks, Dad. I need to go share the good news with Ivy. And I promise that I will not let you down. I'm excellent at my job."

Mom laughed. "You always bossed around your stuffed animals and dolls. I thought at one point you might become a teacher."

She laughed, too. "I remember that. Well, I've become very good at bossing people, as well. Only I'm clever enough to make it sound more like a request. I'll see you back at the house for dinner."

Harper went next door to the tasting room, where Ivy was walking two couples through a tasting. She took a seat, listening to her sister, hearing what a natural she was as she pointed out the notes of each wine and told what to look for in taste. Once each of the wines on the flights had been sampled, the two pairs bought half a dozen bottles of the wines they had tasted. Ivy rang them up and thanked them for coming, encouraging them to recommend Lost Creek Winery to their friends.

After they left, her sister came and took a seat at the small table. "How has your day been?"

"Fabulous. Tasting Manager, meet the new Event Coordinator for Lost Creek Winery."

3

Harper walked Ivy through an abbreviated version of what she wanted to do at Lost Creek Winery, seeing her sister's thoughtful nods as she took everything in.

"This would take a lot of capital, Harper," Ivy said. "With the new expansion of vines Mom and Dad have planned, this may not be the right time for them. Even if it is for you," she added apologetically.

"I know. I actually have what I'm going to term a 'settlement' from Ath, which would cover everything I need. I would pay Mom and Dad to rent the land I would use to erect a facility on.

She explained the money her former fiancé had left in their joint banking account for her.

Crinkling her nose, Ivy said, "I don't know if I could use that money. It sounds like a payoff. I'm not judging you, Harper, but I couldn't touch it."

"That was my first instinct, but I reconsidered quickly. The money would mean everything to me. I could start my own business with it and maintain my independence. Am I still upset? Miserable? Angry? You bet. But at least this money gives me an opportunity to move forward with my life. Frankly, I can't work in Austin anymore with the two of them there, much less open an event planning business there. I would have to deal too much with the people who run in their circles.

"But this wedding business could make a huge difference for our family, Ivy. Mom and Dad wouldn't have to spend a dime of their own money. Weddings by Hart would be *my* venture. I told them I'll take out the necessary loans to build the structure. I would be the one who planned every aspect of the weddings booked here, including working with local businesses to cater the receptions. I could hire local bands to provide the music."

Harper paused. "That leads me to a little more of the ideas I've brainstormed. Things I haven't shared with Mom or Dad yet, but I'd like to run them past you."

"Go on," Ivy encouraged.

"I would love for Lost Creek Winery to be a destination for people on the weekends. Dad already shot down the idea of giving tours of the facilities, and I totally understand that. They could be a pain. What I do think we should do, though, is make visiting Lost Creek Wineries more of an experience than simply hitting up the tasting room and buying a few bottles of wine on the way out the door. I would like to have a picnicking area built, with tables and a cover to lend some shade. People could bring their own food, or we could have baskets available for purchase, along with the wines they buy."

"That would mean setting up a bartender and staff to clear the tables once visitors left," Ivy pointed out. "I can actually see this, though. Other wineries do it."

"I could hire local musical talent to play on weekends. We could have a simple stage erected with some sound equipment, and people could bring a date or even their families. Sit on the lawn in chairs or bring blankets and nibble on the food they brought or something we provide as they sit under the stars, listening to music, relaxing, sipping wine. It would be a way to draw people to the winery and spotlight local talent, as well."

"I like where you're going with this, Harper. I think I want to jump on your bandwagon and add a few suggestions."

"Like what?" she asked eagerly.

"It was an idea I've been toying with. I just hadn't been ready to share it with anyone yet, but I'll run it past you. I want to expand our tasting room. We've obviously got the room to do so. One thing I would like to add to it would be a gift shop, where people could purchase merchandise with the Lost Creek Vineyards label on them. T-shirts. Ball caps. Sweatshirts. Koozies."

"I like this," Harper said, her enthusiasm growing. "And how about small items related to wine, such as those metal wine charms that ID which glass is yours? We could carry wooden logo bottle stoppers or even wine sippy cups. Corkscrews."

"Wait a minute," Ivy said. "What if we created blank

labels? We could write in names in calligraphy for special occasions. Anniversaries. One for the wedding couple themselves."

Harper beamed. "Some couples like to give parting gifts to their guests. We could design a koozie with our Lost Creek logo and the couple's name and date of the wedding and distribute those to all the guests. Or if they were willing to spring for it, couples could present guests with a bottle of wine with customized labels bearing their name and wedding date."

Grateful that her sister was onboard with these new ideas, she said, "Ivy, these are some fantastic things to discuss with Mom and Dad. Yes, they would have to hire a few more people to run a gift shop, but it would be a way to get the Lost Creek Vineyard's name out there even more. Even our own workers could wear caps and T-shirts with our logo. You could also do so in the tasting room. That might encourage people to head to the gift shop when they finished their tasting."

Ivy thought a moment. "What about the tastings them-selves? I've actually been to a few tasting rooms which offered food along with the wine."

"Such as?"

"I would keep it simple. A cheese plate, for example. One which paired a cheese with the optimal wine. Those plates could be premade and stored in a nearby fridge in the tasting room. We could have one plate for whites. Another for reds. And a third for the blends we're known for."

"That's incredible," Harper praised. "You're really on to something. We have a great cheese shop here in town. I'm certain they would enjoy partnering with us in a venture such as this."

Harper hugged her sister. "This is really exciting. I'm so glad Mom and Dad were open to me starting a wedding business here on the grounds. They'll love your ideas, too, Ivy."

"I think it would really boost sales, and the weddings and receptions would expose a lot more people to our Lost Creek wines."

"We haven't talked yet about your painting. I know you've only been here a week, but have you had time to start a new canvas yet?"

Ivy smiled. "I have. I've also had time to simply drive around and do some sketching. Yes, I'm working full time in the tasting room, but the hours are so spread out, and I also have other people to depend upon. It's not like when I was at the gallery and worked ninety-hour weeks and had all the responsibility on my shoulders. I truly feel I'm going to be able to immerse myself in my art again."

"That's the best possible news," Harper told her sister, glancing toward the door as it opened, a couple in their mid-twenties entering.

Ivy rose. "I'm back on the clock. I'll see you at dinner."

Her sister greeted the couple as Harper left the tasting room and headed for her SUV. She paused, studying the building which served both the tasting room and the offices for Lost Creek Vineyards. If they were going to expand the tasting room, they might want to consider building a separate structure for it instead of simply adding on to the current one. That way, she could use the tasting room itself, refiguring it so that she would have ample office space, along with a consulting room in which she could meet with her clients and vendors. If she took over the current tasting room space, her business would be separate from them, even allowing her to have her own logo outside the building. Ivy had done some freelance graphic art work over the years, and Harper would pay her sister to come up with a design distinguished from the Lost Creek Vineyards label but still complementary toward it.

As she drove back to the main house, she ran several ideas in her head, knowing she would soon need to hire an architect to bring her vision to life, as well as get an estimate from him on what the building would cost. Based upon that, she would know whether or not she would need to seek a bank loan.

Trey Watson came to mind. Even though the architect had been Ath's best friend, he was a better man than her former fiancé would ever be. Trey had sent her a single text while she'd been in Bali, telling her again how sorry he was and offering his help in any way if she ever needed it.

Harper decided she would schedule an appointment with Trey once she and Ivy firmed up their ideas for the tasting room and the event facility. Her sister could capture those ideas on paper, allowing Harper to bring those illustrations to Trey in order to give him an idea of what she wanted built.

She pulled in at home and locked her SUV, feeling lighter than she had since that night at the steakhouse when her world came crashing down. Though all her plans had unraveled with the wedding being called off, Harper had stopped things from spinning totally out of control. The trip to Bali with Ivy had been healing in itself, and now she had decided to start her own business here at her family's winery. All considered, things were looking up.

Entering the kitchen, she poured herself a tall glass of her mother's refreshing lemonade, thinking it might be something that could be offered in the picnic area besides wine. She decided to retrieve her laptop and start capturing her ideas through detailed notes regarding all the things she had discussed with her parents and sister.

Going down the hall to her old bedroom, Harper was startled when the door to the bathroom opened. A man stepped out, wearing nothing but a towel slung low on his hips. She gasped—even as her eyes couldn't help but roam over the stranger's muscular body and flat belly. He looked nothing like Ath, who was two inches shy of six feet and had dark hair and brown eyes and was fairly skinny. This man was at least two inches over six feet, with dirty-blond hair and sky-blue eyes, which flickered with amusement in them.

"This is a little awkward," he said, his voice a low, sexy rumble, his lips sensual and inviting. "I didn't realize anyone would be in the house now. You must be Harper. I heard you were coming, and you're a younger version of Cecily."

Obviously, this stranger must know her parents since he was here—and practically naked—but she still asked, "Who are you? I feel I'm at a disadvantage since you know about me, and I haven't a clue who you are."

He smiled lazily at her, and tingles ran through her. No, she was done with men. Even a hot, blond stranger who ran around the house half-naked and whose smile made her feel things she shouldn't be feeling.

Taking a step toward her, he offered his hand, saying, "I'm Braden Clark, the new viticulturist for your family's vineyards."

She took his hand and shook it, ignoring its warmth and his intense gaze which made *her* feel half-naked.

Withdrawing her hand, Harper asked, "Why are you here? In the house."

He chuckled. "I'm living here until my first couple of paychecks come in. You might be familiar with the sordid story, so I'll give you the condensed Braden Clark version of it."

Hearing his name again, she recalled seeing the news about a scandal at a California winery a couple of years ago and asked, "Clark Vineyards' Braden Clark?"

Nodding, he said, "I see you're familiar with the name."

She shrugged, trying to tamp down her physical reaction to this man. "Well, it was all over the news. Even here in Texas. What's your spin on it?" she asked, not recalling many of the details.

"Long story short? My dad did a helluva lot of bad

things and got caught. No one in the family had a clue what he was up to. He's serving a lengthy prison sentence. My mom divorced him and remarried quickly enough to make the gossips' heads spin. She was never the nurturing kind, and she told her three boys she was done with us. I haven't seen or spoken to her since. My promising career as a winemaker went down the toilet. My fiancée jilted me. I've been out of work for two years, and I'm flat broke."

He paused, and though he was making light of his massive troubles, Harper could see the pain etched on his face.

"Your dad was decent enough to give me a chance," he continued. "Your mom, knowing I spent my last few bucks getting from California to Texas for the job interview, offered to advance me a couple of paychecks to get on my feet."

"But you were too proud to take the money, weren't you?" she said knowingly.

"Damn straight. I did take up Cecily on her offer to live here at the house for a month. Until I had enough to put down a deposit on an apartment and move into Lost Creek. End of story."

His gaze searched hers. "Why are you here, Harper? Your parents only said you would be coming to stay a for a while."

"Longer story made even shorter," she said crisply. "Event planner in Austin. Betrayed by best friend and cheating fiancé. Quit my job and came home to lick my wounds, but I've decided I'm going to open up my own business here at the winery. Weddings by Hart. Lots of brides want a unique setting for their wedding, and I think there's a market to have weddings take place here at Lost Creek Winery."

He nodded. "Might need some indoor space for that. I've heard Texas weather can be unpredictable. Can't have a bride passing out before she can say 'I do.'"

Harper laughed. "We've run the air conditioner on both Thanksgiving and Christmas Day in the past. Then again, we've had frost during the spring sometimes. I was at a soccer game once when it was ninety degrees and sweltering. A storm moved in with a fierce, howling wind. The refs paused the game during halftime. When the storm passed through and play started up again, it was fifty degrees colder, with a nasty wind coming out of the north."

His eyebrows arched. "Seriously?"

"Happened in Georgetown. Fortunately, being a Texan means always being prepared. Fans had blankets and jackets in the car and watched the rest of the game comfortably bundled up."

"Who won?"

Grinning, she said, "Why, Lost Creek High School did. It was the state championship game. You didn't think we'd roll over, did you? Not with me playing forward."

Braden Clark burst into laughter, a rich, vibrant laugh. She couldn't recall a single time when Ath had ever laughed so openly and unguardedly.

Stop it, Harper.

Just because this man was incredibly attractive, it did

not mean she had changed her stance on men. Braden Clark was nothing more than an employee at Lost Creek Vineyards. She refused to get involved with him in any capacity.

Even if she did wonder how he might kiss.

4

Braden might have seemed to be casually speaking with Harper Hart, but inside, his heart slammed against his ribs, almost making him short of breath. She looked nothing like Freya Gallagher, the fiancée who'd abandoned him shortly after his father's arrest and kept the ring he'd scrambled to pay off as things got worse and worse financially. Where Freya was short, curvy, and brunette, this woman was tall, with an athletic frame, lively blue eyes, and shoulder-length auburn hair he longed to run his fingers through.

Getting involved with another woman was the last thing on Braden's mind. The fact that Harper was his new boss' daughter made her the absolute last choice even if he ever did change his mind and want to date again. Nope. Dating was a thing of the past. He had a career to revive, one he wanted to thrive in. A woman would just distract him and keep him from reaching his goals.

Even if she was as intriguing as Harper Hart.

"I played a little soccer myself. Also forward. Tried a year as goalkeeper and sucked at it. Didn't have quick enough reactions."

"Same," she said easily. "I started at goalie when I was five. Tried it again for a few games again in third grade when our goalie went down with a broken arm. It just wasn't my thing. Coaches moved me around between midfielder and forward until middle school. That's when I settled in at forward for good. It just felt right."

"I know exactly what you mean. It's like wine, especially blends. When I hit on the perfect combination, it's magic. Same with finding your position in sports. When it's right, you're firing on all pistons. Just in a groove that can't be explained." He paused. "So, you have a state championship ring?"

She chuckled. "Somewhere. Mom will know where it is. I was stupid enough to wear it to college. I already knew not to wear my letter jacket when I got to UT. I don't know about California, but certain things just aren't done in Texas on a college campus. I didn't know wearing my state championship ring was one of those no-no's, though."

"I'm surprised anyone even noticed it."

Harper chuckled. "Spoken like a typical guy. Guys don't notice anything. Girls, on the other hand, notice *everything*. Especially about other girls. The fact that I wore it didn't fly right with a few of the girls on the team."

"Team?" he asked. "Intramurals?"

"No. The UT girls' soccer team. I went to college on an athletic scholarship."

Braden looked her up and down. "I'm impressed. Soccer is a tough sport to play, especially the more you level up. You must've been really good to land a scholarship to a major university."

"I was good. Not be on the US national team or go to the Olympics good, but I still held my own in college. It allowed me to meet a lot of people I wouldn't have otherwise. Travel to see some different campuses. It also made me attractive to some of the sororities."

Braden shook his head. "I never went to college, so I know next to nothing about Greek life. My older brother went, though. He was in a fraternity. Beta something. Why did they want you because of the sports thing?"

"Whether they admit it or not, many sororities look for certain profiles to fill quotas. They need girls with a great academic GPA to help boost the entire sorority's GPA. They want some pledges who sing well so they can be featured in Greek life productions. They like to have a few athletes, cheerleaders, and students in government positions. I happened to be smart, athletic, and pretty. They liked that combination and courted me. I had my pick of sororities when I rushed."

"So, you joined one?"

"I did. I wasn't as involved as some of the other members, mostly because I spent so much time at practice and traveled quite a bit for games and tournaments. Still, membership opened new opportunities for me, and I made some good friends. When I graduated and put out résumés, the woman who hired me had been in the same sorority at UT ten years before me. I'd spoken with her at a few alumni events, and we felt comfortable with one another."

"But you're not working for her now."

"No," she said, a shadow crossing her face. "I resigned recently. I worked as an event planner in Austin for six years. I didn't want Sandra to lose business because of me, and I sure didn't want to work with some of our clients because of their connections with Ath." She paused. "My ex-fiancé."

"Your *cheating* ex-fiancé," Braden emphasized. "Why?"

Harper shook her head. "That's a whole different can of worms I don't want to open right now, Braden Clark. I'm sure you're probably cold and would like to go get dressed."

He hadn't remembered he was wearing nothing but a towel. And he certainly wasn't cold. He ran hot all the time.

And felt even hotter now because of the beautiful woman standing just a few feet from him.

"I'll go throw some clothes on. Why don't you meet me in the kitchen? I need to start dinner."

When she looked puzzled, he added, "I'm a good cook. No joke. I told your mom I'd cook dinner every night as part of staying free in the house."

She laughed, a musical laughter that warmed him from head to toe. It was taking everything Braden had not to pull her into his arms and kiss her. The funny thing was, he had never responded to any woman like that.

Until now.

"Maybe I'll learn something," she said, more laughter bubbling up. "Mom tried to teach me how to cook. I just never had much interest in it. I wind up at enough events where I just nibble my way through them. And I have a ton of takeout places on my favorites." She sighed. "Guess I can take those off my cell now."

"Meet you in the kitchen in ten," he told her, turning and heading down the hall.

Braden entered the bedroom he was staying in and quickly closed the door. Ditching the towel, he quickly dressed in a pair of jeans and long-sleeved T-shirt. He ran a comb through his hair. Though he'd planned to return to the bathroom to shave, he would go with the stubble for now. Maybe Harper would like it.

Cursing under his breath, he stopped moving, willing himself to be utterly still. He didn't have time to meditate and clear his mind, but he could get in a few, deep yoga breaths. Focusing on his breath, he let his mind go blank a moment, only feeling his breath, letting it flow in and out, calming himself. After five full inhales and exhales, he glanced into the mirror above the bedroom's dresser.

"Better," he told the image that stared back at him. "You're just horny. That's all. You've been without a woman for a long time, and Harper is a very attractive one."

But Ivy Hart was also extremely pretty—and he hadn't had the slightest reaction to her when they'd met a few days ago. Braden had just started his job at Lost Creek

Vineyards when Ivy turned up, telling her parents she had resigned from some art gallery and that she wanted to be considered for a job at the winery. Immediately, Cecily had said her daughter belonged in the tasting room. Bill had agreed, praising Ivy's nose. Braden knew how important it was to have a sensitive nose in winemaking, and it also came in handy for those who walked others through wine tastings. Since the Harts were losing both their tasting room manager and viticulturist—a married couple—to retirement, Ivy's timing couldn't have been more perfect.

Why hadn't he been attracted to Ivy? Why Harper?

Why now?

He was just settling in to his new position as viticulturist. It was a key position at a vineyard, one which set up the winemaker to be the best he or she could be. As a viticulturist, Braden handled all fertilizing and irrigation. He monitored and controlled pests and disease which affected the vines, as well as canopy management and supervising the continual pruning which went on. It was his responsibility to monitor the grapes' development and decide when it was time to harvest them.

As a viticulturist, he worked intimately with the vineyard's winemaker—the enologist—since it was his vineyard management which would reveal the ultimate characteristics of the grapes and provide the basis for the winemaker to work his magic. So far, he liked the small but professional crew at Lost Creek Winery. He had spent hours in the fields and also with Bill, tasting previous years of wine and discussing the future of Lost Creek

Vineyards. He wanted nothing to divert his time and interest.

Especially the boss' very attractive daughter.

As it was, Harper Hart had seen her own share of heartache. It surprised him how they both had opened up to one another so quickly, divulging the circumstances which had caused each of them deep, lasting pain. Obviously, they hadn't gone into the bloody details of their sorrows, but as much as he'd hurt when Freya walked away from him, Braden knew just how raw and vulnerable Harper was right now. And it hadn't just been her duplicitous fiancé who had hurt her. She'd been hoodwinked by her best friend as well, a double-whammy. No wonder she had left Austin and come home to the Hill Country to try and recover from all the deception and lies.

He wondered how long she would be here. Since she'd been an event planner in Austin, she was used to moving in pretty lofty circles, even if she were only the designated help. She would know all kinds of wealthy individuals, having planned their life celebrations and business events. He wondered if that's how she had met her fiancé and then decided it was none of his business. It was her past. Just as he didn't want to talk about his, he assumed she would be the same.

Maybe they could be friends, though. He was sorely lacking in those.

Heading for the kitchen, he found her already there, filling a glass with ice and pouring lemonade over it. Cecily's lemonade was the best beverage Braden had ever sampled that wasn't wine.

Harper handed over the glass. "If you're cooking, I thought you might need some sustenance. I'm assuming you've been out in the fields most of the day."

"Yes. Vineyards make for early risers."

"I know. I used to prune vines before school. We'd get up and be in the fields by three in the morning. Put in two-and-a-half or three hours before coming in to shower and leaving for school. It was all hands on deck back when I was in elementary school and the winery was in its early years. Dad and Jerry Hiller were partners then. They'd been roommates in college. Both earned business degrees, and they both were obsessed with wine. Jerry had a hefty inheritance from his folks and bought all the land Lost Creek Winery sits on today. They kept their day jobs and began planting vines, Mom helping them. Jerry and Dad also built this house on weekends, and we all moved in together."

"Two families?" Braden asked, getting out a 9x13 glass baking dish and all the supplies he would need to make manicotti.

"Jerry never married. I didn't really understand at the time, but he was gay. He was just like an uncle to us. He and Dad put in hours and hours before work. After work. On the weekends." She paused, assessing him. "You know how it is. You do the research, figuring which grapes will flourish in the climate and soil you have. Then you do your first planting, deciding upon the number of rows and how to orient them. How to space and trellis your vines.

Which grapes will get the bulk of real estate and which other ones you'll plant smaller amounts for blendings. They went mostly with Malbec back then, but I know they added Petit Verdot over the years."

"My family's vineyard had been around since my great-grandfather's time," he said, putting a pound of ground meat in a pan on the stove to cook and setting the oven temperature, allowing it to warm up. "So, a lot of that was already established. I did see some of the newer fields being planted once, but I didn't have as much to do with those."

"Well, I remember how they babied those vines. We used cartons and covered them to provide warmth and protection as the vines began to grow. The hard part was waiting for that first harvest," she admitted. "As a kid, you're all about instant gratification. Young vines need a lot of attention and care, though. You have to watch your watering. Constantly prune. Keep an eye out for disease. And wait while doing that for three years, until your vineyard produces full, delicious bunches of grapes."

Harper stopped talking. "Here. I can sit and brown meat. That's not cooking. Get everything else ready for whatever you're making."

"Manicotti," he told her, retrieving a box of shells from the pantry.

She looked at him in surprise. "This'll take forever. Mom and Dad like to eat early because they get up so early."

He smiled. "Ah, but this is my no-boil recipe," he

revealed. "I cut out all the heating water, plus boiling the shells, and stuffing them."

Harper frowned. "How?"

"The secret is in the chicken broth. And string cheese. I do make a mean manicotti, stuffing the shells with a blend of mozzarella and cottage cheese. This is my cheating way. Place a piece of string cheese inside each shell. Put the shells in the baking dish and dump the meat and sauce over them. Then pour chicken broth over the sauce and sprinkle with seasoning. While it's baking, the shells soften in the chicken broth."

Grinning, she said, "That even sounds like something I could do."

"You can help by stripping all those string cheeses of their wrappers."

"Yes, Chef!" she barked out, which made him laugh.

Braden finished browning the meat and drained the grease from it. He added a jar of spaghetti sauce and let it warm. By then, Harper had finished with the shells, so he spooned the meat sauce atop them.

"Shake some Italian seasoning all over. Dribble shredded mozzarella cheese on top. Add a little Parmesan to that. Voila! You're ready to bake."

He covered the pan tightly with foil and placed it in the oven.

"How long?" she asked.

"Forty minutes. I used to put this together— or my lasagna, using basically the same ingredients— and then open a bottle of wine to breathe. I'd hit the shower after a long day at work. By the time I was cleaned up and back in the kitchen, I could toss a salad, then dinner was ready."

"Did you always cook?" she asked, her curiosity evident.

"I told you my mom wasn't the nurturing type. She was also not the domestic type. We had someone who cleaned our house. Someone who looked after us kids when we were younger. Someone else to cook. That's who I learned from. I like cooking. It's as much an art as it is a science."

"Like winemaking?" she said, a smile playing about her lips.

Lips he longed to touch with his own.

"Exactly. Mom eventually let the cook go. She said I'd learned enough to keep my brothers fed. She and Dad went out a lot. To the country club. To dinner with clients. I didn't mind feeding Stan and Beau."

"You said there were three of you. Were you close with both brothers?"

Braden leaned against the counter, crossing his arms over his chest. "Yeah, actually I was. Stan was three years older, so I always looked up to him and tried to be like him. Beau was five years younger than I was. He and Stan weren't close at all—too much of an age gap—but I liked looking after Beau. He was a sensitive kid. Didn't change as an adult."

"What are they doing now?" Harper asked. "Did they go into the family wine business like you?"

He hesitated a moment, and she said, "No, that's okay. You don't have to share with me. I was just asking a getting-to-know-you question. We're not speed dating here."

Braden decided he wanted to tell her. At least a little bit.

"Stan was our brand manager. He was the one who wined and dined the clients, along with my parents. He took it hard when the news came out. By that time, Beau was one of our viticulturists. He really had a difficult time accepting everything that happened. It's hard, having your job and identity so wrapped up in your family. And when one of them does something that lowers the boom like what happened to us, it can be devastating."

"Ivy and I always liked growing up at a vineyard, but we never really thought about working at producing the wines. We were eager to leave our small town and the winery behind and do something different." She paused. "And yet here we are, both back now, ready to be a part of the place again."

Her words intrigued him. "I know Ivy wanted more time for her art. That she's the tasting room manager now. What do you see yourself doing here, Harper?"

"I'm going to open my own business on the property. Weddings by Hart. I'll plan the entire wedding and reception for couples. Work out all the details. Hire the vendors needed. Caterers. Cake baker. Photographer. DJ or live band. I may have missed out on getting married myself, but I've planned hundreds of events over the years, including my fair share of weddings. I think holding the ceremony and reception here and serving Lost Creek wines will really raise our profile in the community and beyond."

"Will you be okay doing that?" he asked softly. "After everything that's just happened to you?"

She smiled, determination evident on her face. "It'll be a while before any wedding takes place. I've got to build an event center. One in which I can hold both the wedding and reception. I'd like to eventually branch out to other events. It's going to take a lot of planning, but I've got nothing but time on my hands.

"And I never plan to get married myself."

5

Harper needed to be blunt, and that is why she said exactly what she had to Braden Clark. Already, she was upset and disappointed in herself for being so attracted to him. She didn't want to be interested in him. After all, he was an employee of her family's business, and with her working onsite now, it would be important to keep a professional distance.

More importantly, though, both of them were emotionally raw and had no business becoming involved with anyone, much less each other. She believed it would be a long, long time before she could ever trust a man enough to let him into her life. To her, love and trust were intertwined, and Ath's blindside had changed the way she saw men and the world.

Braden placed the pan of manicotti into the oven and set the timer. She excused herself, saying she would return for dinner. Retreating to her bedroom, Harper grabbed her laptop and furiously tapped away at the keys, trying to capture everything she had spoken about with her parents, as well as the ideas she and Ivy had batted back and forth.

By the time she had completed her task, she decided to make her way back to the kitchen. Ivy was already there, laughing and talking with Braden and their mother. She joined them, along with her dad, seeing the table was set, with the wine opened. A large salad bowl sat in the middle. The manicotti was sitting atop the stove, the foil still on it, resting. Braden returned to the oven and removed a loaf of crusty Italian bread.

"I think we're ready," he announced, and they took their seats around the kitchen table as Braden transferred the manicotti to the table and took a seat.

Todd's seat.

A lump rose in Harper's throat, and she glanced at Ivy, who nodded sympathetically at her, acknowledging their shared loss.

Once her plate was filled, she took a bite of the dish, finding the noodles tender and delicious.

"Nice job," she complimented, not wanting for things to be stiff between her and Braden.

"You could make this," he told her.

Ivy burst into laughter. "Seriously? I would say you needed to try something Harper has attempted to cook, but Dad isn't providing you with combat pay."

"I'm not *that* bad," she said, laughing, defending herself. "Why, I could have tossed that salad. And I actually watched Braden put the entrée together. I think I could do it."

"You can do whatever you put your mind to, honey," Mom told her.

Harper shook her head. "Who am I trying to kid? The three of you have suffered through my few attempts at cooking. I think I'll leave that to others."

"I've been spoiled this past week," Mom said. "Braden has taken on preparing dinner while he's staying with us." She smiled mischievously. "We might have to withhold his paycheck just to keep him around longer."

"I'll stay as long as you need me to, Cecily," Braden said.

As the conversation continued, Harper saw just how comfortable Braden Clark was with her parents. She didn't know what his relationship with his father had been like, but he spoke with ease to Bill Hart after only a week's acquaintance. Braden had revealed that his mother wasn't very hands-on, and so he might even view Cecily Hart as a kind of substitute mother. As it was, her mom always mothered others. Suddenly, it rankled her that Braden had come in and so quickly become a part of things.

"Have you told your sister about what you want to accomplish here at Lost Creek Winery and your new role?" Dad asked.

She and Ivy looked at each other and giggled, with Ivy saying "Dad, you could be creating a monster. The plans already go far beyond what Harper talked to you about."

Taking turns, she and Ivy told their parents about their

ideas for expanding the tasting room. The optional plates to accompany tastings. The gift shop. Even housing the tasting room in a different building altogether.

"If you agree to actually building a separate, larger tasting room, I could take over the current space for my office," Harper shared. "I'm going to need an office for myself and dedicated space to meet with clients and vendors. Who knows? I might even be able to one day add on an area where brides could try on sample wedding gowns and order their bridal dress from Weddings by Hart."

"That's awfully ambitious," her mom pointed out. "But I like it."

"You've said Weddings by Hart," Braden said. "You might want to consider the name Weddings with Hart. *With* speaks to more of a collaboration. It also plays on your surname better and how you'd show care and compassion to your clients."

"Weddings with Hart," Harper repeated, trying it out. Her gaze connected with Braden's. "I like it. Quite a bit." She glanced to Ivy. "I'm going to hire you to create my logo, along with graphics. And my website, too. Which do you prefer—by Hart or with Hart?"

"I like both," her sister said. "Let me try both, and you can see which design you prefer. Saying something aloud is good, but seeing how it appears on the page or a website is even better."

"I'd like it to complement the Lost Creek Vineyards image and logo. Possibly in use of color or font."

Ivy nodded to herself. "I'll get started on that tomorrow. I have the day off from the tasting room and can devote plenty of time to the project."

"What exactly do you want in this wedding hall?" Braden asked. "The reason I'm asking is because we had a similar facility at Clark Vineyards."

"You did?" Harper asked with interest. "Oh, I'll need to pick your brain, for sure."

He grinned. "It'll only cost you a consultations fee. Enough to get me out of Bill and Cecily's hair."

"Oh, Braden. You're no bother at all," Mom said reassuringly.

Laughing, Dad teased, "You just like having dinner on the table when we get home at five-thirty each day, Cecily."

Harper focused on Braden. "I want more of an event hall. Not strictly for weddings. Eventually, I could see us holding other social events held at the winery. Parties for a special wedding anniversary or someone's retirement. A family reunion. Because of that, I want the hall to be a large, open space. I'll focus on weddings to begin with, however, so I want the space to have dual purpose. Weddings on one side and reception tables and chairs set up on the other. What did your winery's hall contain?"

"It was similar to what you're talking about, along with a decent-sized kitchen. I'm sure caterers will bring food in, so you'll need lots of counter space for their warming trays. We had an unusually large island, where they would plate everything. We also had a walk-in refrigerator stocked with wines to be served and a walk-in freezer, as well, though it wasn't as large."

"If you don't mind, I would love for you to sketch that layout for me," she said. "I want to get my ideas on paper for exactly what my wants and needs are before I meet with an architect. I don't know if they charge by the hour or the project, but I want to make good use of our time."

"I can do that for you," Braden said. "Make sure you have enough restrooms. I would also plan for a large room in which a bride could change her clothes. A sofa. Some chairs and a table. I recall we had brides who would change from their long wedding gowns to something shorter so they could move about and dance with ease."

"That's an excellent idea," she said. "It would need to be large enough to accommodate the bride and all her bridesmaids. In fact, they actually need a place for them to get ready before the wedding. We can't have them driving out in their gowns and having them wrinkle in the car."

"That means equal space for the men," Ivy piped up. "A place where they can get ready and hang out before the ceremony. Maybe even place a TV in the room so they can watch sports before the ceremony starts."

Braden said, "Yes, we had something similar to that. We even offered plates of sandwiches and beer and champagne prior to the wedding to the bridal party. Though I didn't have anything do with the weddings held at the winery, I still remember things like that. If you'd like, I can make a list and give it to you," he offered.

"Maybe we could sit down and brainstorm together," she suggested. "I can keep a running list of the ideas and then have Ivy sketch out what I decide upon."

"You'll need to go into San Antonio to find an architect to design your building," Dad said.

"I've already given it some thought," Harper said. "Although Austin is farther away, I think I'm going to bring in Trey Watson for this project."

She glanced at her mother, seeing her surprised reaction. She turned to her father and saw disappointment in his eyes.

"Before you can shoot it down, you need to know that Trey is no longer friends with Ath. He cut all ties with him after... what Ath did to me. Trey refused to stand up with Ath at the wedding." She was able to muster a small smile. "He told me he's Team Harper all the way."

"Those two have been thick as thieves since they were small boys," Mom said. "I'm surprised to hear that Trey ended his friendship with..." Her voice trailed off.

"You can say his name, Mom. Ath. If I can, you can. Yes, I want to move past the whole sordid mess, but I also know Trey is a good man and an excellent architect."

"It's your decision," Ivy said supportively. "If you trust Trey professionally, then I'd go with him. This is going to be a huge project."

"I'm also hoping it could morph into even more down the line. I had an idea about someday putting in cabins on the grounds. Maybe eight or ten. Enough to house the bride and groom and either the bridal party or family."

"Whoa," her dad said. "Rein yourself in, Harper. I know we have a lot of land here at the winery, but I'm always thinking about expansion. We're in the midst doing more of that right now."

"Don't worry, Dad. You won't wake up and find cabins erected overnight," she teased. "Tell me more about the expansion."

Her dad and Braden took turns describing the area of the property where new vines would soon be planted.

"We're becoming known for our outstanding blends, and Braden has solid experience in that area. I may be the winemaker at the moment, but I am counting on Braden to lead this next expansion and the wines which result from it."

Annoyance filled her again. Her parents were being way too welcoming to this guy. Yes, he might come from a winemaking tradition and have experience, but her dad was singing Braden Clark's praises way too loudly for only having known him a short time. Even treating him like family. This man was *not* family.

"It seems that you are putting a lot of faith in a brand-new employee," she cautioned, glancing to Braden. "Don't get me wrong. I'm not saying you don't know your stuff, but you've barely been here a week. You shouldn't be given the keys to the kingdom."

Dad glared at Harper, but she ignored his gaze, keeping hers on Braden.

"I know it's hard to trust someone outside your family when everything's been in-house for so long," he said. "I do have the training and experience, though, to lead this project, Harper. Your dad is giving me a chance of a lifetime to prove myself. Not just to him, but to the wine industry in Texas and even vineyard owners across the U.S. The important thing is that I will not let Lost Creek

Vineyards down. More importantly, I won't let myself down."

Braden paused. "Because I know what that feels like to trust someone—love someone—and be kicked in the teeth."

"Apologize, Harper," her dad demanded. "Now. I raised you to be better than this."

Before she could speak—and it was not going to be an apology—she saw Braden raise a hand.

"Harper has every right to question me, Bill. Lost Creek Vineyards is part of her identity, even if she left it behind and has been working elsewhere. The winery is woven into the fabric of her being. It's part of who she and her family always have been. She's toiled in the fields. She's tasted the results. I understand I need to prove myself to her and everyone else at this table, not to mention the other employees. I don't want or expect an apology from her at this point."

His gaze pinned hers. "What I do need is a fair chance. The time it'll take to prove myself. I can't do that overnight."

"I get that," she said. "And you're right. You understand better than most what a family business entails. Lost Creek Vineyards *is* a part of me, something close to my heart. I just don't want Dad stepping away too quickly. His fingerprints have been on everything from the beginnings. The business that I'm starting will also be tied to the winery. I'm just looking out for the family business and its reputation."

"I can appreciate that. I will never make a major decision that I don't talk over with your parents first. I will give them my best advice and put in the time necessary to not only helm this expansion but to also put out the best crop of wine this vineyard has had since it bottled its first wines." He paused. "Good enough?"

"Good enough," she agreed. Glancing around the table, she said, "Ivy and I can do the dishes. Everyone else is off the hook."

Though they had a dishwasher, washing and drying the dishes had been a part of their childhood. Many confidences had been traded and souls bared while she and Ivy had cleaned the kitchen each night.

"Sounds good to me," Braden said, rising and excusing himself.

The minute he had left the kitchen, Mom warned, "Don't chase off a good man and hard worker simply because you're mad at the world, Harper." She picked up her wineglass and the bottle sitting on the table and exited the kitchen.

Dad gave her a look Harper knew all too well, and she lowered her eyes at his scrutiny.

"Mind your manners, young lady. I don't care how old you are."

"He's not a guest, Dad," she said sullenly. "He works for you. And you've put him in charge of a lot."

"Are you questioning my judgment?"

The question hung in the air.

"No, sir," she said, meeting his eyes. "You've worked too long and too hard to throw it all away. I'll apologize to Braden."

"You do that," he said, leaving the kitchen, wineglass in hand.

Ivy blew out a long breath when it was just the two of them. She leaned over and put an arm about Harper. "You okay?"

"Yeah. I guess."

"You were thinking about Todd, weren't you?"

Her sister knew her so well. "Yes. He should be the one who is the winery's viticulturist. The man who should be the one who steps into Dad's shoes. I can tell that Dad's ready to hand over the entire operation to Braden."

"I think he is. At least the winemaking and day-to-day business of growing grapes," Ivy agreed. "I overheard him and Mom talking about it that first night I got here. I went to the kitchen for a late night cup of tea. They were sitting at the table talking. I didn't want to come in and interrupt. But, yes, it seems Dad is tired of the physical aspects of the job. He wants to concentrate more on the actual brand and clients. He's juggled doing both for years."

"He's earned a rest," Harper said. "At least to cut down from two fulltime jobs to one. It's just hard to think of him stepping away from the actual winemaking. It was something Todd was supposed to do. Follow in Dad's footsteps. Yes, we know a lot about the vineyards and how to care for the vines and harvest them, but neither of us ever developed enough of an interest to become the viticulturist or winemaker for the label."

"We should be glad Braden is here," Ivy said quietly. "I did a thorough internet search on him after I got here. He's the real deal, Harper. We're lucky to have found him."

"You seem comfortable with him."

Her sister shrugged. "He's easy to talk to. And no, I don't have any kind of romantic interest in him. I just want Braden to do a terrific job and keep Lost Creek Vineyard's reputation strong and consistent. I want him to guide the workers and produce some wonderful wines. You and I can't take on that kind of leadership role. He's got the background, experience, and drive. He wants to succeed badly. I can't imagine how difficult the last few years have been on him."

Harper hugged Ivy. "You're right. I was being really hard on him. I like him, too. He does seem like a nice guy. Want to wash or dry?"

Ivy laughed. "If you're letting me choose, it's dry all the way."

The sisters put away the leftovers and washed and dried the dishes, talking more about the event hall, along with colors and fonts to use for Harper's new business. She turned the lights out and headed to her bedroom, where she claimed a light jacket. Sitting on their front porch in a rocker had always been her place to think, and Harper went there now.

Closing the door behind her, she took a few steps.

And realized Braden Clark had beat her to her favorite chair.

6

Harper froze, seeing Braden's eyes closed. She didn't know if he was thinking. Asleep. Or meditating. That would be such a California thing to do. She studied him a moment, thinking how handsome he was, rugged in a way Ath never had been. Feeling guilty for doing so, she turned to go. The porch beneath her creaked slightly. Immediately, Braden's eyes flew open.

"You can stay," he told her. "I'll go." He rose.

"No, you were here first. You stay."

"It's your house. I'll go."

As he passed her, she caught his elbow. "Maybe we both can stay. It's a big porch and a big sky. I think there's room for the two of us."

He nodded and turned, this time taking a seat in a different rocker. Because her favorite had now been freed up, Harper moved past him and sat to his right. The chair was still warm from his large body, feeling good to her in the cool of the night.

"I'm not certain that I should have taken the job here at Lost Creek Vineyards," Braden said, surprising her.

Her gaze met his. "Because of me?"

"Yes," he said tersely.

The word hung in the air, and she let it do so for a moment. The air between them seemed to crackle with electricity. It took everything Harper had to hang on to her senses and not plop into his lap and begin exploring his sensual lips. She had a feeling he knew what she was thinking.

Deliberately, she blinked a few times, breaking their eye contact. "You've told me this is your last chance at making your mark in the wine industry. Being around the vines is something you love. I'm sorry I was so abrupt before. I think I was spoiling for a fight—and I don't want to fight with you, Braden. I think you're a good man who's been pushed to the brink, things spinning out of control for you. I promise I'll play nice from now on. We won't even see each other that much. Yes, we'll both be working here at the winery, but we have very different jobs, and our paths shouldn't cross all that much. When they do, I will be polite."

His gaze searched hers. "What did I do wrong, Harper? I thought we were getting along fine, and then out of the blue—bam! You just turned on me for no reason."

She swallowed, locking her fingers together and squeezing tightly. "I... think I resented you for a moment."

He seemed baffled by her response. "Why? I know you worked in the vineyards when you were younger, but it's not as if it's been your burning desire to be involved in the making of the wines here."

"No. That was my brother's life goal. Todd," she said softly. "He was the one who was meant to take over for Dad someday. When I saw the camaraderie between you and my parents, how easily they've accepted you, how well you've fit in, something inside me just… snapped."

"You felt as if I were usurping your brother's place, both in work and family."

"Yes. You even sat at his spot at dinner, and it really bothered me. I know that sounds crazy, but we all grew up knowing that Todd would be the winemaker for Lost Creek Vineyards someday. Ivy has a great nose, but it's nothing like how delicate Todd's was. He—probably like you—had an affinity for wine. And a terrific palate."

"Why didn't he take over?" Braden asked. "Especially if he loved it so much."

"Todd's dead," she said flatly, obviously startling him.

They sat in silence, Harper gathering her thoughts before speaking again.

"As much as Todd loved this land and the grapes, he had an adventurous spirit. He wanted to see the world, and his best friend Ry Blackwood felt the same way."

"Blackwood BBQ," he murmured. "I've seen it on the main street in town."

"Yes, that's Ry's family's business. Todd and Ry were inseparable from the time they were in diapers. They were both so full of life. Mischievous. Fun-loving. Both were incredibly smart and super-lazy students in school. They just didn't want to put any effort into book reports or projects. They both did enough to get by and graduate, and they knew they were destined to work in their families' businesses. Neither thought college would be a good fit, so they enlisted in the military to see the world for a few years."

She hesitated, deciding she couldn't leave Braden Clark hanging.

"Todd was killed in the Middle East. Not by the enemy," she said bitterly. "By friendly fire. I was nineteen when it happened. His death gutted me, losing my brother and one of my closest friends. We all grieved in our own way. Ivy painted portrait after portrait of Todd, and then she tore up every canvas. Dad threw himself into the business, working longer hours. Mom went through the house and removed every picture of Todd, as if hiding those from sight would help. I asked her once about it, and she said it was too painful to be sitting on the sofa and look up and see Todd in a family picture during happier times. I pressed her, and she said she still has all of those pictures. I hope someday she'll be able to display them again."

She sighed. "It just hurt me deeply when I saw the easiness between you and my parents. It was almost as if Todd had been erased and you had replaced him. I realize you didn't even know he existed or what his role would have been in our family and at the winery. I simply took out my anger on you. For that, I'm sorry, Braden."

He reached and took her hand. His was large and engulfed hers, the warmth comforting her.

"I would never want to take Todd's place at the winery, much less in your parents' hearts. I can back off."

"No, you shouldn't have to do that," she told him. "I understand you're great at your job, and so you'll get along with them no matter what. I am happy that they're being open and friendly with you. It's nice to see them that way again. Mom is a nurturing soul, and Todd's death hit her hard. You yourself said your mom was not the maternal type. If it brings her a little comfort to mother you some, I can deal with that. I just wanted to tell you where I was coming from and apologize for being so rude previously."

"Thank you for filling me in," he said. "I never want to cause this family any kind of stress or add to your grief. I only want to make the best damn wines that I can from your grapes. Being here at Lost Creek is going to give me that chance."

He squeezed her hand. "Truce?"

Harper smiled. "We're not enemies. We never have been. After all, we'll be working together at the winery."

Braden released her hand, and for a moment, she felt bereft. She told herself not to latch onto this man as a substitute for Ath and all she had lost. Maybe they would become friends. Maybe that would be impossible. But she could not become involved with him romantically.

"We really won't see each other much," he said. "I rarely saw our event coordinator. I was either out in the fields or in the building where we made the wine. That's where my office was. I only went inside the event center a handful of times." He paused. "I do hope we can be friends, though. I'm in need of a friendly face. Ivy has already been great to me. I never had a sister, and I feel brotherly toward her."

He didn't say if he felt brotherly toward her or not, and Harper decided to let that sleeping dog lie. She had a feeling that Braden Clark felt the spark between them and hoped he'd be wise enough to keep his distance from her because of it.

"Thank you for sharing about your brother with me, Harper. I never would've known since there isn't a trace of Todd in the house."

"Maybe it's time I approach Mom again and see if she's willing to set out a picture or two of Todd. After all, it's been a long time since we lost him. Changing subjects, Ivy told me you may not be the viticulturist for long. That Dad is at a point in his life where he's ready to step back from the physical aspects of winemaking and solely concentrate on the business end of things. I know it's been a strain on him, doing both jobs all these years, especially after Jerry died in the car wreck, leaving Dad in charge of everything."

"Bill did tell me it's a distinct possibility. I was fortunate enough to come along when his viticulturist was retiring. That job has quite a bit to do with the wines that are finally produced. Of course, we won't harvest until the end of July and beginning of August. By then, your dad should have a better idea of his timeline, and he'll either have gained trust in me or not."

"Why don't the two of you produce this year's wines together?" she suggested. "That way, Dad would get to see you in action and keep his hand in things a final year. If he likes what he sees and how the wines turn out, he could then turn the winemaking reins over to you."

"I'm not going to worry about it now," Braden said. "My focus is on the job at hand and the grapes. I've always enjoyed being outdoors and in the fields with the vines. It just feels good to be around a vineyard again."

"I can't imagine what it must have felt like. Losing your dad. Your livelihood. The family vineyards. Your home." She hesitated and then added, "And your fiancée."

"Funny enough, Dad and I were never that close. My grandfather and I were more like father and son. Pops is the one who taught me everything I know about grapes. He said a person has an affinity for grapes deep in his bones. Either you have it, or you don't. Apparently, my own dad never did. He always was into the business end of things. I thought he was really good at it. Little did I know he was running it into the ground. It surfaced that he had not one mistress, but two. Spent lavishly on both of them. He also had a gambling habit, and a lot of the money was lost that way. That's when he got involved with loan sharks and money laundering."

Seeing the hurt on Braden's face and not wanting him to focus on the negative, Harper said, "So, you worked beside your grandfather, making wines."

His face relaxed, a gentle smile of remembrance touching it instead. "Yes, Pops and I did everything together. not just make wine. We fished. Went skiing. Watched old movies together. Pops was my best friend."

"When did you lose him?" she asked.

"About five years ago," he revealed. "It was a tough time in my life, but Pops told me I was ready to take over —and I was."

"I'm glad you had Pops."

"He taught me about so much more than wine. About people. About life." Braden grinned. "He even taught me yoga and meditation."

Harper laughed. "That sounds so California. Were you meditating when I first came out tonight?"

"I was. I try to do so both morning and evening. It really grounds me and calms my soul."

"Did you ever surf?" she asked. "The reason I'm asking is because you look like such a Californian. Tall. Blond. Athletic."

Chuckling, he said, "No. Napa is nowhere close to the ocean. I've never been on a surfboard in my life. Now, a snowboard? That's a whole different thing. I started snowboarding and skiing when Pops and I would go to Colorado every year for our annual ski trip."

"Did anyone else in the family go with you?" she asked. "Your brothers?"

"It started out as a family trip when I was really young. Mom didn't ski, though, and Dad didn't have much interest in it. Neither of them like the cold and snow. Stan and Beau went for a few years, but Stan broke his leg skiing a black diamond run. He lost interest after that. Beau was never very athletic, and when Stan said he didn't want to go, Beau opted out, too. That's when it became a trip just for Pops and me. To be honest, I liked it so much better that way. I was probably fourteen by then, and I craved the time with my grandfather."

"You haven't said much about your brothers and their role at Clark Vineyards. Have they also had trouble finding work in the wine industry? Or did they leave it altogether?'

A stillness settled over Braden, and instinctively, Harper knew she was treading on thin ice.

"Neither of them is in the wine business now," he said cryptically, and she knew to leave well enough alone.

Trying to lighten the mood, she said, "Walk me through your event facility again. I know you didn't deal with that part of the business at the winery, but you've already mentioned a few helpful things. Close your eyes," she encouraged. "Describe it to me. Walk inside and tell me what you see."

Braden did just that, his long lashes against his chiseled cheekbones. He told her about the parking and land-scaping outside the building before describing the structure himself. He took her inside and painted a very clear picture, thinking of little details along the way.

Opening his eyes, he said, "We also had outdoor weddings on the property. They took place next to one of the vineyards."

"Mom suggested we have a covered area for outdoor weddings since it gets so hot in Texas. Bench seating. Concrete floor."

He nodded. "That would work. We didn't have that.

Just rows of chairs placed on some of the flatter ground. One thing you haven't mentioned is something I recall seeing. Brides in their gowns having their portraits made. They would come out mid-week with a photographer because it wasn't as crowded then."

Excitement filled her. "I can see that now. The sun on the vines. The fields as the background for the bride. We also have a small creek running through the property. A bridge going over it. That would make for a stunning background for bridal portraits. In fact, it's on the other side of that bridge that I was thinking we could erect the event center. Maybe you and Dad could go out with me tomorrow and look it over."

"I'd like that, Harper. A lot."

She rose. "It's getting a little chilly for me. I'm going to go and make myself a cup of hot tea and work some more on the ideas to present to Trey."

Harper smiled at Braden. "Thanks for not chasing me off or letting me chase you off earlier. I'm glad we talked."

"Same," he said, smiling at her.

As she made her way to the kitchen, Harper knew she would have to tread a fine line with Braden Clark. Not only did she feel drawn to him, but he was one of the good guys. Where other women were drawn to bad boys, she had always lost her heart to the Boy Scout types. Braden had been through the wringer, though, and needed to get his professional footing and recover financially.

As for her, she had been on an emotional roller coaster, losing the life she had planned with the man she loved, as well as her best friend. Quitting her longtime job also factored into the formula, as well as her new goal of starting her own business. The time simply wasn't right to get involved with anyone, especially Braden Clark.

Yet Harper couldn't help but wonder if down the line, something might grow between them.

7

Braden finished up irrigating the last field. He had set up a rotating schedule so that all fields in the vineyard would have a complete watering once a week, staggering which sections were watered by type of grape. It was important to keep the grapes in prime growing condition during these sunny but cool days. He would alter the schedule accordingly as the weather warmed up.

He had been studying for several hours a day, trying to familiarize himself with the grapes grown at Lost Creek Vineyards, in particular, as well as others in the Hill Country and also various areas of Texas. Not only did he have to account for temperatures and rainfall, but he also had to factor in climate change, which was heating up the entire planet. Fortunately, he had Bill Hart as his chief reference, beyond the internet and books. Bill had owned and operated his vineyard for over twenty-five years and had seen it all.

His boss was a great storyteller, and Braden had listened to Bill talk for hours about starting the winery and those early days of doubt and worry. Bill had also allowed Braden to dig through the meticulous records kept at the winery, ones which noted the weather daily, with temps and rainfall count, as well as winds and the direction they came from. Braden was able to read about each acre of land and the particulars related to it.

The ledgers were even better regarding the wines fashioned each year. Bill and Jerry, his partner, had started slowly, building over the years from one wine to two to four to a dozen. The two winemakers had recorded everything they tried, listing their thoughts and predictions as they went along. Braden was able to read details regarding each individual vat, which had been given names instead of numbers, and bore a placard with their name and personalities, which he found amusing.

He would continue to study these accounts, seeing the adjustments Bill and Jerry had made to various batches of grapes over different years. One thing he was really interested in were the blends Lost Creek Vineyards had started producing close to a decade ago. They had started slowly and gradually built to a half-dozen kinds now. Braden had sampled each of them, talking over with Bill what he liked and didn't like about them. The winemaker enjoyed hearing his new employee's opinions and picked his brain about what Clark Vineyards had done.

While his winemaking skills seemed to be on par with Bill's, Braden's experience with grapes was very different in Napa than what he would face here in Texas. The unpredictable weather was a huge part of that, as well as the cooler temps. He would need to baby the grapes at Lost Creek more than he ever had at his family's winery. He told Bill he was counting on the older man's experience to guide him through this first harvest and fermentation season.

By now, Bill had let Braden know that Braden would be taking on the task of winemaker when the grapes were harvested in late July and the first couple of weeks in August. Bill was happy to work alongside Braden a final time as together, they created this year's vintages. After that, Bill would be focusing strictly on the business side of things. Cecily already handled all the bookkeeping, but Bill would concentrate more on developing long-term customers and the relationship between them and Lost Creek Vineyards. He would also work on marketing the brand. Ivy was already designing new labels for each of the kinds of wines they produced this upcoming year, freshening the look of the overall brand.

He pulled off his gloves and pocketed them, removing his phone to check the time because he never wore a watch in the fields. Actually, he'd had to pawn his watch, one which Pops had passed along to him. It had nearly killed Braden to let go of it, but at that point, it had been sell—or starve.

Maybe one day he might be able to track the watch down and buy it back.

His phone dinged with a text from Harper, sent to both Ivy and him.

> Trey should be here in a few minutes. Told him to meet us at the tasting room. See you then!

Harper had taken all her notes and sketches and driven into Austin a few days ago to meet with Trey Watson. She said their appointment had lasted three hours, as they tossed ideas back and forth, reviewing Ivy's sketches. When she came home, Braden saw the sparkle in her eyes and had to wonder if it was the project or Trey Watson who had put it there.

"Don't be an idiot," he muttered under his breath as he left the fields and headed toward the tasting room.

If Harper liked this Watson guy, more power to her. Of course, if anything came of it, she wouldn't be hanging around Lost Creek winery for long, not with Watson's office being in Austin. Maybe it would be for the best. Ever since Harper had arrived, Braden thought a lot about her. Too much, in fact. She was a beautiful woman, vibrant and enthusiastic. She had an energy about her, so much that it seemed her body hummed with it. He fought a daily battle to keep his hands off her. Not just because she was his boss' daughter, but because she was still a fragile, wounded bird. He had no business kissing her.

Or anything else.

Besides, he wasn't of her world. He had learned more about her and her career in event planning over the past week. At dinner. Sometimes as they walked around the land. Or sipping a cup of hot tea at night before turning in. Harper's company had managed all kinds of events for corporations and individuals. Even he was familiar with some of the names she casually tossed out.

It was Ivy, though, who had told Braden that Harper's fiancé was the son of Lieutenant Governor Army Armistead. Ivy said the Armisteads moved in pretty lofty political and financial circles. It would have been impossible for Harper to have planned an event without her client being personally or professionally acquainted with Atherton Armistead's family. No wonder she had left Austin.

He reached the tasting room, seeing no cars in front of it. He greeted Melanie, who worked in the tasting room along with her sister Sarah.

"Hey, Braden," Melanie said. "How are the grapes?"

"The grapes are good. Gotta go wash up."

Going to one of the two available restrooms, he thoroughly washed his hands and looked into the mirror. He was finally getting some color back in his face. He'd gone pale after not working outside for the past two years. While waiting to land a job in the wine business, Braden had worked in a furniture warehouse, taking items off the trucks and seeing they were logged in, while placing sold items on trucks that delivered the furniture to customers. The work had kept him in good physical shape, but the pay had been lousy. Most of it was eaten up by the rent he paid and the food he ate, with nothing left over for insurance or other basic needs.

Returning to the tasting room, he found both Ivy and Harper had arrived.

"Ladies," he said, touching his fingers to his ball cap. "Ready for Mr. Watson's visit?"

Ivy held up her sketchpad. "Ready to draw at a moment's notice," she quipped.

He liked Ivy. Enjoyed being around her and teasing her. She truly was just like a little sister to him. Braden had even gone out driving with her so she could show him some of the Hill Country. They had stopped several times for her to sketch something which caught her eye.

And yet nothing flared between them.

Because Ivy wasn't Harper.

Harper held up her phone. "Fully charged. Ready for me to take notes."

He'd gotten used to Harper pulling out her cell in the middle of a conversation and tapping a note to herself. Sometimes, when she was really excited, she simply used the speaker and recorded her notes because, as she said, her fingers simply wouldn't type as fast as her mouth was moving.

He wished his mouth could move on hers.

Blinking, Braden looked as the door opened. In walked a guy a couple of inches over six feet, with a solid build and handsome features. As he drew near, Braden could see that the man's warm brown eyes were the same shade as his hair. He smiled a smile that would have women take notice of him.

Harper wrapped her arms around him. In that

moment, the first pangs of jealousy hit Braden hard, a feeling he'd never experienced before.

And had no right to be feeling.

"I'm so glad you could come, Trey," Harper said, her smile wide. Pulling away, she indicated her companions. "You may remember my sister Ivy."

Trey shook Ivy's hand. "You were at the engagement party."

"Oh, the one where Bethany Armistead ran over everyone?" Ivy said sweetly.

Trey laughed. "Oh, I like this one, Harper."

Braden plastered a smile on his face as Harper said, "And this is Braden Clark, our viticulturist. With the next harvest, he'll be moving up to enologist. Winemaker," she added as Trey looked blankly at her.

"Ah, the magic-maker," the architect said, offering Braden his hand.

"Braden used to work in his family's vineyards in California," Harper continued. "They had an event facility on the property, so I've picked his brain on the topic. He and Ivy are going to join us if you don't mind."

"The more, the merrier," Trey said agreeably.

They walked about the vineyards a bit, with Harper pointing out things to Trey, who said he wanted to get a feel for the property before committing to a design.

"That's why I had to come see Lost Creek Winery in person. Anytime I can go on-site and view where my work will be built, it's a plus."

They came to the area where the bridge was and crossed it.

"This side is where I'd like the event center to be constructed," Harper shared. "Dad, Braden, and I walked the entire property, and this seems the most likely place. It's large enough and also far enough from the grapes currently being grown."

Trey took out his phone and snapped several pictures from different angles. Then he peppered not only Harper but Ivy and Braden with questions. Since they were all so familiar with Harper's project, the next hour passed comfortably as they talked about what should go into the center and what it should look like on the outside.

"I think I have everything I need. Do you have an office we can go to? I want to draw a few things for you. Talk about building materials before I head back to Austin."

"The conference room in my parents' office would be ideal," Harper volunteered. "I don't think there are any client meetings on the books today. Let's go there."

They arrived, with the Harts welcoming Trey Watson, whom they obviously had met on previous occasions.

"If you aren't too busy, Mom and Dad, come to the conference room for us to talk about Trey's ideas and how he'll marry them to the ones we've shared with him."

Both Harts accompanied them, with Bill grabbing cans of his beloved Dr. Pepper for all.

Trey had gone to his truck and collected his briefcase before they came to the conference room. He now pulled out sketches Ivy had made, along with a book of CAD ones he himself had done. As he talked to the group, his pencil flew across a blank page, and a building began to appear.

"This is what I'm thinking about, Harper," the architect said. "I want to incorporate the landscape around the building. That huge oak on the left is something that has to remain. It's too beautiful to cut down."

Trey spoke of the materials he would like to see used in construction, especially the Texas limestone which was found in the area.

They passed around his sketch as Trey said, "I will definitely draw up something more formal, but I wanted to give you an idea of what the outside could look like."

He took up his pencil again, whipping out several different versions of floor plans. The group examined those, as well, making suggestions, with Trey making adjustments to his sketches.

Finally, the architect said, "I think I have everything I need. I'm seeing something really spectacular in my head. I can't wait to commit it to paper. I'll work up a formal presentation for you, Harper. Can you—or anyone else— think of something we're missing?"

"I think we've covered everything, Trey," Harper said. "I knew you were the right man for this job." She paused. "Once you've committed the final plans to paper and I've signed off on them, what's our next step?"

"I'll give you an estimate of what the project will cost. You'll need to work with your bank regarding financing. Then it's all about hiring a construction manager and crew," Trey responded. "That'll be a little tricky. The ones I use are in the Austin area. That's where all my designs are brought to fruition. I've never had a client two hours out. Let me make some calls. Get a feel for who in this area might be able to tackle such a project. I'll get back to you."

"Sounds like a plan," Ivy said. "I'm so glad you'll be working with Harper, seeing her new company come to life."

Trey frowned. "I thought this was for your family, Harper."

"Actually, I'll be renting the land from my parents," she revealed. "I'll be the coordinator for all the events which take place. Weddings with Hart will have an office on the property, but it's a totally separate business. While you're here, though, I want to hit you up with more."

They went to the tasting room, where Harper gave Trey an overview of how she would like that space reconfigured.

"Where will the new tasting room go?" the architect asked.

"Let's go look at that," Ivy said, leading the six of them outside.

Again, they walked around, discussing ideas for the tasting room and adjoining gift shop. Trey made several notes, and they discussed the types of building material and landscaping.

"This project will be on Mom and Dad's dime," Harper said. "But they've given Ivy and me the authority to move ahead as we see fit."

"We'll handle the financing for the project," Bill said. "Cecily's already run the numbers and been in touch with our banker. Once we get a better idea from you, we'll meet with him and take out the loan."

Trey ran a hand through his thick hair. "Okay. I'll also get busy on the plans for the tasting room. Do you want both projects occurring simultaneously, or does one take priority over the other?"

"It might be better to see what size construction crew you can get before you make that decision," Braden noted.

"Good idea," Trey seconded. "I guess I'll head back to Austin now."

He hugged both Harper and Ivy goodbye, and Braden said, "I'll walk you back to your truck."

The two men headed toward where Trey had parked, while Harper and Ivy remained where they were, still enthusiastically talking over ideas with their parents.

"Are you interested in Harper?" Braden asked bluntly.

Trey chuckled. "As a client, absolutely. As relationship material, not at all. She was my... my friend's fiancée. I think of Harper as a good friend." He paused. "Why? What is she to you?"

"A friend. One I don't want to see get hurt," he said firmly.

"Hey, I would never hurt Harper. I am not Atherton Armistead," Trey said vehemently. "Harper is special. Ath didn't know what he had in her. Believe me, Braden, I want Harper protected. I'm glad she got out of Austin. It would've been too painful for her to continually run into the happily married couple. Already, they're all over Austin, popping up at events left and right."

"Married?" Braden asked. "What are you talking about?"

Trey looked at him funny. "Harper didn't tell you?"

"Tell me what?" he demanded.

Sighing, Trey said, "He went through with the wedding. Ath just traded out one bride for another."

Braden halted. "He *what?*"

Grimly, Trey said, "You heard me. Ath never canceled the wedding. He had me to tell Harper things were off between them, but Ath married Cynthia that next day in his parents' church. I'm sure the place was filled to the rafters."

He felt as if Trey had punched him hard in the gut. If he felt so blindsided, how had Harper managed to get through it?

"I've never wanted to kill someone, but if I ever meet Ath Armistead, he better watch out," Braden growled.

"I feel the same," Trey said. "I know the time will come when I run into him and Cynthia somewhere. I'll be civil for the sake of my parents. My dad and Army started a law firm together. Dad still works there with Ath, but he doesn't have anything to do with him."

They reached Trey's truck, and the architect thrust out his hand. Braden took it, and they shook.

"Don't mention any of this to Harper," Trey said. "If she wants you to know it, she'll tell it to you in her own time. Just keep an eye out for her."

"I will," Braden promised, watching Trey get into his truck and drive away.

More than anything, he admired how resilient Harper

was. Braden didn't know anyone—man or woman—who could have endured the humiliation Harper had and then bounce back so quickly. She was forging a new life for herself. Starting up her new business. He promised himself not to be a distraction to her. To protect her.

And if he ever did meet Atherton Armistead?

Braden wasn't certain what he might do.

8

Harper combed her hair and applied a fresh coat of lipstick, pleased with her appearance. She and Ivy were going to have an early dinner tonight with her sorority sister Finley Farrow and Finley's roommate Emerson Frost. The two teachers rented a small house a few blocks off the town square. While she had talked to Finley a few times on the phone since she had returned to Lost Creek, this would be the first time they had seen one another in person since her bachelorette party.

She brushed aside the feelings that cropped up, thinking about the fun they'd had that night, the last time she had enjoyed being with Cynthia before learning of her best friend's betrayal. She realized, though, that she didn't have quite the same level of bitterness when thinking about Cynthia and Ath. Yes, it still hurt, but she was so involved in the new business she was creating. This would never have happened if Ath hadn't ended things and freed her to be the new Harper Hart she was becoming.

Trey had completed his plans for both the event center and new tasting room and insisted he return to the winery so that he might share the designs with her, Ivy, and her parents for final approval. They had been thoroughly impressed with his blueprints and mockups for each building, both unique and drawing from the Texas Hill Country for inspiration.

He had made the tasting room much larger, with different pockets. There was a walk-up bar with stools where tastings could take place, but he had incorporated a few other areas to be used for that purpose. One section had two long, rectangular tables which seated up to eight each, while another area held four tabletops of two each for tastings. Trey had places designated for wine storage, along with an area for a large refrigerator to store both wines and the cheese plates Harper and Ivy thought would become popular at tastings. Trey had left plenty of room for stemware and plates to be stored and even created a small kitchenette to wash out the glasses and dishes used in tastings.

Attached to the tasting room—but having its own separate entrance as well—was the gift shop. Cleverly, the restrooms were located at the rear of the gift shop. Anyone wishing to use them would have to walk through and see all the Lost Creek Vineyards merchandise available.

She had found a local vendor to take on personalizing and stocking their clothing and hats, and Ivy had tweaked the current Lost Creek Vineyards' logo, making it cleaner and slightly brighter. Her parents had loved the idea of employees wearing the vineyard's logos on both hats and T-shirts. Her dad had even suggested moving a step up beyond T-shirts and sweatshirts and carrying a golf shirt in stock. He said he would wear that every day himself.

For the merchandise involving items such as wine openers and cork stops, they would use a San Antonio firm. She and Ivy had made the trip to San Antonio and seen the goods in person, feeling comfortable both with the quality and price. A contract had been executed, and the first of those items bearing the Lost Creek Vineyards' logo would soon arrive at the winery. Ivy had said she would make room to display samples of various at the tasting bar and could ring up any sales.

It had been Ivy who came up with the idea of including a wineglass with the winery's logo with each paid tasting. They would move up the price of a tasting by a dollar to help cover their costs, but Ivy had said it would be unique for customers to leave a tasting with a wineglass advertising Lost Creek Vineyards. She also suggested for every bottle of wine they sold on-site, they should include a free wineglass, as well. Ivy believed it would encourage more sales, and their parents had been onboard with the idea. The first wineglasses should arrive early next week.

Harper had also found a vendor whom she would work with on custom labels for the bride and groom. Things were rolling along smoothly. She had been to the bank and taken out a small business loan to complete the event center. She had yet to decide upon a rental agreement with her parents, but she wasn't worried about that.

Ground had been broken two days ago, in the morning on the event facility and in the afternoon on the tasting room and gift shop. The construction crew would move back and forth between the two projects, pouring the foundation of both at the same time and installing electrical and plumbing and erecting walls simultaneously. The construction manager thought it would be a more efficient use of his crew's time and their resources to do so, and Harper had agreed with him.

She couldn't be prouder of the progress being made in such a short amount of time and couldn't wait to share all her news with Finley and Emerson. She stopped by the kitchen to remind Braden that she and Ivy would not be home for dinner this evening and caught him with his back to her, stirring something at the stove. She couldn't help but admire the worn, tight jeans molded to his lower body and felt guilty for ogling him.

"Hey," she said brightly, causing him to turn, wooden spoon in hand. "Remember that Ivy and I are going to be gone tonight. We're having dinner with my friend Finley Farrow and her roommate Emerson Frost."

Braden's smiled. "I've met the delightful Miss Frost. Stopped in at The Bake House last weekend for something to satisfy my sweet tooth, and she talked me into a couple dozen boxes of cookies."

"You brought back cookies and held out on me?" she teased.

"I had planned to serve some for dinner, but after the

vineyard workers got their hands on them, nothing was left. Not even crumbs in the boxes."

She laughed. "I've had Emerson's cookies before, as well as a few other sweet treats. She knows her stuff. Well, I guess I'll see you tomorrow."

"Goodnight, Harper," Braden said. "Have a nice night with your friends. You deserve a little time off after working as hard as you have."

"Thanks," she said, retrieving her purse and heading to her SUV.

Ath had never acknowledged her job and the effort she put into it. Others sang her praises, remarking on how unique the events she created were and how smoothly they unfolded. Ath seemed to take all that for granted. She had finally figured out it was a rich-people thing. They told others what they wanted done, and then they expected things to magically unfold exactly as they'd asked, not ever thinking about all the work that went into pulling that off. Rich people never seemed to think of the time and effort that went into an event. They just threw the cash at you and expected perfect results.

On the other hand, Harper had always complimented Ath on his work ethic. She had even gone and sat in a few times during one of his trials, admiring his commanding presence in the courtroom and how he could make language sing. He exuded confidence, and his juries were drawn to it and his good looks.

Harper shook her head, trying to clear it as she drove to the tasting room, texting Ivy she was on her way. By the time she reached it, her sister was waiting outside, a bottle of wine in hand, and she quickly jumped into the car.

"I like how the new tasting room will have a large porch," Ivy commented, buckling her seatbelt. "I would have preferred waiting for you sitting in a chair with a converted wine barrel holding flowers next to me. Trey really has done a nice job of including all the little details in his designs for us."

"Not only that, but he won't accept a dime from me," she shared.

"What? You're kidding!"

"Nope. He said it's all part of the service to Team Harper. That's not only for the event center, but it's for the tasting room and gift shop, as well. Dad about had a fit when he learned about it, wanting to pay Trey for his time. Dad even pulled Trey aside, and they had a talk over a few beers. In the end, though, they came out smiling, shaking hands, and Dad told me he would not be paying for the plans Trey drew up."

"You should have thought about marrying Trey instead of Ath," Ivy joked. "He really is a nice guy."

"I always knew he was, but Trey's the kind who prefers working in the background and letting others take the credit. Of the two, Ath obviously had the stronger personality and sought the limelight more than Trey. I liked Trey —but I've grown to truly appreciate him. And his friendship."

"Do you think something could be there between the two of you?" her sister asked.

Harper laughed aloud. "Not at all. Trey is more like a

brother and good friend than a romantic prospect. Besides, it wouldn't be smart to become involved with him. His firm is in Austin, as are his clients. My heart and soul are being poured into my business here. I don't need any distractions or romantic entanglements."

Though her mind went straight to Braden Clark as she uttered those last words.

"I know Finley some, especially after your crazy bachelorette party. Can you tell me a little bit about Emerson?" Ivy asked.

"I've only run into her a few times over the years. She was a scholarship student at UT, and that's why she didn't rush a sorority. Their initiation and membership fees would've been out of her league. She roomed with Finley their freshman year, and they both stayed friends, being elementary ed majors and having classes together. I've found Emerson to be pretty reserved."

They approached the town, and Harper adjusted her speed accordingly, adding, "Emerson worked at a bakery in college. Finley told me that now Emerson is working Saturdays during the school year and summers at The Bake House."

"For Ethel Frederick?" Ivy asked. "She must be a hundred years old by now because she was ancient when we were kids. Or at least she seemed really old to me."

"People like Ethel live forever. I can't imagine what'll happen to The Bake House when she's gone."

As they passed the local cheese shop, Harper said, "I've made an appointment for us to talk with the owner at The Cheeses Connoisseur on Monday morning. I checked the schedule and made sure you were off from work. I want us to talk to them about adding to some of the catering at the wedding receptions held, but I want your input on the small cheese plates we want to offer during tastings. Also, if they would consider partnering with us to provide cheeses for those picnic baskets I've mentioned."

"I'd be happy to talk over things with them," Ivy said.

"I definitely need you there because you know more about wines than I do and what cheeses pair well with them. We're supposed to meet them at nine o'clock. That way, you'll still have the bulk of the day off for your painting."

"Fine with me," her sister said brightly, clearly liking the idea.

After a few more turns, they reached the house her friend was renting. Harper cut the engine, and they got out of the SUV. It surprised her when one of the Lost Creek Vineyards trucks pulled in behind. Braden got out of it. He was carrying a rectangular pan covered with foil.

"What are you doing here?" she asked, shocked to see him here.

"You had mentioned your friend was making enchiladas the other day. I didn't want you to show up empty-handed, so I put together a seven-layer dip. I forgot to give it to you before you left and thought I'd bring it over instead of making you come back for it."

He handed her the dish. "Let me grab the chips to go with it."

Harper was stunned. In all the time she had been with Ath—or any other man—no one had ever been so thoughtful. Her throat swelled with emotion, one she wasn't ready to try and pin down.

Braden returned, passing the bag of chips to Ivy, who said, "This is great. I could make a meal off this dip alone."

Harper's gaze met his. "This is a lovely gesture. Thank you very much."

He shrugged, something she had picked up on that he did when he wasn't sure what to say.

"I know Finley and Emerson will appreciate this," she continued. "If you don't mind, I'll leave any leftovers with them and pick up the pan later."

He smiled. "Fine by me. I've got to get back to cooking."

They said goodbye to him and headed to the front door. Harper sensed that Ivy wanted to say something but held her tongue.

Finley opened it and smiled. "Ah, you come bearing gifts. And here I thought you'd only bring wine."

"No. It's seven-layer dip," she revealed.

As her friend accepted the dip and ushered them in, Harper said, "Why did I even bother to make enchiladas? We could have simply nibbled on this all night. Come on into the kitchen. You can set your purses and jackets on that chair."

They did so and followed Finley into the kitchen, where Emerson was pulling out a baking dish from the oven.

"Hi. Right on time," she said.

"Emerson, I don't believe you've met my sister. This is Ivy."

"I hear you're creating a sensation at The Bake House," Ivy said.

Emerson blushed. "I enjoy baking. More than I do teaching if I'm being honest." She set the enchilada pan on a trivet which sat on the kitchen table. "Hope you both would like a glass of sangria. My secret recipe. Even Finley has never been able to get it out of me."

Finley laughed. "She does allow me to slice up the lemons and oranges to float in it. Let me grab the pitcher from the fridge. We can save the wine for after dinner."

While Finley poured large glasses of sangria for them, Emerson removed the foil from the enchiladas. Harper sighed, seeing the were sour cream chicken, her favorite. Ivy took the foil from the dip and located a spoon for it. Soon, they were seated at the table, their plates full.

Finley raised her glass and said, "To Harper, the strongest woman I know. You should be a role model for every female on the planet."

The four women clinked their glasses together and dug into their food.

"Tell us more about this business you're starting," Finley encouraged.

Harper shared her ideas for weddings at the winery, while Ivy told them more about the expanded tasting room and gift shop. Then Harper elaborated on the patio and picnic grounds that would also be put in, giving people a place to relax.

"I see Lost Creek Winery as a destination place on the weekends," she shared. "I want to hire some local talent and have bands play every Saturday night. I'm also going to talk to a few people in town about catering the receptions, chiefly Blackwood BBQ. They're the first restaurant which comes to mind when you think of Lost Creek."

"I agree," Finley said. "If you want a true Hill Country wedding, the reception needs to be plates of barbecue with all the fixin's."

"That leads me to cakes," she said, turning her attention to Emerson, who had been quiet for most of the meal. "I've devoured your cupcakes before, and they were heavenly. So moist and rich. I was hoping you might agree to provide wedding cakes to my clients."

"Me?" Emerson said, looking startled. "I have made a few wedding cakes while I've been at The Bake House. Actually, I really had fun designing them and playing with different kinds of frostings." She paused. "It would really depend upon my schedule, Harper. I'm already working a full shift on Saturdays for Ethel. And I've got school during the week."

"I know how expensive a good wedding cake is, Emerson," she said. "I don't know what you're earning for those Saturday shifts, but you could charge a healthy amount for both a wedding and a groom's cake. It would more than cover your time and the baking supplies used. Maybe you could even give up working at The Bake House to be Weddings with Hart's exclusive cake vendor. Would you consider it? Obviously, I don't need an answer anytime soon. It'll be several months before the event center is ready to host weddings and I start bookings."

Emerson nodded thoughtfully. "I'll keep it in mind, Harper. Your offer is very tempting. Even if I only baked one cake a week, I would definitely earn more than I bring in with my part-time job now. Would you have a kitchen on-site, or would I need to do my baking here? If I did that, I'd need help transporting the cakes. They sure won't fit into my Mini-Cooper."

"My SUV would be large enough to move a cake of several tiers. I know the cakes would have to be protected, though. You'll know about the kind of boxing to preserve its integrity. Just think on things."

"I will," Emerson said, and Harper believed she would sign the baker as her cake vendor. She now turned to Finley. "I want to hit you up about hiring on as the center's photographer."

"Really?" Finley asked. "Remember, I'm not a professional, Harper. I just do some photography on the side."

"I've seen your work," she said. "You are talented, my friend. You have a great eye and capture unique angles and moments. Mom said you're doing senior portraits for students?"

"Yes. I take them out different places. To the lake. The cliffs. The hills. Lost Creek Rock. Different packages allow for a certain number changes of clothing. Some want to wear their cap and gown. Others like Sunday church clothes. Most of them want to be shot in their uniforms. Band. Football. Drill team. I've had a lot of fun doing them, and my side business is growing."

"See," she said. "You *do* have a business. That's being a professional. What if we could beef it up? Have you shoot bridal portraits at the winery, as well as weddings."

Finley frowned. "I'm not sure about that. Most brides

do those during the week. I couldn't take off school for that. My students need me."

"Well, I also need you. Again, it's just food for thought. Finish out the school year. Take all those senior portraits this summer. Then we can talk."

Ivy drained her sangria glass. "We've finished the sangria. Should I open the wine so we can get down to gossip?"

Everyone laughed, and Emerson said, "Let's clear the table. Bring the wine and the rest of this dip into the living room. We can catch both of you up on what's been happening lately in Lost Creek."

Over the next two hours, Harper truly relaxed. She enjoyed being with her longtime friend and believed she was well on her way to making a new one in Emerson. Starting her own business was turning into a satisfying part of her life.

Not marrying Atherton Armistead was turning out to be the best thing that had happened to Harper.

9

Braden knew payday was today. It would be the second check he'd cleared since coming to work at Lost Creek Vineyards.

Which meant it was time for him to move out.

Cecily had assured him he could stay as long as he wished in order to get back on his feet, but he needed space.

In other words, he needed to be away from Harper. And thoughts about kissing her.

Every day, his attraction to her grew. Yes, it was definitely physically in nature, but that was only a part of it. Harper was bright and personable and easy to be around. They hung out after dinner several times a week, sometimes talking about business, but often about all kinds of topics. She was definitely opinionated when it came to politics and sports. Above all, no one trash-talked her beloved Dallas Cowboys.

The longer he stayed, the harder it would be to leave. If he moved into town, which wasn't but ten minutes away, he wouldn't see her nearly as much as he did now. It would kill him—but it would be a good thing. Maybe he might finally get over this idiotic crush he had on her. The one thing Braden knew was that he could never act on his feelings toward her. She'd made it clear she wasn't interested in anything romantic, even declaring she never wanted to get married. He knew that was just her wounded pride talking and that someday, Harper would be ready to make that commitment again to some guy.

Just not him.

He needed to keep from mixing business with pleasure. He was at Lost Creek Winery to work. To put out the best damned wines he could. To keep the Texas flavors and yet possibly bring a bit of California spin to the blends. Concentrating on wine and work was all he should be thinking about. Besides, if he moved into town, he might make a few friends. That would help keep his free time occupied. He did like the workers at the winery, but he'd learned in the past that work friendships needed to stay at work. For his own mental well-being, he need friends outside of work. To have a drink. To watch a game. A separation from the long hours he put in at work needed to occur in order for him to be in the right frame of mind to create wines.

Before heading to the house, he went to the office in order to pick up his paycheck from Cecily. He'd set up an account at Lost Creek Bank after he'd received his first one and needed to sign a paper she had that would allow automatic deposits into his account. That required a permanent address, though, and it was time he got one beyond the winery, even if it was a rented apartment.

As he entered the building Cecily caught sight of him and waved him her way. Braden poked his head in her doorway.

"I've come to collect my paycheck."

"Got it right here," she said, opening a drawer and removing an envelope.

He accepted it. "Thank you. I'd also like to fill out that form I need in order to have my pay placed into my account at the bank. That requires an address from me." He hesitated. "It's time I move out, Cecily."

She frowned. "You've only had a month's worth of pay, Braden. You don't want to jump the gun too soon and stretch yourself too thin."

"I know. I do want to look at a few places in town tomorrow, though. I'm hoping to find something furnished. Else it'll mean buying a sleeping bag at Walmart and sitting in a lawn chair for a while," he joked.

"I respect that you crave your independence, Braden, but you're not an inconvenience to us," she emphasized.

"I know. You've been so gracious to me. I appreciate everything you and Bill have done."

"Well, Bill thinks you walk on water. He's always trusted his gut, and he likes you as a person and respects you as a winemaker."

"Even though I haven't made any wines yet?" Braden asked, grinning.

"You know what I mean. He's seen you in the fields.

Asked you a thousand questions. The two of you have sampled wines from years past and discussed them to death. Bill knows you're a professional, through and through. When it comes time for the two of you to make this year's wines, he'll place his complete trust in your judgment."

"That's nice to know. I respect Bill. He's knowledgeable. Flexible. Curious. Those are all great traits for an enologist to possess. Besides, Bill's just a nice guy. A good boss and family man. I'm enjoying working for him."

Cecily smiled. "He's definitely a wonderful guy. Unless he's snoring. I'm ready to make an appointment for him with his doctor and see about getting him a CPAP. It's either that or I start sleeping on the couch."

"See? You need my bedroom as a back-up. If you don't mind, I'll borrow one of the trucks tomorrow to drive into town and check out a few places."

"Fine with me. It's a slow time of year for the grapes."

"I'll see you at dinner."

Braden returned to the house, where he mixed up a meatloaf and placed it in the oven. He scrubbed potatoes, piercing and wrapping them in foil, and put them in next to the meatloaf. The corn could be boiled in another half-hour.

Harper came into the kitchen. "Hey." She began rooting around in the fridge.

"Looking for something?" he asked, knowing she liked to nibble.

"A snack. I'm starved. I didn't have time for lunch

today. I snagged Ivy, and we went into town to look for somewhere to live."

He frowned. "I thought you were happy here."

"Braden," she said, looking and sounding exactly like her mother in that moment. "I haven't lived at home since I was eighteen. I *need* to get a place of my own. Actually, with Ivy. She feels the same way. We've never been wild girls, but we don't want to be living with parents at our age."

"You'll both have to commute back to the winery each day," he pointed out.

She snorted. "So? A ten-minute commute is nothing. Besides, I want to be in town. I want to start renewing old acquaintances. Become a part of things. Join the Chamber of Commerce. See Finley—and Emerson—more."

"Did you find a place?"

"We did. We first looked at two different apartment complexes. Neither came furnished, which would be a problem. I didn't have anything in Austin. Cynthia... she was the one with the good taste and made our apartment a showplace. Ivy's apartment in Houston was furnished, so she has nothing, same as me. In fact, she's going down next weekend to visit with a couple of friends and pack up the rest of what she left there since her lease is about to run out. Clothes. Shoes."

She removed a can of sparkling water and a block of cheese. Opening the can, she took a deep swig as she got out a cutting board and sliced some of the cheese, fetching crackers and some grapes to make up her snack.

"Since the apartments didn't work out, I thought about

maybe renting a house. Lots of times, they come furnished. Then out of the blue, Finley texted me. Their neighbor, who lives two doors down, just accepted a job offer in Ft. Worth earlier this week. He's got to report Monday morning, and so they packed the car last night and left first thing this morning. Since Finley knew I wanted to get a place, she gave me the heads-up, along with the landlord's cell number."

Harper paused to take a couple of bites. "Anyway, I texted him, and he was free to meet us since it was lunchtime. Needless to say, we loved the place and told him we'd like to sign a six-month lease. We're going back over to the house tomorrow morning to do so. We'll get the keys and be good to go."

She gobbled another cheese cracker. "I am going to miss your cooking, though. Probably most of my meals will be snacking like this. Or cereal. I absolutely adore cereal."

"Which apartments did you look at?" he asked.

She told him. He'd intended to look at both tomorrow, but since neither came furnished, he wasn't sure what he would do. Lost Creek was a small town. Maybe he could find a furnished room to rent in someone's house.

"You look disappointed, Braden. What's up?"

"I was hoping to get out of your parents' hair and had planned to look at those apartments. I don't have much of a nest egg built up yet, though. Maybe I'll stay here another month or look to find a room to rent."

"You need your space. I get that. It must be hard living with your boss." She paused, and he could see the wheels in her head turning. "Why don't you move in with us? The house has three bedrooms. It's totally furnished, including linens and dishes. We could split the rent three ways instead of two, which would be really nice. If you continued to cook, Ivy and I would take on the house-cleaning. What do you say?"

He should say a flat no. Not even consider her offer. The biggest reason he wanted to move out was to get away from her. Being in the bedroom next door to her had been torture.

Yet Braden heard himself saying, "I think I'd like that."

"Like what?" asked Ivy, coming into the kitchen and stealing a piece of cheese off her sister's plate. She placed it on a cracker and popped it into her mouth.

"Braden is going to join us in the house," Harper told her sister.

"That's terrific!" Ivy exclaimed. "And cheaper for all of us."

"He'll cook, and we'll clean," Harper continued.

"That's the perfect arrangement," Ivy declared.

"Wait. I haven't agreed to it. It sounds good."

The sisters looked at one another, a conspiratorial look that only siblings used.

"We can draw for straws for the primary bedroom," Ivy said. "It comes en suite. The other two can share the other bathroom in the hall."

"You are too messy to share with anyone," Harper said. "I know that better since we shared for years. In fact, Ath was a terrible mess in the bathroom. I almost didn't marry him because he could be so careless and sloppy."

Harper paused—and then both sisters burst out in laughter.

"Oh, you're really getting over him, Harper," Ivy declared. "I can see it. I can hear it."

Harper grinned shamelessly. "And Cynthia is the queen of neat. I hope she's tearing her hair out—and his—over their chaotic bathroom."

"Maybe she'll divorce him over it," Ivy said, holding her hands up, as if she framed something. "I can see the headlines now. 'Realtor to the Rich divorces Hot Mess of a Lawyer over bathroom disorder. Irreconcilable differences stated as cause for divorce.'"

That got Harper to belly-laughing, with Ivy joining in. Braden watched them, amazed, thinking them so different and yet joined together in sibling love—and their mutual loathing for Atherton Armistead.

"Okay, I'm in," he said. "But you've got to calm down."

His words only caused them to dissolve into giggles. Harper stopped hers by stuffing grapes into her mouth. Ivy followed suit, and the kitchen fell quiet. He watched them chew their grapes, swallowing, finally composed again.

"The house has a den," Harper told him. "Eat-in kitchen. No dining room. Well, it did, but it's used as an office. No dining table or chairs in it."

"And a decent backyard," Ivy mentioned. "We could get a grill. Have some friends over. Convince Emerson to bring cupcakes or baklava or some other kind of pastry. The good thing is that the bills are included in the rent.

Water. Electricity. And Mr. Keller said his teenaged son comes over to mow and edge."

"Ready to draw?" Harper asked. "You *are* in, aren't you, Braden?"

He was insane to think this was a good idea, but he only said, "I'm in."

"We'll see how it's going after six months," Ivy said. "If anyone wants to bail, you can. No questions asked. If we all stay, maybe we draw again for the primary."

"Good idea," Harper said, removing three toothpicks from the holder on the Lazy Susan, which sat in the middle of the table.

Braden watched her break one of the toothpicks so that it was shorter than the other two.

"Short straw gets the primary," she said, wrapping her fingers around the three toothpicks.

"Do you know which one it is?" Ivy demanded.

Harper grinned. "I'll never tell." She held her fist up to her sister. "Draw."

Ivy did so, removing an intact toothpick. "Darn it."

Harper swung her hand to Braden. He debated a moment and then pulled out a toothpick. The broken one.

"Winner, winner, chicken dinner," Harper said. "It makes sense for Braden to have his own bathroom. If he had to share with you, he'd break the lease and never look back."

"I am not *that* bad," Ivy protested. "Well, maybe a little bit bad."

Harper turned to him, offering her hand to shake. Braden took it, feeling a rush of desire pour through him.

His gut told him he was making the biggest mistake of his life.

And yet he felt powerless to change his mind.

"Congrats, Mr. Clark," Harper said. "You've got yourself two roommates. Let's just hope we all get along together."

"We will," Ivy assured them. "We already do now." She chuckled. "Mom is going to be so jealous that we're stealing her cook. She'll probably invite herself over once a week, saying she wants to see us, but really wanting to eat Braden's food."

Harper threw away the toothpicks and finished the last of her snack, putting away the grapes and placing her plate in the sink. His eyes followed her orderly movements, and Braden couldn't believe he had allowed her to talk him into living with her.

It was going to be a long six months.

10

_____

A week had passed, and Braden had fallen into a routine with his housemates. He continued to cook dinner with the occasional help from Ivy, who said she enjoyed cooking but never had really had time for it when she worked at the art gallery.

Ivy had driven to Houston yesterday afternoon, though, leaving Braden and Harper in the house alone last night. Fortunately, Harper had made plans with Finley and Emerson and had not come in until almost eleven o'clock. He had been in bed but had heard her arrive.

He had decided he would kiss her. Once. Get it out of his system. One kiss—and then he would move on. When and where that kiss might occur had yet to be determined.

This morning, he sat at the breakfast table, sipping his coffee, not quite sure what he was going to do with himself on this Saturday. Bill had expressly told Braden not to come to the winery today because of the long hours he'd already put in this week. He was thinking about walking into town and checking out the shops on the square. Maybe grab lunch at Lone Star Diner or stop at Hill Country Hangout, the sports bar, and eat while he caught a ball game on TV.

Harper appeared, already dressed, even though it was only six-thirty.

"Ah, you're up. You have any plans today, Braden?"

"Not really," he said casually, wondering why she was asking.

"Would you like to go to Austin with me?"

Maybe that kiss might happen today.

"Sure," he said. "What's in Austin?"

She placed a pod in the coffeemaker and slipped a mug beneath it, pushing the brew button. "I want to collect the rest of my things from the storage unit I rented. It's just a couple of boxes of odds and ends I've saved over the years and my work clothes."

"Will it all fit into your SUV, or should we take the truck?"

Bill had given him use of one of the vineyard's trucks, which Braden appreciated. It would be a long time before he would be able to put the money together to make a monthly car payment.

She wrinkled her nose. "Definitely not the truck. Everything should fit. I rented the smallest indoor storage space they had, and it didn't fill up even a third of it. I guess I travel light."

"Then why do you need me if there's nothing heavy to lift?"

"I'm not asking you to go for brawn, Braden," she told him. "I'm asking for your company."

"Oh. Okay." He took a sip of his coffee because he didn't know what else to say.

"I thought I would show you Austin. *My* Austin. You said you flew in to it, but I doubt you were there long enough to see very much."

"No, I got up the next morning and came straight to Lost Creek."

"Then you're going to get an Austin education from someone who lived there for a decade. When can you be ready to leave?"

"As soon as I finish this cup of coffee and shower," he replied.

Braden took his mug with him to his bedroom and jumped into the shower. He shaved and dressed in a T-shirt and jeans, returning himself and the empty coffee mug to the kitchen twenty minutes later. Harper still sat at the kitchen table, scrolling through her phone. She glanced up as he entered.

"You are fast. Let me go brush my teeth and get rid of that coffee taste. Then we can be off."

Ten minutes later, they were leaving Lost Creek as it came to life on a Saturday morning. He had suggested they swing by The Bake House to pick up something for the road, but she said she wanted to leave plenty of room for Mexican food and ice cream when they reached their destination, telling him about the famous Amy's Ice Cream, telling him about some of her favorite flavors.

They didn't talk much for the first half hour, simply

enjoying the peaceful landscape of the Hill Country. He pointed out a hill and large oak tree that he thought might be a good one for Ivy to paint.

"I agree," Harper said. "Ivy could do that vista justice. It's such a relief to see her in good spirits and excited about her art again. That had almost been beaten out of her during her years at the gallery in Houston. It was a soul-sucking job. It's been different for you and me," she continued. "We've always been able to do something we loved."

Braden didn't bother to mention the last two years he had not worked in the wine industry, but he understood what she meant.

"We need to have a picnic out at the lake so I can show you Lost Creek Rock. It's not quite as famous as Enchanted Rock, which is a little north of Fredericksburg and a bit hit with tourists, but ours is just as pretty. When we get warmer weather, we could even rent a boat or jet skis or wave runners from Hill Country Water Sports. Finley's brother and wife run that outfit."

"I do want to start learning more about the community," he said. "How is construction going?"

She brightened. "Really well."

Harper talked about the progress which had been made during the next few minutes and about the website Ivy was designing for her.

"I've already bought the domain name. Weddings with Hart, thanks to you. You were right. *With* was the way to go. It's those little touches which can make such a difference. I appreciate your contribution to my new business."

They reached Austin a little before nine, and Harper played tour guide for the next few hours, driving them around and pointing out various places of interest. He liked seeing Moonlight Towers, a group of seventeen iron towers that were a part of the city's first street lighting system, installed in the late nineteenth century. Braden also enjoyed visiting Treat Oak, a tree which was about five hundred years old, one which was the last of a group of fourteen trees where the Comanche and Tonakwa tribes met together.

"You'll really enjoy this next thing if you like quirky," she told him, driving by the Cathedral of Junk and a group of murals, which included one which read *You're my Butter Half.*

"I like what you're showing me. It's not typical."

"Austin definitely marches to its own beat. The state is pretty conservative as a whole, but Austin is as liberal and free-spirited as they come."

He enjoyed the view of Lady Bird Lake, and Harper said they would have to come back another time and hike or bike the trails around it. She drove him down the famous 6th Street, full of bars and restaurants and funky shops.

"This is South Congress Avenue," she told him, making a turn onto the street. "Locals call this area SoCo."

Braden spotted more murals in this area, chuckling at the one promoting *Willie for President* and seeing a flurry of tourists having their pictures made next to another which read *I Love You So Much.*

"The view of the Capitol is amazing," he noted, glancing ahead of them.

"We don't have time for a full-blown tour, but let's go inside for a few minutes."

They parked and walked toward it, with Harper explaining, "It's built in an Italian Renaissance Revival style, modeled after our national capitol, but this is all local red granite that you see on the exterior."

Inside, they paused in the rotunda area under the open dome, a true wonder of architecture. At the very top of the dome was a single star.

"The Lone Star of Texas," he ventured.

"That's right. You need to come back for a guided tour. Or better yet, have Trey walk you through. He knows about every nook and cranny in this place and can tell you about it."

They left the building, returning to her SUV.

"One more stop before lunch. The iconic Ann Richards Congress Avenue Bridge."

As she pulled from her parking spot, Braden asked, "What's so interesting about this bridge? And who is Ann Richards?"

"Ann Richards was the Governor of Texas. About as smart and feisty as they come. It's not the bridge itself I want to show you. It's the bats under it."

"Bats? That's creepy."

"This colony of bats—Mexican free-tails—has about a million-and-a-half bats in it. They gather under the bridge during daylight hours starting in mid-March to a little after Halloween. They come out every night and blanket the sky as they fly out to forage for food. The females give birth and raise their babies during their sojourn in Austin."

"What time do they fly out from the bridge's protection?"

"Around dusk. People gather every single night to watch. It's about the quirkiest thing you can see in Austin, but once you do, you'll never forget it. We don't have time to wait until tonight, but I at least wanted to show you where it is."

Harper drove to the bridge, slowing down so Braden could get a look at it, then she continued on.

"I definitely want to see that happen sometime," he said. "What's next? I think you mentioned eating?"

Her stomach grumbled loudly. They both laughed.

"I'd say lunch is in order. It's almost one now. I have the perfect spot in mind. It's close to the UT campus and my favorite hole in the wall. It's the best Mexican food in Texas, hands down. I've eaten many a meal here."

She greeted the hostess by name and did the same with their server. Harper introduced Braden and said it was his first time to eat at Alamilla's.

Grinning, the server told him, "You are in for a treat. It's not every day a person can discover Alamilla's for the first time. Where are you from?"

"California," Braden said, watching the server frown immediately. "I know, Cal-Mex is as mild as it comes, but I do like a kick to my food."

"Braden is a terrific cook," Harper bragged. "We'll simply have to broaden his repertoire and have him add some classic Tex-Mex dishes to it. Let's start with two ice teas and The Platter, Javier, and then go from there."

"Right away, Harper," the server said.

"What is The Platter?" he asked, scanning the menu and not seeing it listed.

"You won't find it there," she said, laughing. "You have to be a regular to know about it. Also, the Friday salsa. Alamilla's mixes a wonderful salsa six days a week, but on Fridays? They jazz it up a bit. You have to know to ask for it, too."

"You must have been coming here a long time to know the people working by name."

"I ate here a lot in college because it was so close to campus, but I never stopped coming, even after graduation. I've even held some events here. Special parties. A few anniversaries. An engagement party. Several landmark birthdays. The Alamilla family is warm and welcoming to everyone."

Javier returned with their drinks and a large basket of the thinnest, crispest chips Braden had ever tasted, along with the Friday salsa. Harper thanked him profusely for making the salsa up for them.

"You are a special customer and an even more special lady," the server said admiringly. "We have missed seeing you, Harper."

A shadow crossed her face, but she smiled. "I'm sure you heard what happened."

"All of Austin heard, Harper," Javier said. "I think you have more people on your side than you realize. That includes Señor and Señora Alamilla."

"Are they here today?" she asked. "I would love to say hello to them."

"No, they are in Bandera this weekend for their niece's wedding. I will tell you, though, they turned away that *estúpido*."

"Ath?" Harper asked.

Javier nodded. "He thought he could bring that woman here. To *your* place. Mrs. Alamilla was at the hostess stand when they came in and told him we had no tables available." He grinned. "We did, of course, and he could see that with his own eyes. He was smart enough not to press the issue, but that *puta* tried to. Mrs. Alamilla put her in her place. They won't be back."

Braden saw Harper's eyes mist with tears. "Would you thank them for me, Javier?"

"Of course."

He made sure to change the topic the moment the server left. "You've shown me all around, but we have yet to see the campus. We're so close. Is that our next stop?"

"First, the storage facility. Then, Campus. I was saving it for last. I'll try not to do too much of a walk down Memory Lane."

Javier returned with The Platter, and Braden thought it was large enough to feed four or more people.

"As you can see, it has a variety of items on it," she told him. Pointing, she went around the platter naming everything. He was familiar with some, such as quesadillas, flautas, and nachos, but Harper mentioned other items that looked both intriguing and mouthwatering.

"I'm not going to need anything beyond this. Not even that ice cream you mentioned."

"We can come back another time and try their enchiladas and tacos. But we are not walking out of here without satisfying our sweet tooth."

They dived into The Platter, and Braden was determined to try one of everything on it. He started with the queso in the center, proclaiming it the best he'd ever tasted.

Half an hour later, he said, "I am stuffed, just like those jalapeño poppers. I hate that we won't be able to take the leftovers home with us."

"The owners are conscious about food waste," she informed him. "After each dinner service, they take any unused food in the kitchen to a nearby shelter. In fact, the shelter has held a few of their fundraisers here."

"Planned by you, I'm guessing."

"Yes. I always did some pro bono work, as a lawyer might, and my boss was very supportive. I was happy to donate my services in helping the shelter raise money."

He didn't tell her that he'd been forced to live in a shelter for a few weeks until he landed the job at the furniture company. Braden didn't want Harper feeling sorry for him.

Javier appeared again. "You liked everything, Braden?" he asked, refilling their glasses.

"*Like* isn't a strong enough word," he said, grinning. "I'm ready to move to Austin just so I could eat here a few times a week."

"The city would be happy to have you," the server declared.

"No, you don't, Javier," Harper said playfully. "Braden is working at the winery now as our viticulturist, and he'll be moving up to winemaker alongside Dad once the summer crop is harvested."

"Then you are much too valuable to steal from Lost Creek Vineyards," Javier proclaimed. He turned to Harper. "The usual now?"

She nodded, and he departed.

"What is the usual? Seriously, Harper, I don't think I can manage another bite."

"Then make room for one bite of each dessert that comes out of the kitchen. It will be sopapillas and flan."

"I'm not familiar with either. Describe them to me."

"Basically, sopapillas are puffy bits of deep-fried dough. Alamilla's revs them up by rolling them in cinnamon and sugar and serving them with honey. Flan, on the other hand, is a pie without crust. Mexican flan is a custard baked with a caramel glaze. Very simple ingredients, but from what I gather, it's hard to master."

The desserts arrived, and Braden chose to sample the flan first. The sweet mixture melted in his mouth.

"I am declaring half of this mine," he said.

"What happened to your one bite?" she teased.

"Suddenly, I have room again."

While he ate his portion of the flan, she tore a small piece of the sopapilla away, pouring honey inside the hollowed part before cutting the pastry in half. By then, he had consumed the flan and pushed the plate toward her.

They traded, and he cut through the sopapilla, dipping it into the honey and taking his first bite.

"Ah," he moaned. "Why didn't we start with dessert first?"

"We can next time," she said. "I like that idea."

Would there be a next time?

They finished their shared desserts, and Javier asked if they would like iced teas for the road.

"Yes, please," Harper said, pulling out her credit card.

Braden no longer had a credit card and reached for his wallet. It was nice to have a reserve of cash in it these days. He only hoped the cost of lunch would be reasonable.

"I'll get it," he offered.

"No, I asked you to come to Austin today. You're giving up your Saturday for me."

He would give up more than a day for this woman.

He would give up a lifetime.

The thought seized Braden, almost paralyzing him. He'd sworn off women after Freya washed her hands of him, and yet somehow, Harper had worked her way under his skin. Braden had yet to kiss her—and yet his gut told him something that seemed impossible.

She was the one for him.

The emotions washed through him quickly, and he was glad he was sitting because he felt unsteady.

"I insist," she told him. "Put your wallet away."

Javier returned with their to-go cups, and Harper tried to hand him her credit card.

"No, Harper. Mr. Alamilla told the staff that the next

time you came in, it would be on the house. You have done so much for everyone here. The shelter, too."

"Thank you," she said. "I'm grateful to have all of you in my life. Thank you for this lovely lunch."

"Yes, thank you," Braden echoed.

"Let them know I'm back in Lost Creek, Javier. Starting my own business. I'll be in charge of events held at the winery, mostly weddings, but I'll expand as I go. I'll be sure to invite everyone at Alamilla's to the grand opening. The facility just broke ground recently, so it'll be several months before it's complete."

Javier smiled broadly. "We will be honored to come celebrate with you, Harper."

The server left, and Braden placed a ten-dollar bill on the table. "For the tip," he said. "No arguments."

They returned to the car, and Harper drove to the storage facility where she had left her things. She hadn't been kidding. She had several trash bags, which she said contained clothes and shoes, and then two boxes.

"You aren't a typical woman," he said, carrying both boxes stacked atop one another to her SUV. They had already brought out several trash bags filled with clothes and placed them in the rear seat and back of the vehicle.

"The clothes I own are all good quality. My work clothes, that is. You haven't seen me in them. Suits. Sky-high heels. Small, tasteful pieces of jewelry. Full makeup. I don't have a lot of clothing, but everything is top of the line. I needed to represent my company, as well as blend in at the events which I managed. Image is everything in event planning, from the venue chosen to the way it's decorated to the look of the food and drinks served."

"I bet you're really great at your job," Braden said, placing the boxes in the back of her SUV.

A look of satisfaction crossed her face. "I was very good at it. And I plan to be even better, owning and running my own business. My parents instilled a great work ethic in me, and I am detail-oriented and more organized than anyone you'll ever meet. I look forward to holding events at the winery and making people happy. That's what these events are that I plan and run. Memories which people will look back on and cherish, be it a wedding or some special party recognizing a milestone in their lives."

He pushed the button, closing her tailgate. "I can see you take pride in what you do. I get that. My work is everything to me. In a way, it's the same as yours. The wines I create are used to make people happy, whether they're celebrating a huge event with others or simply coming home after a long day of working and sipping a glass of wine in solitude, relaxing and regrouping."

"We have a lot in common," Harper said, looking up at him.

"We do," he agreed, his voice husky.

It was now or never.

Braden placed his hands on her shoulders, lowering his head until his lips touched hers. Either Harper would respond to his kiss—or he'd be walking the entire way back to Lost Creek.

11

She had never been kissed in a parking lot.
And it felt glorious...
Harper leaned in as her lips met Braden's. The feel of his fingers on her shoulders brought a rush of powerful emotions. She hadn't known what to expect today when she had invited him to come to Austin with her. She had sensed the strong connection between them and had tried to ignore it—and then decided to pursue it.

He didn't rush the kiss, which she appreciated. His kiss was deliberate, like the man himself, full of purpose. Slowly, his mouth moved over hers, getting to know it. She clasped his waist to steady herself because she felt herself go lightheaded.

He increased the pressure slightly in response. She inhaled the clean, masculine scent of his soap and his essence, glad not to be overwhelmed by cologne. She feared he would break the kiss and tell her it had been a mistake, so she moved her hands to his back and pressed the front of her body against his incredibly hard one.

His lips left hers, and she sensed defeat until his tongue slowly swept back and forth across her bottom lip, sending delicious tingles up and down her spine. He took his time, using the tip of his tongue to outline the shape of her mouth, ratcheting up the desire building within her. When his mouth returned to hers in a firm, committed kiss, Harper opened to him.

And the magic...

His tongue swept inside her mouth, leisurely exploring her. Once again, deliberate and steadfast. Braden was a thoughtful man, intentional in his speech and actions. She only hoped this kiss might lead to more between them.

Wanting to show him her level of desire, she became an active participant in the kiss, her tongue mating with his, battling for control, in a fight where both could be named winners.

His fingers slid from her shoulders, moving slowly along her back, drawing her close. She lost herself in the kiss. In his taste and scent. Relishing the feel of his broad, strong back beneath her palms. This was a man who had performed physical labor his entire life. One who never backed down from a challenge. A man she hoped to come to know even better than she already did.

Braden broke the kiss, his lips hovering above hers. Harper was afraid to speak—to even breathe—and break the spell between them. He started to pull away, and she couldn't bear the thought of it.

Her gaze met his, seeing his sky-blue eyes darken with desire.

"More," she said boldly.

A slow smile spread, his sensual lips a thing of beauty.

"Gladly," he murmured, a moment before his mouth seized hers again.

This kiss was richer. Deeper. More demanding. It caused Harper to experience sensations she never had with any other man. She couldn't believe she had been foolish enough to want to marry Ath because he had never inspired what ran through her now. Braden's kiss promised things not yet vocalized between them—and guaranteed things to come—if she were open to them.

She didn't know how long the kiss went on. She was lost in this moment in time, a willing participant, learning about herself even as she learned about Braden. She had thought she liked kissing, but kissing with Braden Clark ramped things up to an interplanetary level.

Finally, he ended the kiss again, gazing down at her, his breathing ragged.

"I'm not going to apologize for kissing you," he said roughly, causing her skin to tingle.

"If you did, you would be walking back to Lost Creek," she declared.

Laughter bubbled up from inside him, rich and deep. "I thought *because* I kissed you, walking would be a definite possibility. And yet I did it anyway."

He still held her close, and Harper found herself wanting to wrap all her limbs around him. To place her ear to his heart and hear its steady beat.

"Why would you think that?"

"Why did you ask me to come to Austin with you today, Harper?" he countered.

"Because I hoped something like this would happen," she responded. "I know you have felt the spark between us, Braden, else you wouldn't have attempted to kiss me. And let me say that was the best kiss of my life."

His satisfied smile filled his face, and for the first time, she believed she was finally seeing the true Braden.

"I have felt drawn toward you," he admitted. "From the beginning. But I knew with what you had just gone through with that asshole, becoming involved with someone would be the last thing on your mind. That was already strike one. Strike two is the fact that I work for your dad, and I doubt Bill would want his daughter to mix with the hired help."

She started to protest, but he placed two fingers against her lips.

"Third strike is that I'm broken myself, Harper. I'd lost everything by the time I reached Lost Creek. My career. My reputation. My family. My fiancée. I am flat broke. It will take years to gain everything back, and I can't ask for you to wait around for that to happen." He smiled sadly. "So, what do you say we close the book? Just enjoy the kiss for what it was—and move on."

Anger sparked within her. "You don't get to decide what I do or how I feel," she said sharply, pushing away from him.

Braden was not letting go yet, however.

"I understand I'm raw emotionally, but I shouldn't

have to close myself off from the world—or from the feelings I have for you. There's no set timetable, Braden. I can't say 'check back with me in two months or two years and maybe we can take a shot at things then.' I have been foolish in regard to my love life, questioning everything about myself because of what happened with Ath. Why wasn't I enough for him? Why couldn't I hold his interest? Why did I—"

"Absolutely nothing is wrong with you, Harper," he said fiercely. "He's the jerk. He was the one who felt inadequate in your relationship. That's why he strayed. Some men can have everything, and yet they want more. Want different. Want to flex their proverbial muscles. They want to be attractive to everyone, men and women. Draw them in. It makes them feel good about themselves."

"You are describing Ath to a T," she said. "And you've never even met him."

"I've met his type. He was never good enough for *you*. You didn't realize that. You might have been dazzled by his looks. His charm. His intelligence. Hell, even by his pedigree. He comes from a powerful, wealthy family. He wined and dined you. That would have been hard for any woman to say no to. But zebras can't change their stripes. Underneath his shiny veneer was a rotten core. You should celebrate that you dodged a bullet and weren't stuck with him."

"I am celebrating that, Braden. I want to celebrate that with you," she said softly, framing his face with her hands and pulling him down for a gentle kiss.

Harper was the one to break it. Releasing him, she

said, "You aren't in any way or fashion a substitute for Atherton Armistead. You, Braden Clark, are an original. I want to get to know you better if you'll let me."

His eyes heated, boring into her, and Harper shivered at their intensity.

"What exactly are you saying, Harper? How far do you want to take this?"

"We're already becoming friends," she said carefully. "I think friendship is the basis for anything that follows between us." She hesitated and then spit it out. "What I'm saying, Braden, is that I'd like to explore a physical relationship with you. To see if these sparks between us are a flash in the pan—or if they catch fire."

"What if we get burned?" he asked, searching her face.

"I want to feed the fire. Let the flames go as high as they choose," she told him. "I need to be with you. To see where this goes."

His lips touched hers again, almost reverently, as if he sealed some unspoken bargain between them. Harper didn't want to think about getting hurt or hurting him. She only knew if she didn't pursue him, she would live with regrets for the rest of her life.

He released her, stepping back, his gaze still searching her face as if he weren't quite certain he should have agreed to anything.

"I know you have been hurt, too. By your parents. By your ex-fiancée. By the industry which turned its back on you. I won't hurt you, Braden. Maybe we are the answer to what each other needs in order to heal emotionally from what's come before. Could you give us a chance?"

Harper waited, watching him contemplate what she was proposing.

"What if this doesn't work?" he asked, his tone tinged with doubt.

"I believe we could remain friends. I like you, Braden. Beyond what you stir within me physically. Yes, it's risky to plunge ahead, our hearts already bruised by others, but I'm willing to give us a try if you are."

His large hands framed her face. Smiling, he asked, "Nothing ventured, nothing gained?"

"Something like that. If we try and it flames out, no hard feelings. But the trying is important." She grinned. "Or maybe we should take Yoda's philosophy. *'Do. Or do not. There is no try.'*"

Braden burst out in laughter. "Are you a Star Wars junkie, Harper Hart?"

"I might be, Braden Clark," she said loftily. "There's a lot about me that you don't know."

His thumbs caressed her cheeks, making it hard for her to think coherently. "Such as?" he asked.

"I am crazy for Buc-ee's barbeque sandwiches and slushes. I'm a purist when it comes to margaritas and don't want them flavored with strawberry or watermelon. I like music from the seventies. And I turn to running in good times and bad, especially when I need to work through a problem."

"I have no idea who Bucky is," Braden began, "but I'm eager to meet him. Only sissies flavor their margaritas. I know squat about seventies music, so maybe you'll introduce me to some new, great bands. As for me? I like old black and white movies. A smoky scotch. Meditating. And a medium rare steak paired with a rich, dark Cab."

He gazed at her wordlessly until Harper felt he saw into her very soul. "But I am very much ready to jump off the cliff with you, Harper Hart. We might crash on the rocks and manage to wind up hurting ourselves even more than how we're already broken. Or we could dive into deep water and learn to swim together, side-by-side. Either way, I'm in. All in."

She breathed a sigh of relief. "I'm glad you're willing to take a chance on me, Braden. On us." Spontaneously, she began humming a catchy song which fit what they were embarking upon, taking a risk—and hoping the reward would pay off in the end.

He looked at her as if she were crazy, and Harper said, "Sorry. That's from ABBA, one of the biggest bands in the seventies. It's called *Take a Chance on Me*." She grinned. "First thing we're going to do is watch the movie *Mamma Mia* together. It's all ABBA songs, and they're totally earworms."

"Earworms?" he asked, clearly puzzled by the term.

"Songs that get in your head and won't leave." She laughed. "It's going to be so much fun introducing you to the seventies. The Eagles. The Commodores. Al Green. Diana Ross. The Bee Gees."

"I've heard of some of them. But I've never really been into music," he admitted.

"Then you will attend the Harper Hart School of Musical Education free of charge, Mr. Clark," she said, taking his hands in hers.

"I look forward to it," he said, his eyes filled with heat.

"Let's go home," she said. "We can take advantage of an empty house."

He smiled slowly at her, causing her heart to slam against her ribs. "Let's see how long it takes you to scream my name."

12

Harper said, "Let's go home," wanting nothing more than to make love with Braden.

"I thought we were going to see the UT campus next. You know, relieve your glory years," he teased.

"That can wait. I want one, glorious night with you instead."

She saw desire flare in his eyes.

"You're on."

They climbed into her SUV, and soon Austin was a speck in the rearview mirror. She wondered what the ride home would be like, but the sexual tension seemed to be placed on hold, replaced by a deep camaraderie and comfort level she'd never known with a man.

"Tell me more about seventies music," Braden encouraged. "Where did you pick that up?"

She laughed. "People in the Hill Country are born with

love for three things. Texas barbeque. The Dallas Cowboys. And country music. It's just in our DNA. I do like country music. I like the stories it tells, but my granddad had a huge record collection. He enjoyed all kinds of music, from jazz to rock to love ballads. Gramps thought the seventies was the golden age of music. At least, that's what he called it. He liked that the decade had so much variety. A lot of times, an era's music can sound a lot alike, but the seventies had it all. Soft and hard rock. Even country rock, with people like Linda Ronstadt. It was filled with Motown and R&B. And let's don't forget disco. Gloria Gaynor's *I Will Survive* or Thelma Houston's *Don't Leave Me This Way* might be the greatest examples of that. I guess I'm just drawn to how eclectic seventies music is. What about you? You said you didn't know much about music."

"I have always liked things quiet. To me, music wasn't something in the background. It's always just been noise to me. Especially with the jobs I held at the vineyard, I enjoyed the peace of silence."

"Then tell me about these old movies you said you like."

She glanced over and saw his big smile, glad she had tapped into something he enjoyed.

"I love 1930s and 1940s movies. Black and white films, to me, were the golden age of Hollywood. Color ruined everything. Of course, I'm drawn to the classics. Movies such as *Casablanca*. *The Philadelphia Story*. *The Best Years of Our Lives.*"

He paused. "You haven't seen any of those, have you? I can tell by your expression."

"No," she admitted guiltily. "I've never really had a lot of time to sit and watch TV or go to movies. Growing up, I was busy with school, sports, and the vineyard. That was intensified when I went to college. When you're on an NCAA Division I sports team, it consists of a lot of travel, which means you miss a ton of class. I'm smart, Braden, but I had to work twice as hard as the average Longhorn student in order to make up for what I missed during my absences for games and tournaments. Usually, my professors were pretty accommodating, willing to work with me and help me fill in the gaps. A few? Not so much, so there were a few classes in which I struggled.

"I mentioned joining a sorority, and when I wasn't practicing or playing a game—or studying—the sorority took up all the rest of my free time. Don't get me wrong. I enjoyed being a part of a community of women who supported one another. We had all kinds of social activities, from mixers to dances to intramural sports, which I coached. We also did philanthropic work in the community, something I believe all students should participate in, whether Greek or non-Greek."

Seeing no one on the highway now, she set the cruise control and relaxed. "After college, I started at my job as an event planner, and that is almost a 24/7 kind of circus."

"Tell me about it. I don't really know much, other than what you've mentioned."

"You meet with potential clients. They tell you about the

event they wish to hold, and you pitch them ideas regarding it. Themes. Venues. Food and beverages. If you click, you sign them to a contract. A lot goes into planning the event."

Harper talked about scouting places to hold events and the vendors she worked with to provide everything from decorations to flowers to entertainment.

"Sometimes, people change their minds. A lot. That can get on your nerves and be time-consuming. They want a different entrée served or they think they've found a better band to play at their event. You go back to the drawing board. A lot of balls are being juggled in the air before the event occurs, and then the day arrives. I had to be present at each event to ensure things ran seamlessly."

"That's a lot of moving pieces on the gameboard. You really know your stuff."

"It was a lot, balancing the clients' wants and the work I put into things. I am good at it," she said, pride in her voice. "I've always been organized to the max, and that's a huge part of being successful in event planning. It helps that I did the job in the same town for as long as I did because I got to know all the available venues. Sometimes, people want traditional, and other times you get clients who thrive on quirky. I was also knowledgeable about area's DJs and bands. Austin has a terrific music scene, and it rivals that of Nashville. That's my next goal."

"What do you mean?"

"I want to familiarize myself again with everything about Lost Creek. It's grown quite a bit since I left for college. New shops. New B&Bs. New restaurants. I under-stand Lost Creek Winery will obviously be the place I hold every event, no matter its nature, but I want to get to know the local businesses. Form partnerships with them. I especially need to start going to hear local musicians play on the weekends so I can have an idea of what's out there for when I do start booking clients."

"I'll be happy to accompany you to listen to singers or bands," Braden volunteered. "We can broaden my musical education that way."

"I'd like that," she told him. "I've already hit up Emerson Frost about baking wedding and groom's cakes. She's considering it. If she doesn't freelance and do these on her own, I'll simply have Ethel's people at The Bake House make them."

"I've met Ethel," he said. "She's getting up there in years but still seems pretty spry."

"That's why I'd prefer having Emerson as my exclusive cake vendor. If I can bring in enough business—and I think I will—she can quit her second job at the bakery and work with Weddings with Hart. I don't want to pressure her, though. I've told her she's got some time before I need a decision from her."

"You've mentioned bringing in caterers. Any ideas who?"

"Number one on my list would be Blackwood BBQ. They have a stellar reputation, not only in this area, but throughout the state. Blackwood regularly makes top-ten lists in various publications and polls in Texas. It's owned by two locals, although Shelly spends all her time at Lone Star Diner, another place the Blackwoods own, and one I'd consider using to cater down-home kind of receptions.

If a bride is thinking about a Hill Country wedding, then barbeque is the natural thing to serve at the reception, though. I think with Blackwood being so close, most people would even expect it. I've got to make an appointment soon to talk with Shy Blackwood about it."

Harper glanced to him. "Enough about me. Let me get to know more about you, Braden."

"My story is a lot like yours, having grown up at a winery. I started working with the vines at an early age. Participated in harvests. They say it takes a village to raise a child, and my brothers and I were raised by all those workers at Clark Vineyards. Mom and Dad were hands-off parents. No helicoptering from them. We never really spent a ton of time with them. Dad was always going off to meetings with clients or potential clients. Mom was one of those ladies who did lunch as her living. Her days were filled with those lunch dates, as well as hair appointments, manicures and pedicures, and spa days. She and Dad were gone to dinner for hours several nights a week and started leaving us alone at what I now know is a pretty early age to do so."

"Even though you were the middle child, it sounds as if you were the caretaker for you and your brothers."

"I never thought of it that way, but you're exactly right. I learned to cook early, and I associated making food with looking after Stan and Beau. I could show them I cared about them by feeding them."

He fell silent, and Harper knew enough not to push him. Braden was an enigma, but she believed he would continue to open up to her, bit by bit.

"As we got older, Stan pulled away more and more, both from the vineyard and the family. He really got into sports and lettered in football, basketball, and track. Because of that, he was never home and didn't contribute much to the vineyard. Then he went away to college in Santa Barbara and rarely came home, even on weekends. He was all about his Greek life and fraternity brothers, even going home and spending holidays with them."

"What did he do at Clark Vineyards after he graduated from college?" she asked, curious.

"Stan worked with Dad, but he was involved in handling all the social media and branding for the label. He didn't have anything to do with the wine itself."

"You said Beau is your younger brother, right? What was his role?"

"Beau was awkward socially," he shared. "I guess nowadays people would say he was on the spectrum. I never thought of him as being autistic, just extremely quiet. Shy around others. With a lot of quirks. Beau did maintain the company's website and was in charge of bottling and shipping the cases out to our clients."

Sensing he needed the topic changed, Harper said, "I'd thought about stopping on our way home and picking up some steaks to grill, but I'm still pretty full from our lunch."

"I would jump at steaks any other time, but I'm right there with you. Mexican food is great, but it sure sits heavy in your belly."

She glanced at him flirtatiously. "I hope you won't be too full to fool around when we get home."

Braden reached and took her hand from the steering wheel, pressing a tender kiss to her knuckles. "I'm not *that* full, Harper. I've been starving for you far too long to pass up this opportunity to be with you." He hesitated. "Exactly how far do you want to take this tonight? I'm good with moving slowly."

"I'm not," she boldly declared, sensing his surprise. "We lead busy lives, Braden. I'm not going to waste time. I've been curious for too long about what it would be like to make love with you. I'm not saying we have to voice any kind of commitment to one another. I'm happy to take things day-by-day, but I'm not willing to pussyfoot around."

"Pussyfoot?" he said, laughing. "That sounds like a Texanism. I suppose that means you don't want to waste time."

"We can work on your vocabulary later," she said, her voice low, desire running through her. "Tonight, I want to learn everything about *you*."

He brought her hand to his lips again, brushing them against her fingers before he released it. The gesture was small but packed a punch. She couldn't wait to explore his hard, muscular body.

They reached Lost Creek and a few minutes later, Harper pulled into the driveway. Turning to him, she said, "Leave my stuff. We can get it later."

"Maybe even tomorrow," he said, innuendo in his voice as mischief danced in his eyes. "Because we might be too busy tonight."

Harper liked the sound of that.

Braden already had his key out and unlocked the door, allowing her to go in first. She set down her purse and heard the door close and lock.

Suddenly, her back was against it.

He had snagged her waist and still held it now, pressing her into the door, his body against hers, his mouth hard and insistent. Desire flared within her, and Harper kissed him back, her hands going to his strong forearms and gripping them. That wonderful, clean scent of his filled the air around her as her body warmed against his.

His kisses grew bolder, commanding her attention, causing her to fire on all pistons. Never had a man's kiss excited her as much as Braden's did. His lips left hers, trailing kisses along her jaw, moving to where her pulse fluttered out of control. Her heart was already beating in double-time, anticipating what would come next.

Braden's teeth grazed her throat, causing her core to tighten. Her nipples also sprang to life as his mouth moved against her neck, sucking, biting, soothing.

Without warning, his hands left her waist, capturing her wrists, pinning them against the wall, high above her head. It caused her breasts to press into him. Again, he ravaged her mouth, demanding more and more of her, need building within her. Her core now pulsed violently, and he had yet to touch her there.

He brought her hands together and gripped her wrists with one hand of his, leaving the other free. It pushed into her hair, his fingers tangling in it, his mouth continuing its almost brutal punishment of hers. Then his hand moved to her breast, and Harper whimpered when he touched it. Already, the nipples were incredibly sensitive. Braden palmed her breast, moving and squeezing gently, causing her breath to hitch.

He broke the kiss, his face close to hers, his gaze intense as he unbuttoned the shirt she wore. When he reached the last one, he parted the shirt. Cool air danced along her skin, as did his fingers.

"Front clasp," he murmured. "Convenient."

One-handed, he undid the bra, moving it so both breasts were exposed, dipping his head. His mouth closed over her left breast, and he began sucking hard, causing her to whimper. She wriggled against him, but he held her wrists tight and kept his lower body pressed to hers.

She couldn't say how long he feasted at her breast, only that he devoured it. She felt the orgasm coming, slamming into her hard, and she bumped against his body, moaning.

He finally lifted his head. "Did you just come?" he asked, low and rough.

"Yes," she whispered, turned on by the intensity of his gaze.

"Damn, woman. I've never had that happen before."

"Same," she managed to say.

A wicked light flashed in his eyes. "Let's see if we can go two-for-two."

His mouth took her other breast now, his tongue flicking across the nipple, his teeth grazing it, teasing her, toying with it. Again, the orgasm began building, and it erupted as she cried out, bucking against him. She closed her eyes, feeling new sensations. Raw. Primal.

When she opened them again, his gaze met hers. A slow smile spread across his handsome face. He released her wrists, and her hands fell to his shoulders, needed to hold onto something so she didn't slide down the wall and plop onto the ground.

His hand cupped her cheek, and Braden kissed her deeply. His other hand cupped her even lower, and she almost growled.

"Bed," she murmured against his mouth.

Though the word was muffled, he interpreted it correctly because he scooped her up. One arm went under her knees, while the other supported her back. He kissed her the entire way across the room and down the hall, bumping into the wall but not stopping. Her arms were locked behind his neck, and Harper kissed him with everything she had.

Slowly, he lowered her to the bed. "Stay there," he ordered, pulling off his shoes and socks before making short work of his T-shirt and jeans.

He stood before her in boxer-briefs, looking like an ad for them. His chest was broad, his belly flat.

"Let me," she volunteered, pushing from the bed and slipping her fingers into the waistband.

She could feel the heat coming off his body as she slid his underwear past his hips and thighs, down to his ankles. He stepped from it and caught her elbows, bringing her back until she stood facing him.

"My turn," he said.

With fingers full of heat and rough with calluses, he pulled her shirt and bra from her and then bent to remove her loafers and socks. He stayed in a crouch, unbuttoning and unzipping her jeans, pulling them slowly down her legs. She placed her arms on his shoulders to steady herself as she stepped out of them.

Now she stood, only wearing her panties, his mouth close to the center of her heat.

"A pretty scrap of lace," he said, dipping his fingers into them and gliding along her ass, causing her body to quiver in need.

Gently, he lowered them, and Harper stepped out of them as Braden tossed them aside. He rose to his full height again, his hands framing her face.

"I'm ready to get to know you, Harper," he said, so low she almost didn't hear him.

His hands began roaming her back, cupping her ass, pressing himself to her, the large bulge making it obvious he wanted her.

Somehow, they wound up on the bed, though she would have been hard-pressed to explain how. Braden's hands were everywhere, exploring her curves, learning how to stroke her, figuring out what she liked. No man had ever taken such time with her, wanting to please her.

In turn, she touched him everywhere, feeling the rock-hard biceps and brushing her fingers against his six-pack, seeing the muscles bunch beneath her touch. They kissed. They touched. They tasted.

Then he stopped, cursing angrily.

Thinking she had done something wrong, she asked, "What is it?"

"I don't have any condoms. I haven't needed one in ages."

She smiled, capturing his face in her hands and placing soft kisses on it. "Don't worry. I've been on the pill since high school. Mom experienced awful cramps, and I'm the same way. We're good, Braden."

He breathed a deep sigh of relief. "Thank goodness." His eyes gleamed at her. "I guess it's back to business."

He kissed her everywhere, and she reveled in his touch. His taste. In these new, fragile feelings that ran through her as he hovered over her, parting her legs, dipping a finger inside her and caressing her. He pulled it out, slipping it into his mouth and slowly pulling it out.

"Oh, yes. You're ready, babe."

He kissed her again, his body against hers now, suddenly thrusting into her. Harper cried out. In joy. In need. Braden moved in and out, each thrust deeper and more satisfying. He used the pad of one of his fingers to touch her intimately, moving it in a circular way, causing another orgasm to begin building. As he pushed into her a final time, she exploded, clinging to him, calling out his name, tears escaping from the corners of her eyes.

Collapsing atop her, he quickly rolled to his side, still in her. His arms came around her, and Harper rested her ear against his chest, his heart beating fast beneath it.

They lay together in silence, their limbs entwined, as their bodies cooled. She had made love with men she liked. Men she cared about. One she even had loved.

This experience came nowhere close to any of those times.

His hand stroked her back. He kissed the top of her head. "You okay?"

"Better than okay," she replied, snuggling against him, her eyelids heavy as she drifted off to sleep.

13

Braden awoke, Harper's nestled against him, her warmth like a blanket of contentment. He could not recall ever being awash with such deep satisfaction after having made love to a woman. Not even Freya.

Already, he had shared more of himself with Harper than he had anyone else. He was a private person and rarely opened up, but Harper had a way of easing bits and pieces out of him. He didn't want to look too far into the future—nor did he want to push her too hard or too fast. He would need to let her set the pace for whatever blossomed between them.

But his gut told him he was in it for the long haul.

He had only felt that way about wine. Usually, he was extremely deliberate, taking his time with trying anything new. The grapes, however, had called to him from an early age. Braden had known his destiny was entwined with them when he was still a small boy. The same felt true now with Harper. Innately, he understood this woman would be his future.

He wanted to slip from the bed to make breakfast for her, thinking how she had said he'd been the caretaker for his two brothers and shown them love through his cooking. He supposed it was the same with Harper, but he was reluctant to leave her now.

She stirred and pressed a kiss to his bare chest. "Good morning," she said, looking up at him with an incredibly sexy smile.

He brushed his lips against her brow. "Good morning, yourself. Want me to make breakfast for us? I'm starved."

Her fingers caressed his cheek. "I'm starved, too. For you."

Breakfast could wait.

Once more, Braden made love to this woman, knowing in his bones how right it was between them. They both climaxed together, and neither of them was quiet about it. He collapsed atop her, kissing her hungrily, wondering if he would ever be able to get enough of her.

Breaking the kiss, he said, "Now, I'll go and make us something to eat. Any requests?"

She stretched lazily against him. "Anything except yogurt and berries. That's my go-to every morning. I'd like something different for a change." She grinned. "Maybe something that involves real cooking."

He kissed her hard. "You got it."

Rolling out of bed, Braden tossed on the boxer-briefs lying crumpled on the floor and went to the kitchen.

By the time Harper arrived, he had coffee brewed and on the table, along with French toast and sausage links.

Her eyes widened. "This smells heavenly. What a feast!" she proclaimed, sitting and glancing at her coffee. "You doctored it for me?" she asked, sounding pleased.

"I pay attention to little things. Especially if they concern you."

He joined her at the table, and they ate a leisurely breakfast, not rushing since they had nowhere to be.

"What would you like to do today?" he asked. "When does Ivy get home?"

"I'm not sure. She said she'd text me when she left Houston. I do know she had brunch plans with some friends. She'll probably leave after that."

"Then I'm taking you back to bed," he said, his tone possessive.

"Why, Mr. Clark, you are a sex machine," she teased, batting her eyelashes at him.

They cleared the breakfast dishes, placing them in the dishwasher, and Braden took Harper's hand, once more leading her to his bedroom. They spent the next two hours exploring one another's bodies, finding what they each liked and running with it. He could see how addicted he already was to her and bit back any words she might be reluctant to hear, simply putting his feelings into each kiss, hoping it conveyed what he was feeling.

"It should be a pretty day today," she told him. "Would you like to go on a picnic at the lake?"

"I'd go to the moon and back if you asked me," he said, liking the slight blush that tinged her cheeks.

"I need to go shower, and then we can put together a picnic. Hike around the lake. Just have the day to ourselves."

She kissed him a final time and left the bed, retreating to her own room. Braden showered and shaved, dressing in a T-shirt and cargo shorts before heading to the kitchen to make sandwiches for their picnic. He found Harper already there, doing that very thing. Her hair was swept into a high ponytail. The only makeup he saw was on her lips, giving her a touch of color. She was a beautiful woman, both inside and out.

"I see you beat me to things," he said, wrapping his arms around her and nuzzling her neck before releasing her.

"Hey, even I can put together peanut butter and jelly sandwiches. I've already placed some blueberries and strawberries in separate containers. I know there's a small cooler sitting on the top shelf in the laundry room. If you'll grab that, I'll put some bottled waters in it."

He returned with the cooler, and she put four waters inside it before placing a Ziploc bag filled with ice atop them.

They reached her SUV and saw all her things still inside it. They looked at one another and burst out laughing.

"We should carry your things in before we leave," he said.

It only took a few minutes to do so, and then they were on their way to Lost Creek Lake. Where the winery was to the west of town, the lake was to the east. Harper said they could reach it in about twenty minutes.

She told him a few stories along the way. How she and her friends used to take wienies and marshmallows to roast at the lake.

"It was so close," she said. "I got spoiled. "Going to the lake was always fun. Swimming. Fishing. Just hanging out."

"You fish?" he asked.

"Sure. Do you?"

Braden shook his head. "Never been. But it's something that appeals to me."

She smiled. "I know. You and your peace and quiet. Well, that's what fishing is. Dad used to take Todd and me. Ivy never showed much interest in fishing. She would rather be with her paints or pastels."

"You and Todd were close."

"Yes. He was the perfect big brother. Teased me unmercifully—but would protect me with his life. Todd always wanted to know where I was going. Who I was seeing. If a person didn't have the Todd Hart stamp of approval as being good enough for me, then I knew it wasn't meant to be. He could read people really well."

They reached the lake and parked, leaving their lunch behind. Harper took them along one of her favorite lakeshore trails which eventually wound through the woods until they reached a hill overlooking the entire lake. They sat, admiring the view, sipping on the water they had brought along for the hike. He decided it was time he opened up more to her.

"Beau's dead," he said abruptly, his throat constricting with emotion, hearing the words aloud.

Harper's fingers found his, and Braden gained strength from her touch.

"He never seemed to be able to connect with anyone but me. Others thought he was an odd duck, but to me, he was just my brother. I loved him. Even though Beau had no social skills, and he couldn't read social cues at all, he was smart. Way smarter than I was."

She squeezed his hand encouragingly. "What happened?"

"Beau was all about routine. Once the FBI raided Clark Vineyards, that was a thing of the past. They seized all computers and cell phones, even Beau's personal tablet. Without his digital connection to the world, he began to flounder. Badly."

"Couldn't you just buy him another tablet?"

"All our accounts were frozen, Harper," he explained. "Not just the Clark Vineyards business account. All our personal ones, too. We had nothing. Friends stopped taking our calls. I told you how Freya walked away, afraid to be tainted by the brush of scandal. The FBI wound up seizing the entire property, as well, after a week. When the house payments couldn't be made, we lost it, as well. Beau simply couldn't handle any of what was happening. Any change to his routine threw him off his game. With no internet, he was a lost soul. I won't get into the nitty gritty details, but he killed himself. He left a note for me, with two words.

"You'll understand."

Harper climbed into his lap and wrapped her arms around him, her head resting on his shoulder. They sat wordlessly for a long time before he could speak again.

"We couldn't even bury him. Or at least, I couldn't. Mom had already filed for divorce and was living with our neighbor, who'd been a famous Hollywood actor years ago. She washed her hands of the entire situation and her three sons."

Hurt for him filled her eyes. "I can't imagine what you've gone through, Braden."

"I won't pretend it hasn't been rough or affected me. Dad went to prison. Mom abandoned us. Beau couldn't face another day of living. And Stan? He... just vanished one day. I don't know where he is. What he's doing. I doubt I'll ever see him again. I lost my entire family. My job. My purpose in life."

She framed his face with her hands. "You have me, Braden. You have Ivy and Mom and Dad. Everyone at Lost Creek Winery. You'll never have to be alone again."

Harper kissed him, a slow, deliberate kiss. He tasted promise in it.

He could only hope she meant what she said. That he was a part of her and life at Lost Creek.

Breaking the kiss, she crawled from his lap, wrapping her arm about his waist and resting her head against his arm. They sat, looking at the lake, and in the tranquility, Braden finally had a glimmer of hope that he could make a new life for himself and leave behind the ugliness of his yesterdays.

"Ready to hike back and eat?" he asked.

"I've definitely burned through that French toast. Which was amazing, by the way."

He grinned. "Wait until you try my pancakes. They are thing of beauty."

She got to her feet and held out a hand, pulling him up. "Then that can be dinner."

"Pancakes? For dinner?"

"Of course," she said, her usual enthusiasm bubbling up. "We had breakfast for dinner at least once a week when I was growing up. Mornings were too busy for anything except cereal. Oatmeal, if we were lucky, but we all liked breakfast foods. Mom and Dad would cook together. Dad was great on the griddle and focused on pancakes and bacon. Mom could fry, poach, or scramble an egg to perfection. She would also make cinnamon rolls from scratch or buttermilk biscuits. If we were really lucky, she'd make hash browns, too."

He slipped his hand around hers, and they started back down the trail. "I can do all of those. Except the cinnamon rolls. Maybe we could ask your parents to come to dinner tonight and serve breakfast."

"That's a great idea. It's about four hours from Houston to Lost Creek, so Ivy will be home by then."

"I think we should tell them about us," he said.

She stopped. "What about us?"

"That we're seeing each other."

Frowning, she said, "I don't need anyone's permission to see you, Braden."

"No, but your dad is my boss. I think it's a courtesy to

let him and your mom know. And Ivy would figure it out in a nanosecond after being around us."

Harper nodded. "She would. But… what do we tell my parents?"

"What do you want to tell them?" he countered.

"You do that. Answer a question with a question sometimes," she told him. "As far as Mom and Dad go, I think we should just say we're seeing each other—and seeing where it might lead. Sound good?"

"Yes. But I want us to be open with one another, Harper. If things aren't working out, we need to talk about it. See if we can fix it—or if we should just let it go and go back to being friends."

Her blue eyes gazed up at him. "I want this to work, Braden. I'll admit it. I have FOMO where you're concerned."

He knew that was an acronym for 'fear of missing out.' "You aren't going to miss anything with me, Harper. If anything, you'll be the one to have to end anything between us."

They continued down the trail and retrieved their picnic from the car. Tables were nearby, and they took their food to one and sat, eating and talking quietly as they looked out at the water. When they finished, they threw away their trash. Harper saw she'd gotten a text from Ivy, who planned to arrive in Lost Creek by five that afternoon.

Braden snagged Harper around the waist and pulled her close, stealing a kiss. "Should we go home and make good use of our time then?"

"I have one more place to show you," she said.

They drove to a large rock formation and pulled off the highway, sitting on the SUV's hood and studying the rock.

"This is Lost Creek Rock," Harper explained. "As I said, it's almost as large as the more famous Enchanted Rock, which is farther south in the Hill Country. But locals like to talk of the legend surrounding it."

"Has Ivy painted it before?" he asked.

"Many times. She was obsessed with it in high school because she was such a romantic back then."

"She isn't now?"

Harper smiled wryly. "I think we've all grown up and seen life—and love—aren't always what we thought it was. Anyway, the Hill Country was populated by the Lipon Apache. They were a fairly peaceful people, even welcoming the Spanish missionaries to Texas. The Comanche were located more to the north and west but eventually, they pushed farther south, hunting buffalo."

"Even I've heard how tough and warlike the Comanche were," he said.

"They definitely did not like white settlers entering Texas and fought many times with them. But the Comanche and Lipon Apache also began fighting with each other. Two of their chiefs met, and the Apache chief offered his daughter Ekta—which means unity—as a bride to the chief's own son, Tosawhi, which means white knife."

"Something tells me this marriage didn't solve the problems the fathers thought it would."

"Ekta had already been promised to Tarak, one of her own people. Her father went against this agreement, angering Tarak and his family, along with other tribe members. Still, he was trying his best to calm things between his people and the Comanche and thought giving up his precious daughter the best solution. Finally, after much protest, it was decided by the two chiefs that the two young braves would have the opportunity to fight for Ekta. It would be a fight to the death."

"Wow. Bet Tarak didn't see that coming," Braden said.

"Tarak could mean star. It also can be interpreted as protector. Though Ekta begged her sweetheart not to fight Tosawhi, Tarak said it was a matter of honor, as well as the way to claim Ekta as his. He told her he would keep her safe and not allow her to become the wife of a Comanche warrior."

"So, did they fight here? At Lost Creek Rock?"

"Actually, on the other side of it. Ekta couldn't bear to watch her lover engage in mortal battle with their enemy, and so she climbed to the top of this rock and deliberately stared out in our direction."

He slipped his hand around hers.

"All morning and afternoon, she could hear the voices of the two tribes' members, shouting encouragement at the warriors dueling to their death. Ekta cried. She prayed. And she waited. Eventually, as the sun was beginning to set, she heard loud shouts. And then utter silence.

"She turned, facing the direction of where the fighting had occurred, waiting to see who would climb Lost Creek Rock and claim her."

Harper paused dramatically, and Braden said, "Quit holding out. The suspense is killing me."

Laughing, she continued. "Tosawhi, the Comanche warrior, was the one who appeared. He staggered toward her, bloody and bruised. Knowing he must have killed Tarak, Ekta told her husband-to-be that he would never have her. Ekta removed the knife she had brought with her and stabbed herself in the chest."

"How very Juliet of her," he quipped.

"But there's more," she said. "Ekta wanted to make certain she died, and so she went to the edge of the rock and stepped off, falling to her death. Little did she know, Tosawhi fell to the ground immediately after, dead himself, a knife protruding from the back of his skull."

"He climbed that rock with a knife in his head?" Braden asked, doubt in his voice.

"Legend has it that Tosawhi had stabbed Tarak in his belly, claiming victory over his opponent, but while the Comanche warrior danced in delight, Tarak moved toward him and slammed his own blade into Tosawhi's head, burying it to the hilt. I don't know how it's possible, but both men began climbing the rock, trying to reach Ekta first, both mortally wounded. When Tarak managed to finally crawl to the top, he found his enemy dead—but he did not see Ekta. He continued dragging himself along the dirt, following the trail of blood she had left, seeing her broken body at the foot of Lost Creek Hill.

"Tarak let out a cry that echoed throughout the Hill Country, one full of anguish, mourning the death of his beloved. He pushed himself to his feet and flung himself off the cliff, landing next to his true love, united forever in death."

"And how does everyone know how it went down?" Braden challenged. "If all three of them were dead."

Harper grinned. "Because Onawa, Ekta's younger sister, had accompanied her and waited through the long vigil with her sister. Onawa wasn't able to stop Ekta from killing herself, nor could she save either brave who had fought for her sister's hand. Lost Creek Rock became known as a haunted place, where Ekta and Tarak would forever stay, bound to Mother Earth, while Tosawhi watched them from a distance."

"Have you ever seen a ghost here?"

She grew thoughtful. "I'm not sure. Teenagers would come out here, trying to see that very thing. I'll admit I was one of those who did. Once, I thought I heard someone crying. Whether it was Ekta, weeping for the loss of her lover, or Onawa, mourning her sister, I'll never know. But I respect the legend all the same."

Braden slipped an arm about her. "Good story. Tragic ending." He paused, gazing into her eyes. "I hope you and I will write a better one, Harper."

She held his gaze. "So do I."

14

Harper heard the front door open, Ivy calling out, "Hey! I'm home."

She closed her laptop and left the kitchen, going out to meet her sister. Ivy had a backpack slung over one shoulder and was rolling a suitcase into the living room.

"More in the car?" she asked.

"Yes. Clothes, shoes, and some art books. I can't seem to let go of physical books. Yes, I have a lot downloaded on my Kindle, but some books need to be held." She glanced around. "Braden here?"

"He's gone to the store to pick up a few things. Mom and Dad are coming to dinner."

"Great." Ivy wheeled her suitcase to her bedroom, saying, "Leave the carton of books for Braden to bring in, but you can help with the rest."

Harper found two more suitcases in the car, ones she

had lent Ivy. She lifted one from the trunk and retrieved the other from the back seat of the car. Her sister met her, taking the handle of one, and they got the luggage inside.

"Good thing this house has some decent closet space," Ivy said. "Else I wouldn't have room for everything. Not that I need a lot of the clothes I brought. Like you, it's a bunch of work stuff. Nice blouses, jackets, suits. Working in the tasting room, I don't need to dress as I did at the gallery. In fact, I'm looking forward to getting the shirts with the Lone Creek Vineyards logo. I'll wear those to work every day with shorts or jeans and then just tool around in leggings and yoga pants on the days I paint."

Harper placed the suitcase she'd brought in on the bed, unfastening the locks and opening it. "Well, I'll need my work clothes. I want to look professional when I meet with clients and especially at weddings and the other events I'll eventually hold."

"You should still think about some shirts with the Weddings with Hart logo on them for days you aren't meeting with clients. Just for puttering around. Going into town to meet with vendors. Even if you get a drop-in, you'd be wearing your logo."

Ivy started opening drawers and filling them with bras, panties, and pajamas. "Did you get up to Austin and clear out your storage space?"

"I did. Braden went with me. I showed him around Austin, and we had lunch at Alamilla's."

"I am so jealous," Ivy declared. "Nothing in Houston compares to Alamilla's."

"I told Javier that when I hold the grand opening of the

event center, I'd let them know so they could come and celebrate."

Ivy touched Harper's arm. "That's so nice. I know all the people who work there have meant a lot to you over the years."

Harper grinned. "Mrs. Alamilla turned Ath and Cynthia away. Even though it was obvious they had empty tables and could have seated them."

Ivy smiled with glee. "I love it. That took guts. Mrs. Alamilla is plenty fiery. I sure wouldn't want to tangle with her over something."

She heard the front door opening again. "Sounds like Braden is back from the grocery store."

"What are we having?"

"Breakfast."

Ivy sighed. "Ah, the best kind of dinner is breakfast. I'll finish all this unpacking later. I'd like to see what Braden will make. I've already picked up all kinds of cooking tips watching him in action."

They went to the kitchen, where Braden was setting down two canvas bags.

"Got everything I needed," he told them, reaching in to claim the items and set them on the counter.

"Harper said you're making breakfast. I am so ready for this meal," Ivy declared.

"I thought you had brunch today," he said.

"You can never have breakfast enough," her sister declared. "Besides, it was mimosas and Eggs Benedict. I'll bet you're serving something completely different."

"Pancakes and bacon. With a fruit compote over

yogurt," Braden revealed. "I make mine with maple syrup instead of sugar. I'll use raspberries, peaches, and blueberries."

"Mind if I hang around and watch?" Ivy asked. "I've never seen a fruit compote being made."

"Sure," Braden said easily. "You briefly cook it on the stove. You just have to nurse it. A compote can't be rushed. You can also dump it atop ice cream as a dessert."

"Whoa," Harper said. "You had both of us at ice cream. Could we do that instead? Dad is an ice cream fiend. He loves to top a meal off with some Blue Bell."

"I'll call Mom and have her bring a carton of Homemade Vanilla," Ivy volunteered. "They always have that on hand."

Harper sat and watched as Braden got to work preparing the pancake batter. Ivy played sous chef, cutting up strawberries and slicing peaches and adding them to the other fruit in the bowl before placing strips of bacon in a frying pan.

Braden dipped a spoon into the fruit mixture and took it to Harper to sample.

"Yum," she said. "And that's before the compote is poured over it. I do love fruit."

"I know you do."

Ivy stopped. Glanced at Braden. Then Harper. Back to Braden.

"Finally," she declared.

"What?" she and Braden asked in unison.

"You're together," Ivy said, a smug smile on her face. "I knew it."

"What do you mean?" she asked.

Her sister laughed. "I shouldn't have to spell anything out to you, Harper. I know what went on while I was gone."

She felt her cheeks warming. "Why do you say that?"

"It's been obvious to me that something was building between the two of you. Mom and I talked about it early on. She didn't think you'd act on it because you would think it was too soon after the Ath debacle. I told her she was wrong. That you were smart enough not to mope about Ath because he was such a royal jerk. I said you and Braden would be together by May—and it's only mid-March now."

"But *how* did you know?" Braden insisted. "We've barely looked at one another since you got home. I thought we were being really cool about things."

Ivy laughed. "I wasn't one hundred percent sure—until just now when you confirmed it. But I caught a few glances. And you took her a bite of fruit to eat. That was a definite move from the friend zone. I guess it's a good thing you drew the primary bedroom, Braden, since they'll be two of you in it."

The doorbell sounded. "That'll be Mom and Dad," Ivy said. "I'll let them in."

Harper quickly stood. "You stay here. I don't trust you to be alone with them."

"Is it a secret?" Ivy asked. "I won't say a word."

"That's why we invited them to dinner tonight," Braden said. "I think they need to know."

"I'll still get the door," she insisted, going to greet her parents.

Mom handed her the half-gallon of ice cream. "Here's dessert."

"Braden is making a fruit compote to pour over the ice cream," she told them.

Dad held up a six-pack of Dr. Pepper. "Just in case you didn't have any on hand."

"We don't," she said, laughing. "None of us want to succumb to the temptation of drinking pure sugar on a daily basis."

"DP is nectar from the gods," Dad proclaimed. "I'll put this in the fridge. I'll take the ice cream, too, and get it in the freezer. And just to let you know, you can keep the fruit. I'll be having a Dr. Pepper float for dessert."

"I'll let Harper start the house tour," Mom said.

She showed her mother around, her dad joining them. Harper felt a little funny when they reached Braden's bedroom and remained in the hallway. She glanced to the bed and thought of what she and Braden had done in those sheets and felt her face flame.

"We should stay out of Braden's room," she said crisply. "Come see my room next. And Ivy's is a mess. She just got home before you arrived, so she's got open suitcases and stuff scattered about."

The tour concluded in the kitchen. Harper saw the table had been set and jugs of milk and orange juice were sitting on the table.

"Oh, it must be breakfast," Mom said, clearly delighted. "Eggs? Waffles?"

"Pancakes," Braden shared. "One of my specialties. If I would've known the Harts liked breakfast at night, I would have served it to you when I was living at the house with you."

He finished stirring the fruit and removed the spoon, setting the burner to the lowest setting. "The fruit can keep warming. I'll start the pancakes now that you're here. Ivy is flipping bacon. Harper, why don't you pour drinks for everyone?"

"I'll get my DP," Dad said. "It goes with everything. Even breakfast."

Minutes later, two tall stacks of the fluffiest pancakes Harper had ever seen were brought to the table, along with bacon fried up by Ivy. Braden had set out a stick of butter to come to room temperature, making it easier to butter their pancakes. She added maple syrup to her stack judiciously, while Ivy poured a river atop hers.

Her sister talked about the friends she'd seen while in Houston. She had also gone by the gallery early Saturday morning to return her set of keys, avoiding her boss, who never set foot in the gallery before late afternoon on the weekends.

"While I'll miss everyone I worked with—minus the boss—just being there for a few minutes let me know how much I'm enjoying running the tasting room. Sarah and Melanie aren't too particular about their hours, which allows me to rotate the schedule, so everyone has a weekend off every month. I enjoy interacting with the customers who stop in for a tasting, and there's no pressure to sell them anything, unlike when people dropped by the gallery. I was always stressed out about pushing hard to make a sale when we had drop-ins. And the pressure to sell to regular clients was unbearable."

"Don't forget, you'll be hawking things from the gift shop," Dad teased.

"That's different," Ivy said. "I'll have some items on display which will sell themselves. Either people will want a T-shirt with the LCV logo or a cap or bottle opener—or they won't. As it is, the wine already sells itself. It's rare when someone comes in for a tasting and doesn't leave with a couple of bottles of what they sampled. I don't have to play pushy salesperson when I have a great product that people want to buy."

"Well, that was delicious," Mom declared. "I've never had such soft, pillowy pancakes, Braden. And your bacon was perfect, Ivy."

"Ready for dessert?" Dad asked, retrieving the Blue Bell from the freezer.

Braden went to the stove and stirred the compote. "This has been warming. We're good to go here."

Bill Hart scooped out ice cream for each of them, generous portions that Harper wasn't certain she would finish. Braden ladled the compote atop the ice cream, making for a delicious combination.

"Harper and I asked you for dinner tonight for a reason," Braden said.

She watched her parents exchange a glance.

"You and Harper invited us?" Dad asked.

"Yes. We wanted you to know that we are seeing each other. We wanted to be upfront about it. I hope you don't

ALEXA ASTON

have any problems with an employee dating your daughter, Bill."

"I don't care if she's dating a president or janitor. As long as my little girl is happy."

"Dad, I'm not a little girl. I'm a grown woman," she protested. "But I am happy. Braden makes me happy."

She realized it was true even as she spoke the words. Braden had no pretense about him, while Ath had always seemed pretentious to her. She'd chalked it up to rich-people syndrome and forgiven him for it, just as she'd overlooked what she now realized were so many things she hadn't cared for. Braden Clark was what her dad called WYSIWYG—what you see is what you get.

"At first, I didn't think I would ever want to have a close relationship with a man again," Harper revealed. "And certainly not so soon after my disastrous broken engagement." She paused, meeting Braden's gaze and smiling. "But it would be foolish to hold myself to some arbitrary timetable when a good man is right before me. One who is honest and full of integrity. Braden has more character and kindness in his pinkie than most people do running throughout them. We simply wanted you to know that we're together. We don't know where it's going. We're making it up as we go along."

Mom patted her hand. "That's the best way, honey. No preconceived notions. Just go with the flow."

She laughed. "That's usually *not* my style. I've always been predictable. Knew exactly what I wanted and went after it, either professionally or personally. This time, I'm floating down the Guadalupe in an inner tube, letting the movement of the water carry me where it wants. Not where I force it to go."

Braden spoke up. "I want you all to know I will treat Harper well. She's already a good friend, and we're exploring beyond friendship now. I can't promise what the future holds, but I will never deliberately hurt her, just as I will always protect her."

Their gazes met, and she thought of the legend of Ekta —and how Tarak fought to his death to protect and claim the woman he loved.

Harper didn't know if Braden Clark loved her. She couldn't answer that question for herself. But she was ready to delve further into their relationship.

Because she suspected he might just be the one she'd searched for all along.

15

AUGUST

Braden rolled out of bed, no alarm necessary, even though it was the middle of the night.

It was the second round of harvesting at Lost Creek Vineyards. The grapes used to make the white wines had already been plucked at the end of July when he'd determined they had ripened. Today began the first day of harvesting the reds.

He dressed in the dark, having already left his clothes out the night before, not wanting to disturb Harper. He sensed she wasn't in the room, however. Maybe she had gone back to her own bed to try get a few more hours of sleep before her own busy day began. Harvesting usually started at three in the morning. It was best to get the grapes off their vines while the temperature was at its coolest of the day. He'd also taken into account the sugar levels which he'd constantly monitored, along with the flavor profile he wished to create for this particular harvest. He'd rapidly discovered the Texas heat could also speed up ripening. He couldn't afford sunburnt grapes, and so today's harvest was actually occurring two days before they'd projected a month ago.

Besides the heat, Braden had had to contend with a spring frost in Texas. He'd kept a constant watch on the night weather back in March and April, and just after bud break, the temps had dropped below freezing. Since Lost Creek Vineyards hadn't invested in giant wind machines, which would circulate the air and keep the cold air from damaging the vines, he'd gone the more risky route— turning on the sprinklers and allowing the water to freeze on the vines. The process seemed contrary to saving the vines, but in actuality, water freezing directly on the vines protected them because the freezing process produced a little bit of heat. He had closely monitored the vines over the next forty-eight hours, and this year's crop of both white and red grapes had been saved.

Going to the kitchen, he found both Harper and Ivy up, dressed for picking.

Harper handed him a mug of coffee as Ivy filled up their water bottles to have in the vineyards.

"Neither of you have to do this again," he told the pair. "You already helped bring in the entire whites. You have other things you can be working on."

"It's a family affair," Harper told him. "We wouldn't miss red harvest for anything. Besides, I'm in a lull. I'll be going to San Antonio next week to purchase chairs and tables, as well as look at table arrangements. Red harvest came at a great time for me to participate."

He already knew from their many hours of discussing business that while some brides preferred fresh flowers, the trend was moving toward candles, mirrors, and fake flowers which almost looked real. Harper would offer three levels of table decorations to clients beyond fresh flowers, which would be provided by the local Lost Creek Florist, one of Harper's approved vendors.

"I'm off from the tasting room today anyway," Ivy added, sipping on her coffee. "And even if I weren't, I would have Sarah and Melanie covering so I could be out in the fields. There's nothing like seeing a grape crop brought in." She grinned. "And sampling a few along the way."

They piled into his truck, and Braden drove them the ten minutes to the winery, seeing the place already alive at a quarter to three in the morning. As viticulturist, he was in charge of this entire harvest, but as the future enologist for the vineyard, he would be present at harvest regardless, if not actually picking the grapes. Besides tending to the vines over the last several months, he had worked closely with Bill Hart on the grapes which had already undergone fermentation from previous harvests.

Even though today's crop took precedence for the moment, many facets were in motion at the winery. They were still keeping a close watch on the new acreage which had been planted in the spring, shortly after his arrival, grapevines which would not mature for another three years.

As for previous years' harvest, Braden was constantly tapping into various vats and barrels at the winery in order to see how those wines were progressing. Whites went straight from the field to the press, being placed in concrete eggs or steel vats. For a Sauvignon Blanc, it took three months before its flavor profile began to emerge. Chardonnays, on the other hand, went straight into oak barrels in order to develop their creamy, buttery richness.

Reds needed much more time to develop and weren't pressed until their primary fermentation occurred. Merlots could take up to eighteen months to two years to develop, while Cabernet Sauvignons might not be fully ready until two years after harvest occurred. Merlot, which was a staple of the Texas Hill Country and Lost Creek Vineyards, was also used in several blends he was currently working on in his lab.

He went to where one of the vineyard workers distributed the sacks and claimed one, slipping the strap over his head. It fell diagonally across his broad chest and rested on his right hip. Braden entered the row he had assigned to himself. He pulled the first grape off the vine and sampled it, nodding to himself.

"We're ready to roll," he called, and workers scattered, each one taking their first row to complete.

He supposed in the past that music had played as workers harvested the grapes, but his preference for silence had become known. Because of that, they worked quickly and quietly. He had already established the picking schedule, and once bags were full, younger work-ers, who had been hired from the local high school, would collect them and hand the pickers empty ones.

The grapes would then be removed from the sacks and

placed into bins, being trucked to the large warehouse. He wouldn't be in the vineyards tomorrow since everything seemed to be going well. Instead, he would start working with the incoming grapes, to supervise the crushing and destemming process.

Since they had already brought in the white grape crop with no problems, he did not foresee any new ones popping up this time. Everyone knew his or her role and worked efficiently.

As he worked, Braden couldn't help but think of the turn his life had taken ever since he'd arrived in the Texas Hill Country. Bill Hart trusted him implicitly, and for all intents and purposes, Braden was now the vineyard's winemaker. He would need to hire his own viticulturist after this harvest because he would be too busy creating the wines from the grapes collected and processed during previous years. The new hire would then keep an eye on the vineyards for him, since he would no longer have the time to devote to the fields. While he would always get out on the land each week and keep an eye on the vines, his focus must turn toward the making of wines for Lost Creek Vineyards.

He had told Bill this very thing yesterday, and his employer said he would begin the search for a new viticulturist in the next few weeks. Bill expressed a desire to hire someone from Texas for the position, preferably the Hill Country, but he would even broaden his search to the Texas Plains, if necessary. Bill had said while Napa Valley viticulturists were talented, since the man who now helmed Lost Creek's winemaking was a Californian, he still wanted to have a bit of Texas influence in the process of creating wines.

Braden had concurred, knowing they would find someone talented and skilled to fill the position. Lost Creek Vineyards had a stellar reputation in the industry. Others would be eager to come onboard.

It was because of this reputation and the numerous awards won in the past, he had suggested that in the new tasting room a section be devoted to where wines and their awards could be displayed. Ivy had enthusiastically seconded that idea, and Trey had designed places for built-ins to be added in various tasting areas so those bottles and their medals might be prominently displayed.

Both the tasting room and event center were coming along nicely. Trey had told them once permits were filed and ground broken, an event center could take anywhere from four months to two years to be built. Because Harper's facility would house everything and not have separate buildings for the weddings and their receptions, construction time and costs had been pared. It helped that when they completed one task at the event facility, the construction company mirrored doing the same at the new tasting room, so electricity, plumbing, flooring, and drywall had been completed at the same time for both places.

Looking at the progress already made, Braden thought they would beat the completion date by at least a couple of weeks. Instead of the center being ready in mid-November, he could see the grand opening occurring in October.

He handed off his gathering sack to the closest

teenager, who quickly handed him a second one, but Braden took the time to drink the entire contents of his water bottle before resuming harvesting. The Texas heat was much greater than that in Napa Valley, and Bill had stressed to Braden and all those picking to remain hydrated.

He refilled his water bottle and continued working, the grapes familiar to his fingers, sampling one every now and then to make certain that section needed to be harvested now. After four hours, he took a longer break, heading to the food truck which Bill hired each year to be at the harvest. The truck came from Hill Country Hangout, the local sports bar, and had breakfast tacos available at this time.

"Migas—and the largest Dr. Pepper you have," he ordered, now addicted to the smooth, unofficial soft drink of Texas.

Rob Owens, who owned Hill Country Hangout, handed Braden a basket with three soft tacos and a large drink. "Is it going well?"

"Pretty smoothly, Rob. I thought our white harvest went like clockwork, but this seems to be going even faster this morning."

He sat underneath the canopy which had been erected to shade workers taking a break, chatting briefly with those there, making sure everything was going according to schedule. After inhaling his tacos, which consisted of scrambled eggs, sausage, cheese, salsa, red onions, sliced avocados, and fresh cilantro, he walked the sections being harvested today, touching base with the workers on each row, encouraging them to take frequent breaks. They would call it a day by noon and halt the harvesting until tomorrow. Rob would have lunch ready for them at that time. Cecily had devised the menu with the sports bar owner, and Braden knew this first day would be cheeseburgers.

He thought of the song *Cheeseburgers in Paradise*, one of the many songs Harper had introduced him to in the five months they had been together. He had found his own paradise with her. A juicy cheeseburger would simply be icing on the cake.

Braden loved her. There was no doubt about that in his mind, but he kept his lips zipped and didn't verbally express his feelings. He believed they were committed to one another, but saying those words would take the game to an entirely different level. He wasn't sure what Harper wanted or was willing to accept from him. She was as busy as he was, supervising construction and lining up vendors for future events, as well as working on marketing and advertising for Weddings with Hart. The website Ivy had designed had recently gone live, with progress of the construction updated weekly, as well as various packages which would be offered and the vendors available to couples.

The two sisters worked extremely well together, finishing one another's sentences, brainstorming with ease. He felt privileged to work at Lost Creek Winery and have Harper as his girlfriend and Ivy as a close friend.

He was also starting to get to know a few people in town, especially Dax Tennyson. The coffeehouse owner was fairly new to Lost Creek, having opened his establishment in early March. Dax was easygoing and fun to be around. He also played guitar and sang and had started doing so on a few weekends a month at his coffeehouse, along with other musicians invited to play. Dax was also seeing Ivy Hart. Ivy was usually open about most things with Braden and had let him know she and the Java Junction owner were seeing one another, but Ivy was holding her cards close to the vest regarding the status of her relationship with Dax Tennyson. Still, Braden sensed the connection between the couple.

Harper had told him that Ivy hadn't dated anyone seriously until college. That one relationship had ended abruptly when Ivy found her boyfriend was a serial cheater. She had only casually dated after that, saying she didn't really want to marry. Braden found Dax to be a solid guy with a strong moral core and hoped things would work out between the pair.

He returned to his next assigned row and finished up, his speed at picking simply faster than others, due to his long years in harvesting grapes. It gave him a chance to walk not only the rows being plucked today but the ones designated for harvest tomorrow. Stopping, he sampled a few grapes from the vines, knowing he was on schedule.

Noon arrived and he called a halt to the day's picking, telling the workers to mark where they left off so they could return to the correct spot tomorrow. Small red flags were provided for this, and workers began pushing them into the ground, close to the vines they were working on, the flag resting against the trellis.

Braden followed the exhausted workers back toward where the canopy stood, the smell of the burgers wafting through the air as they got closer. Rob had two workers grilling just outside the food truck. Braden joined the back of the line waiting by the truck and collected a large cup of iced tea and the biggest order of fries he'd ever seen, placing them at one of the tables and returning to grab two of the cheeseburgers coming fresh off the grill.

Harper and Ivy joined him, along with Bill and Cecily.

"How are things going?" Cecily asked. "I almost feel guilty, staying in an air-conditioned office to keep the business portion of things running, but it's my preference."

He gave the couple a status report, estimating how many tons had been picked this morning and how much longer the harvest would continue.

He and Bill then began discussing the red blends they had started working on, while the women moved to other topics. Bill was continuing their work in the lab while Braden supervised the last harvest of the season.

"I have a line on a new viticulturist," Bill told him. "One from a vineyard just outside of Fredericksburg."

Being plugged into the wine community of the Hill Country for so many years, it didn't surprised Braden that Bill already had a lead.

"I haven't touched base with him yet," Bill continued. "I will if you want me to—or I can leave it up to you. In the end, Braden, it'll be your hire. Not mine. You'll work hand-in-hand with whoever assumes your position. The partnership you form together will be what our label's reputation stands upon."

"I appreciate the faith you have in me, Bill. If you want to put feelers out to this candidate, do so. Tell him I'd like to meet after the harvest here is completed."

"Will do."

Braden saw most of the workers were finishing their lunch. Rob and his crew began closing up the food truck, and he waved to them. "See you tomorrow."

"It's back to the office for me," Cecily said. "You girls have had enough sun today. Go home and get some rest."

"I'll take a quick shower, but then I'm heading into town," Ivy said. "I've got a project I'm working on."

"Anything you want to share?" Harper asked.

"Not yet. When I know more, you will."

He stood. "I'll give you and Harper a ride back to the house and then hit the lab."

"You aren't going to stay?" Harper asked. "You've been up and doing hard labor for a long time, Braden. Those barrels aren't going anywhere. You can check on them and tinker some tomorrow when you're supervising pressing."

"You're right," he said. "And a shower would feel pretty good."

They headed to the car, bringing their iced teas with them. Harper crunched on what was left of her crushed ice.

"You take the first shower, Ivy," Harper said.

They had learned the water pressure in the house wasn't the greatest, and so it was smarter to only have one shower at a time going.

"Let's sit at the kitchen table and cool off," he told Harper. "I'll get us some lemonade."

He had talked Cecily into sharing her lemonade recipe, and Braden had encouraged Harper to offer it as an alternative to iced tea at the event center. He'd also told her to place it on the limited menu of drinks which would be available once they started hosting musical events at the winery. Both kids and adults would go wild for Cecily's lemonade.

She wet paper towels and they held them to their faces, removing the Lost Creek Vineyards ball caps they'd worn while plucking the grapes.

"This Texas heat saps all my strength," he told her.

"*All* your strength?" she asked flirtatiously. "And here I thought once Ivy left, we might be able to shower together."

Braden sat up. "I suddenly have a burst of energy flowing through me."

"Good. Because I want to take advantage of having the house to ourselves."

And they did.

16

H e was going to tell her that he loved her.

They had been together five months, and Braden wanted to be the first to say those words to Harper. He still didn't know how she might respond to them, but he could no longer keep silent. He loved her with all his heart and needed to let her know where he stood. To assist him, he was going to talk things over with Ivy, Finley, and Emerson. He had gotten to know the two teachers fairly well since they only lived a couple of doors down. At least once a week, he cooked for the group or Finley did. Her specialty was Tex-Mex dishes, and Braden had learned quite a bit from her, putting his own California spin on several recipes he got from her.

Pulling his truck up to the curb at home, he saw Ivy's car was already in the driveway. Since it was almost five-thirty, he walked down to Finley and Emerson's house and knocked on the door.

Emerson opened in. "Good to see you, Braden. Come on in. Ivy just opened a bottle of wine for us."

He followed Emerson to the kitchen, feeling at home with these women who were close with Harper.

"Hey, Braden," Finley greeted. "The pizza will be here soon. I decided that would be easier than cooking. Today was a rough one for Emerson."

Ivy set the full wine glasses on the kitchen table, and they gathered around it, Emerson sharing about her day and a lost little boy who was angry at the world.

"I don't know if I helped him. I'd like to think I have. His world has been shattered, though, by his parents' divorce, and he's coping with it by lashing out. Sometimes, I think he's pressing the boundaries with me, testing me. Waiting for me to reject him like he thinks his parents have."

"Remember, I had a little girl who did pretty much the same thing last year," Finley said. "The harder she pushed me away, the more I clung to her, trying to make her feel safe. Divorce is rough on kids. They don't understand it's not their fault. They take it personally, as if they are the root of all their parents' problems."

The pizza arrived, and they removed slices from the box, all eyes now turning to him.

Ivy said, "You called this meeting, Braden. Specifically asking that Harper not be present. What's up?"

"I love her," he said simply. "I think I did from the very beginning. I've never told her, though."

His gaze met Emerson's. "You tell her every day, Braden. You just don't use words. I've seen how you look at Harper. How lovingly you treat her. She knows what's in your heart."

"That's not enough anymore," he declared. "I want to say those words. Tell her how committed I am to her. Let her know I'm not going anywhere. I haven't before now because I didn't want to chase her away. When we met, she was coming off the Ath situation. I didn't want to pressure her."

He paused. "In fact, one of the first things she told me was she never wanted to get married."

"Is that where this is leading?" Finley asked. "You say you want to tell her that you love her. Are you looking for a commitment which will lead to marriage?"

"I would marry her tomorrow if I could, Finley, but I think Harper is still a little too fragile to entertain a marriage proposal. It may be overwhelming enough for her to hear that I love her. I will say that I plan to play it by ear. If I think she's ready to hear a proposal? I'll toss that into the mix. For now, though, I'm going into it just with a declaration of love and letting her know that I'm not going anywhere."

"So, why have you called us together?" Ivy asked. "You don't need our permission to tell Harper you love her."

"I want to do something special for her. Something different. We're both so busy, but I want her to know I've put some thought into this." He shrugged. "I'm a guy, however. Not very good at this kind of thing. I never have been. Can you think of somewhere around here that I can take her? I don't mean just a nice steak dinner at Lone Star Chophouse. Somewhere memorable."

The three women thought a moment, and then Finley said, "I have an idea. I did an engagement photo shoot not too long ago near a bed-and-breakfast. The Inn on Lost Creek. It's close to Lost Creek River. There's a bridge on the property which crosses it. I took some wonderful photos there. It's a wonderfully romantic setting, Braden. All green and lush. You could take her to stay at the B&B. Go for a walk and stop on that bridge. Say what you need to, then bring her back to the B&B. They have a few rooms, but they also have two cottages for rent. The cottage might be better. It would offer you more privacy. You could go back to it and have a picnic there."

"I could pull a few wines for you," Ivy volunteered. "You could stop at The Cheese Connoisseur and pick up one of their platters."

"Or a charcuterie board," Emerson said. "And I could contribute something for dessert."

"That sounds terrific," Braden said. "Give me the name of the B&B again, and I'll call and see if they have a vacancy in one of the cottages."

"You might want to try and do this during the week. Weekends are probably booked up through the fall," Finley said. "It's Monday. How about this Wednesday?"

"I can find some excuse to get Harper there," he said.

"Let us handle everything," Ivy told him. "I'll pack a bag for Harper and drop it off at the B&B. I can also stop at the cheese shop and deliver the charcuterie board."

"I'll come up with something special, Braden," Emerson promised.

"I can swing by and pick it up," Ivy said.

"I'll call Miss Bradley now and see what she has available," Finley volunteered.

Finley made the call, and within minutes, all arrangements had been made. Ivy suggested that Braden also pack a bag once Harper left for work. She would take both over to the B&B and pick up the key for him so he could take Harper straight to the cottage.

"I can't thank you enough for your help," he told the trio. "Harper is a special lady. I want her to feel special. She's always doing for everyone else. It's about time she let others pitch in for her."

HARPER LEFT THE EVENT CENTER JUST BEFORE THREE o'clock and returned to her temporary office where her parents' offices were located. Construction was coming along faster than they anticipated. The tasting room was almost complete. Fred Patterson, the construction project manager, had promised that his crew could then come in and reconfigure the old tasting room, using plans Trey had drawn up to give her the office space she needed.

Other pieces were also falling into place. She had determined which software to use to process invoices and bought it, familiarizing herself with it. She'd also invested in a customer relationship management system to keep track of her clients and their information. She had all her vendors lined up, from ones who would provide goods and services at the event center to ones she would recommend to clients, such as the local jeweler and hotels and B&B's for guests to stay in.

She sensed a presence and glanced up, seeing Braden standing in the doorway, his tall, rangy body tan from the time he'd spent outdoors in the Texas sun. Every time she saw him, strong emotions filled her. Harper realized how lucky she was to have this sexy, smart, hardworking man in her life.

"Hey, you," she said. "What are you doing here?"

"I have somewhere I want to take you. Are you up for playing hooky in the middle of the week?"

She wanted to ask if it could wait, but then she decided work could be what waited. They were busy people, but if he had carved time out of his schedule for them to spend some time together, she could do the same.

"You bet," she told him, opening the desk drawer and removing her purse from it. "Where are we going?"

"That is a surprise." He glanced down. "Good. You have comfortable shoes on."

"Are we going hiking?"

"Curiosity is eating you up, isn't it?" he teased. "I will tell you that I think a stop at Sonic is in order. Happy hour is still going on."

She laughed. "You are hooked on Sonic's crushed ice, aren't you?"

"That I am, Ms. Hart."

They left the building, waving goodbye to her mom, and Braden opened the truck door for her. She liked that he was such a gentleman. He came around to the driver's side and slid behind the wheel.

Braden pulled in at Sonic a few minutes later, where her dad used to take all them for happy hour after school once a week. The drive-in burger joint discounted its drinks and floats from two until four every afternoon, and it had been a treat to leave school and make a Sonic run. Harper had always opted for root beer, enjoying the taste of it poured over the crushed ice, which she loved to chew. Braden ordered a root beer for her and a DP for himself, and they sat in the car, enjoying their drinks, catching up on their day.

"I'm ready to roll on production on a really special wine," he shared. "I believe it's the perfect blend. More merlot than cab. Very mellow. I think I've knocked it out of the park. I'll have your dad taste it first thing tomorrow morning to get his opinion, but I think he'll be pleased."

"I am so proud of you," she said. "I've already tasted several of your wines now, and you are more than holding to the Lost Creek Vineyards' standard. You taking over the winemaking end of the business and letting Dad cut back to only handling clients and marketing has really taken a burden off his plate and let you thrive. Dad has devoted most of his adult life to the grapes. It's time he and Mom got to play a little and enjoy the fruits of owning a successful business."

"Your dad not only gave me the best position in a winery, but he also helped restore my faith in myself," Braden told her. "I had beaten myself up for so long. Couldn't find a job at any vineyard, much less an award-winning winery. He's given me the greatest gift—the responsibility of creating my own wines. Bill gave me a new outlook on life."

He reached for her hand, squeezing it. "You've done the same, Harper. Your dad believed I was a talented enologist and gave me the freedom to follow my instincts—and my heart."

Bringing their joined hands to his lips, he brushed a tender kiss upon her fingers. "And you let me know I was okay personally."

"I've enjoyed our time together," Harper said, wanting to tell this amazing man that she loved him. That was too much to put on his plate now, though. Braden was at a busy time of the season, working on the flavor profiles for this year. She decided Christmas would be her target date to open up and share her feelings with him. By then, the event center would be open and hopefully, weddings would have been booked.

He released her hand. "We've got places to be."

Braden started up the truck, and they left town. After a few minutes, he slowed the truck and turned in at The Inn on Lost Creek, a local B&B.

"Mr. Clark, have you booked us a room?" she asked, excited by the thought of having him all to herself.

He smiled enigmatically. "You'll see."

They didn't stop at the B&B, which puzzled her. instead, he headed down a small road, parking in front of a free-standing cottage. Another cottage sat opposite it, about twenty yards away.

"We're going to stay here tonight?"

"I thought we deserved a getaway, Harper. We've both been putting in long hours, and that's not going to ease up anytime soon."

He got out of the car and came around to her side, opening her door and helping her out.

"I should text Ivy and let her know we won't be home tonight."

"Ivy's not going to worry about anything," he promised. "Come on inside."

The cottage had a porch with two rockers on it.

"Maybe we can sit on the porch tonight and watch the sun set," she said. "Sip on a glass of wine. Relax."

"Maybe. If I don't have you in bed."

A thrill shot through Harper, and anticipation flooded her. She had never been so physically attuned to a man. Making love with Braden Clark each time was an adventure.

He took out a key and unlocked the door, causing her to comment, "My, you are prepared."

Motioning for her to go first, she entered the cottage. The room was cozy, with a loveseat in front of a small coffee table, and two club chairs nearby. She didn't see anywhere to eat other than a breakfast bar with two stools sitting at it. A kitchenette was on the other side, with a small fridge, microwave, and hot plate.

"Let's check out the bedroom," he said, leading her to the open door off the main room.

Again, the bedroom was small, a queen-sized bed dominating it. She saw her weekender sitting at the foot of the bed.

"You packed for me?"

"I would never have attempted that," he said, laughing. "Ivy put together what she thought you might need."

Harper slipped her arms around his waist. "Thank you, Braden. A mid-week getaway is exactly what I needed." She corrected herself. "What *we* needed."

He kissed her lightly, disappointing her. She was ready to tear his clothes off him.

"Want to go for a walk?" he asked.

"All right," she agreed. "Now I see why you were happy to see me wearing tennis shoes."

They walked the property, which had a lovely flower garden, as well as a vegetable garden. Everything was still green this September afternoon, from the grass to the thick trees. As they approached a bridge, she could hear rushing water.

"We must be close to the river."

"We are," he assured her.

Strolling hand-in-hand, they reached the bridge and stepped onto it. Braden led her halfway across before they stopped, leaning on the rail and looking down at the moving water below. His hand cupped her nape, his thumb gliding up and down the side of her neck. Harper's heart began to beat rapidly as Braden's other hand touched her waist, turning her so that she faced him.

"Harper," he said, his voice low and rough, causing butterflies to begin beating inside her. "I've told you I was broken—but you've fixed me."

She placed a palm against his broad chest. "No, you did

that yourself, Braden. You had everything taken from you, but you never gave up."

His thumb continued to caress her neck. "Still, you've been a big part of putting this Humpty Dumpty back together. Yes, my confidence is soaring now that I'm working again as a winemaker and doing a damn fine job of it. But I was depleted emotionally. I never thought I would ever be close with a woman, much less love her."

Her breath hitched. She swallowed. "Love?" she echoed.

"I love you, Harper Hart. I love how you draw up to-do lists and systematically work your way through them. I love how you care about everyone around you. How many people would think to bring popsicles to the crew putting on a roof in the hot summer sun? But that's you. You care about others."

He tugged her close, his thumb now stroking her cheek. "I love how smart you are. How open you are. How willing you are to do the hard work and make the tough decisions."

Braden kissed her softly. "There isn't anything I would change about you. You are perfect to me. I love you, Harper. I love us together. We're like one of the blends I've experimented with, tweaking it until it's absolutely perfect. We go together, just like those blended wines do. I wanted you to know that. To understand that I'm committed to you. That I want to continue to grow with you. To learn more about you. To spend every free moment I have with you."

His words moved her, and her throat thickened with

emotion. "I have loved you for what seems like forever, Braden," she revealed. "I didn't know when to say those words to you. I wasn't sure if you were ready to make that kind of commitment to me."

"I would do anything you asked of me, Harper. Go anywhere you wished. I just needed to let you know that I'm in this relationship for as long as you want us to be."

She touched her fingers to his face. "What if I want a really long time with you?"

A slow smile spread across his face, his eyes lighting up. "I would say that makes me very, very happy."

Knowing she was going out on a limb, Harper asked, "Are we talking marriage, Braden? A dog? Kids?"

"If you see that as our future, I'd be happy. If that's too much for you, I'll still be happy just being with you, babe."

Fear gripped her for a moment. At one time, Harper had thought Ath would be her husband. The father of her children. The man she spent every day beside. But that dream had crumbled in an instant, and she had been afraid to resurrect it.

Only now, she looked at Braden and saw he held more love for her than Atherton Armistead ever had. Braden was selfless. Giving. Wise.

And she wanted him with her forever.

"I love you," she said sincerely. "I cannot imagine my life without you. I do want kids someday, Braden. For now, I'd be happy simply to be called your wife and give my everything to you."

She saw the tears fill his eyes, moving her greatly. Her own tears began to fall down her cheeks.

"Will you marry me, Harper Hart?" he asked, searching her face. "Will you continue to help me grow as a person and us as a couple? "

Joy filled her. "I will marry you whenever and wherever you wish," she said, happiness spilling from her."

A shadow crossed his face. "I can't afford a fancy engagement ring. I won't be able to take you on some exotic honeymoon, Harper."

"I don't need either. In fact, I would prefer a simple wedding band. No engagement ring is necessary."

He frowned. "Shouldn't a woman planning weddings be wearing a huge rock on her hand?"

"It's not the diamond in a ring that's important," she said. "What tells of love is the eternal circle that makes up that ring."

Braden smiled. "You always know the right thing to say. When can I slip that ring on your finger?"

"How about if we're the first wedding that takes place at the event center?" she asked.

He laughed. "You want our ceremony and reception to be the dress rehearsal for all the events to come?" he teased.

"I want our wedding to be the gold standard. For brides to see how in love we are and know the origins of our love led to the first wedding to take place at Lost Creek Winery."

"You're on," Braden said, his mouth coming down on hers, his kiss demanding.

They kissed for an eternity on the bridge, the birds sweetly chirping around them, the water of the river rushing below. The kiss told of the promises they were making to one another, even before the legal ceremony occurred.

When Braden broke the kiss, she said, "I will never forget this moment. The moment we shared how we felt toward one another. I see our future together, Braden, and I know how special it will be. How safe I feel in your arms and how much love I have for you."

He kissed her again. "I love you. It's so liberating finally being able to say it out loud."

Harper grinned. "Do you think you could say it again while we're naked in bed?"

He released her fast, grabbing her hand, running along the bridge. They rushed back to the cottage and bounded inside, the door barely closed before they were tearing off their clothes. Braden finished first and helped her fling the last of what she wore to the floor.

Scooping her up, he carried her to the bedroom, where the bed was already turned back.

"I'm going to love you so much, you'll never want to leave here," he promised.

The sex was hot. Dirty. Fast. And very, very satisfying.

17

Harper stood next to Ivy, their fingers linked together. Braden held her other hand. Her parents were also present, just as eager to see the final results of months of hard work. Finley had already been allowed early access and had even dressed the tables, shooting numerous pictures, both inside and outside, and would join them at the tasting room.

Fred Patterson had asked them to be present today to do a walk-through of all three completed sites. Harper had worked from home the last two weeks, staying out of the way of the crew as they finished up the events facility and tasting room and the redesign of the former tasting room, which would now serve as the offices for Weddings with Hart.

"I have to tell you, Fred, the outside looks terrific," her dad said. "Your use of limestone, wood, and glass are the perfect marriage."

"Thank Trey Watson for his design efforts," the construction manager told them. "It was Trey's vision. We just brought it to life." He smiled. "But yes, I'm really pleased at how things turned out."

A generous-sized parking lot had been paved so that guests would have ample space to park at events. A cobblestone sidewalk led up to the event center, with landscaping which used the best elements of the Texas Hill Country. The large oaks present had been left intact, while tastefully scattered patches of salvia, lacy oak, Texas Gold Columbine, and cape plumbago brought color to the setting.

They walked across the bridge, rebuilt and widened, and headed inside. Fred had asked Harper for a map of how she wanted things placed for a typical wedding. She had provided three different set-ups, not knowing which Fred would choose and Finley would dress.

Inside, she removed her sunglasses, her eyes roaming, taking in everything.

"It's beautiful," she said, tears misting her eyes.

Moving about the room, she saw where weddings would occur, the backdrop an entire wall of glass which looked out over one of the fields which grew red grapes. Receptions would be on the other side of the building, and tables had been set up, both round and rectangular, for a guest list of one hundred and fifty, giving her a clear idea of the space. Already, she was reconfiguring the setup in her head, changing it from seventy-five to one hundred to two hundred and twenty-five, the maximum allowed. She could see that last number really pushed things, and so she would advise clients accordingly.

"Walk us through, Harper," Mom encouraged.

"Okay. Obviously, here are the seats for the ceremony. The slight platform is only six inches high, but it will allow everyone a good view of the bride and groom, while attendants can be lined up here."

She continued around the room, pleased at how the tables had been completely set, with the dinnerware, silverware, and glassware she had purchased in San Antonio at a restaurant supply place. Centerpieces were also on display, and she couldn't help but sigh at the beautiful Chiavari chairs at the tables.

"It's stunning," Ivy declared. "The table decorations are spot on."

"Finley changed out a few of the tables when she was photographing the room," Fred told them. "She wanted to get examples of each type you were offering, as well as the entire room."

"Keep going," Dad encouraged. "I want to see the rest."

"You just want to find the bar," her mom teased.

Harper took them to the bar and an area which housed a photo booth. They went to the area housing the two rooms where the bride and her attendants and the groom and his would get ready for the ceremony.

They headed back and explored the kitchen, which had a large walk-in fridge and a smaller freezer.

"Plenty of room for a caterer to set up and plate everything," Mom noted.

"Oh, I forgot to show you the area designated for the

cake cutting and the tables for that," she said, leading them back to the reception area.

"I know you'll want to do a more thorough walk-through," Fred said. "Test lights. Flush toilets. That kind of thing."

"We can come back and do that after we see the other buildings," Braden said. Looking to her, he asked, "Are you ready to go and see the rest?"

"Yes," she agreed.

They returned to the parking lot and drove to the new tasting room. Again, the exterior looked as if it belonged in the Hill Country. To the left of the tasting room was a large, covered patio with plenty of tables and a bar area. Beyond it, more tables appeared, from picnic to small metal two-tops. What Harper liked best was the way old wine barrels had been used. One of the construction team members dallied in furniture making, and he had been tapped to create all kinds of pieces from old wine barrels. Now the patio held barrels full of beautiful blooms, as well as barrels which served as the base for long tables. Some barrels had been cut in half and served as a coffee table to hold drinks and food, while a few seating areas had rockers composed entirely of various barrel pieces.

"This captures exactly what I was hoping for," Harper said.

"Let's go inside," her sister said enthusiastically.

The interior of the tasting room was even better. The tasting bar ran a good twenty feet, and two other areas had been designated to use for tastings. Another two groupings of chairs were for guests who either were waiting for their tasting to begin or for ones who had already gone through the process and chose to stay a while and visit, sipping on wine.

Throughout the tasting room were displays of various Lost Creek wines on floating shelves, highlighting the medals they had won. Large wine racks also held numerous bottles of wine which could be purchased.

They all went behind the tasting bar and saw the storage space, which contained wineglasses for both red and white wines, all stamped with the winery's logo on them. Racks stored the reds, while if you stepped through a door, a large fridge chilled the whites and blends which needed cooling.

"This is amazing, Fred," Ivy said. "Even better than what I imagined."

"Shall we tour the gift shop?" he asked.

They moved toward it and found Finley inside, photographing some of the merchandise.

"Hey, everyone," she said. "What do you think?"

"We love it," Harper said.

"Seeing a dream come to life is a powerful thing," her dad added.

They walked through the gift shop and also checked out the restrooms. By then, Finley was replacing items on shelves again.

"I'll be taking updated photos for the website," she told the group. "I've already got great shots of the exterior and interior of each building, but I need to do headshots for everyone who works at LCV. Should I coordinate that with you, Cecily?"

"I'm happy to set up the times, Finley," Mom told her. "Let me know what your calendar looks like. We can try to get them done in one or two days and not have you coming out several times."

"I appreciate it," her friend said.

"We should move on to your offices, Harper," Fred said.

They returned to their cars and drove the short distance. Pride filled Harper as they pulled up and she saw the Weddings with Hart sign displayed in front of her portion of the building. Inside, they saw her office and the large conference room where she would meet with potential clients. A second office was designated for bookkeeping, and she'd already purchased the accounting program her mom used, with Mom giving her lessons on how to use it as she set up everything for Harper. For now, Mom would help Harper get her feet wet with it before completely handing over the reins. She hoped one day to be able to turn enough of a profit to hire a business manager to handle all the invoicing, bookkeeping, and taxes. For now, though, she would be in charge.

She took them to the small kitchen. "I'll store samples of bride and groom cakes here. I haven't yet worked out the food samplings. I think it might be better to send clients into town to the restaurants I'll be using."

The last place they saw was a storage area, where Harper had samples of various decorations and table settings.

"I'm really pleased, Fred," she told the construction

manager. "We'll take our time and go through everywhere again now."

"I'll leave you to it, Harper. Call me if you run into anything that needs tweaking." He offered his hand. "It's been a pleasure working with you."

Fred shook all their hands and left. Harper retreated to the kitchen, signaling Braden to accompany her. They came back a few minutes later with trays bearing champagne flutes.

Raising her glass, Harper said, "To the next chapter at Lost Creek Winery. May we be successful and have the time of our lives."

"Hear, hear," Dad said.

They all downed their champagne, and she told Braden, "I don't know if I'm giddy from drinking the champagne too fast or if it's simply the joy I feel now."

"It's becoming reality, babe," he said, pressing his lips to hers.

"All I have to do now is go through and see which pictures of Finley's need to be uploaded to the website, and then I'll be open for business and ready to book events." She paused. "What about us?"

"You mean being the first wedding in the place? Let's get the license and set the date."

"You mean it?"

He smoothed her hair. "You know I do. I know we won't be able to take off any time for a honeymoon. I couldn't afford it, anyway. Maybe we can take a trip into San Antonio for a day or two. You're always talking about how much you like the city."

"Hey, my money is your money, honey," Harper told him. "I don't see the point in separate bank accounts once we're married."

She saw the stubborn look in his eyes, though. Braden Clark was not a man who would want to be dependent upon his wife—or anyone else.

"We can look into what it takes to get a license," she said. "Then we can talk about a date." She looked at the others. "Braden and I are headed back to the event center to do a slow, thorough walk-through. Ivy, you do the same at the tasting room and gift shop. Help her out, Mom. You've got a great eye for detail."

"I guess that leaves me to go back to the office and sip a DP," Dad said, smiling. "Come with me, Finley? I have a few ideas for some new marketing. I'd like to run them by you and see if you could photograph some things for me."

"Sure thing, Mr. H," Finley said.

Harper went to Braden's truck to drive back to the event center.

"I have an idea. A little bit out there," she said.

"What is it?"

"You know I've planned to throw a big party for the grand opening of the facility. Family. Friends. Locals. Vendors."

"Yeah, you mentioned that to Javier when we stopped for lunch in Austin."

"What if it started with a wedding—and then the reception *was* the party?" she asked. "Yes, there would be some people we're not super close to at our wedding, but we could still celebrate. It would give the vendors I've signed—and the ones I'm trying to talk onboard—a glimpse at how an event could turn out."

"Would you be able to manage the celebration and get married at the same time?"

"Oh, please. I could organize and run it in my sleep," she said, only half-teasing. "This is what I've done for years, Braden. Instead of slipping through and around people, I'll just be the bride and go around the room, greeting guests and checking on things a little more openly."

"I don't care if we have twenty or a hundred and twenty at our wedding. As long as it's you and me, saying those *I Do's*, I'm good."

They went through the facility at a much slower pace, with Harper's eye for detail taking in everything. She whipped out her phone and made a list of four things that needed attention, all minor in nature.

"Fred and his crew really did an excellent job," Braden said.

"I would definitely recommend them to anyone," she seconded. "I'll need to call Trey and let him know we've seen everything and how pleased we are."

Heading for the truck again, she texted the list to Fred, saying if she had anything additional, she would let him know. Braden told her he needed to get back to work and would see her at home, so he dropped her at the new tasting room.

Ivy had gone through the place with a fine-tooth comb and said, "I only found one small detail I need Fred to fix."

Harper asked what it was and made a note of it. "When will you start using this space?"

"Tomorrow," her sister said. "It's stocked and ready to go. I've already called The Cheese Connoisseur, and they'll deliver the tasting plates first thing tomorrow morning. Sarah and Melanie will be coming in early to familiarize themselves with the layout and the gift shop. I also have two interviews tomorrow for gift shop clerks. I'm on things!"

"It sounds like it. I'm happy you're pleased with how everything has turned out."

"I am." Ivy paused. "I thought I'd call Dax and see if he wanted to come over and check it out."

"Great idea," she encourages. "How are things going with the two of you?"

"Good," Ivy said casually, not elaborating.

Harper decided when her sister had something to say, she would. For now, Harper would not bring up Dax again and wait for Ivy to do so.

"Want me to drop you at your new place?" Ivy asked. "It's really nice. Clients will be impressed."

"I can walk," she said. "It's a pretty day, and it's not that far. It's not as if I'll be meeting with anyone from the public."

She set out, walking briskly, arriving at her office in a little over twenty minutes. Once more, she went through the entire space. The only thing she found wrong was one outlet which wasn't working. The top plug worked fine, but the bottom one didn't. Harper supposed it was a loose wire and could easily be remedied.

Texting Fred again, she heard back from him immediately. He told her everything would be in working order by noon tomorrow. He hoped they could meet then, let her approve the last bit of work, and then she could sign off on the paperwork. She agreed, telling him she would be at the event center at noon.

Hot from her walk and the warm sunshine, she went to the bathroom and splashed cold water on her face, dabbing it with a paper towel. The restroom was a little sterile for her, which meant clients would also view it the same way. She would buy a few items to spruce it up a bit. She hoped in a week, all pictures would be up on the website, and she'd be in a position to meet with clients. She also wanted to start planning her own combination wedding and reception and grand opening party.

Her first call would be to Blackwood BBQ. She wanted them to be her go-to caterer. Before she could book them, though, she needed to check on how to get married in Texas. She doubted anything had changed in the months since she and Ath had applied for their own license and was right. Bexar County, where San Antonio was located, was the closest county clerk's office to them. They could fill out the online form and submit it, but they would still need to go in person to complete the process.

She thought they might as well fill out the form and submit it tonight when they got home from work. Once they applied in person, they would have ninety days to get married. Since she wanted to hold the grand opening in about a month, having the license in hand would be one less thing to worry about. It made her realize it was time to line up a couple of officiants to conduct weddings at the winery, and she made a note of that.

Turning to her calendar, she looked a month ahead, thinking she could get the invitations emailed to everyone in the next week and hold the party three weeks after that. She wouldn't make a mention of the wedding. That would be the surprise once guests arrived. Doing it that way would cut down on the time to have invitations printed and mailed out, as well. She would need to talk with Mom about a guestlist. While Harper would be inviting a few friends and others she wished to work with in her new business venture, she knew her parents would have a certain number of people they would wish to invite.

She decided to head next door and chat with her mom about what the grand opening celebration would entail. She'd also need to talk with Emerson ASAP about baking the wedding and groom's cakes. Harper had grown to really like Emerson quite a bit. She felt her new friend's heart really wasn't in teaching and hoped to encourage her to turn her sights to baking as a career.

Standing, she slipped her tablet into her tote and placed her sunglasses on before starting out of her office. The door opened, and her heart sped up for a moment, thinking she might already have a client. Then she saw who it was and was happy her eyes were hidden by the dark glasses.

Because her visitor was none other than Atherton Armistead.

18

S he wanted to slap him. Scream at him. Punch him in the nose. Kick him in the balls.

But Harper did none of these things.

Instead, she reined in her temper. Any display of emotion would make Ath think that she still had feelings for him—when the opposite was true. She also knew he was petty enough that if she laid a finger on him, he would slap her with assault charges. She couldn't afford to go to jail and shake off the bad publicity which would result from the incident.

Looking at him coolly, she asked, "What do you want?"

Ath gave her that million-dollar smile, one which reflected his father's image. It made Harper question what she had ever seen in him. Yes, he was incredibly handsome but far too polished for her taste. Comparing Ath to Braden, with his rugged good looks and sterling character, made her rejoice that she had been fortunate enough to find Braden when she was at the lowest point of her life.

"Why do you think I want anything, Harper?" he asked, his tone suggestive and flirtatious.

She removed her sunglasses and looked at him dispassionately. "You always want something, Ath. Something that benefits you. And I don't see myself giving anything to you—whatever that is. How did you even find me?"

"You left Austin pretty quickly. I can understand why. I suppose I left you in a pretty awkward position."

"Awkward?" she asked, her voice rising. Harper tamped down the anger racing through her and stared at him without emotion.

"It wasn't hard to track you down, Harper. After all, I've visited Lost Creek before. Plus, your old boss was bragging on you. How you'd pulled yourself up by the bootstraps and that you were creating your own event facility at Lost Creek Vineyards and would plan and host events."

She wanted to ask him again why he was here but decided to wait him out, merely staring at him without speaking. Ath was someone who was never comfortable with silence, and she knew he would fill it.

"I've missed you," he said, reaching out and touching her arm.

Immediately, she jerked away, taking a step back. But only one. She didn't want him to think that he intimidated her.

"I want you to leave. Now," she said firmly. "We have nothing to discuss."

"On the contrary, we have a couple of things we need to talk over together."

He smiled again, and she was completely unaffected by it. It was liberating to be immune to the charm which used to suck her in. Ath must have figured that out because his smile quickly faded.

"You are the best event planner in Austin," he complimented. "I need to draw on that now."

Frustration filled her. "Do you really believe I would take you on as a client? Besides, I don't live and work in Austin anymore."

"But you could," he said, confidence in his tone. "You see, I'm going to run for Land Commissioner next fall when Dad runs for governor."

"What would that have to do with me?" she asked sharply, tired of disguising her feelings.

"Everything. I've got my family name and good looks, but I need more. The secret sauce. Eventually, the story would get out regarding how we called off our marriage."

Harper snorted. "There's no *we* in that equation, Ath. It was all you. And you were so cowardly, you couldn't even man up enough to tell me we weren't getting married. That you still planned for the ceremony to take place—but you had replaced me as the bride."

Contriteness filled his voice and face. "I am sorry about that, Harper. You're right. I should have spoken to you in person, long before it ever came to that."

"So, let me get this straight. You know your image will be damaged when reporters barely have to scratch the surface and find out you jilted me for Cynthia. That one bride was out the door and another one stepped in without having to change the date. Yes, that will make you look pretty bad in the eyes of voters. Particularly, female voters."

He nodded enthusiastically. "That's it. You understand my dilemma. If I can get you to come back to Austin and plan my campaign fundraisers and other events, it's a win-win for us both. People can see that there are no hard feelings between us, plus I would have the best event planner in Austin handling my affairs. Why, you could even—"

"Stop right there, Ath. I don't know what kind of fantasy world you're living in, but I would never lift a finger to help you win office, and I would certainly never vote for you. You're the one with the terrible character who dumped me. I've heard how you and Cynthia have made the rounds as the golden couple of Austin. Well, I want no part of that. I'm not going to sell the lie that you're a good man whom the public should trust and vote into office, much less that I forgive both you and Cynthia, and she's once again my closest friend. You both walked away from me. Ties have been severed, Ath. Those fences will never be mended between us."

She saw the worry which filled his eyes. "Are you going to talk to the press once I announce my candidacy?" he asked anxiously.

"I won't actively seek out reporters, but if any come knocking on my door? They will receive the unvarnished truth."

Immediately, he switched tactics. "You know that I still love you, Harper, don't you?"

She burst out laughing because he was being so obvious. "Do you believe I'm so foolish to believe any lies that come from your mouth, much less nonsense such as that?"

"I will admit to you that I made a mistake. Mom thought Cynthia would present a better image than you as my wife, especially once I decided to declare my candidacy."

She should have known Bethany Armistead had a hand in what took place.

"Your mother never liked me much, did she?"

"Cynthia comes from an old, moneyed family. She has the looks and charm. She's someone who is willing to set aside her career and campaign for me. You never would have done that."

Was he right? Would she have refused to do so?

Harper didn't know—because she had never been given the chance to find out. Although she should have suspected it, Ath had never mentioned a word to her about running for state office. She had been in love with him, though, and most likely would have set aside her own ambitions and career path in order to support him.

With Braden, she would never have to make that choice. He understood her completely.

"No, you don't still love me. I'm not certain you ever did. No, I will not play nice and pretend to have forgiven you and my former best friend for blindsiding me with the toughest blow of my life. It did show me, however, that I am made of strong stuff, Ath. Stronger than I ever knew. I've started a new life. A new business. I'm looking forward. Not to the past."

She paused. "If reporters come calling, I won't air your dirty laundry with them, but I won't disguise the facts."

He took a step toward her. Harper held her ground. Ath even reached out and clasped her elbow. His touch did nothing.

"What if I told you I realize now that I made a huge mistake in listening to my mother and marrying Cynthia? Please, come back to Austin. We can pick up where we left off."

"You are not going to turn around and divorce Cynthia so quickly after having married her, especially if you're running for public office."

"No," he said quickly. "I didn't mean to insinuate that. I just thought... we could begin seeing one another again. Capture that old magic."

She shook her head in disbelief. "So, the woman you asked to marry you—the very woman you had someone else dump—is now the woman you want to cheat on your wife with?"

Harper took his forearm and removed his hand from her in a calm, deliberate fashion.

"I knew you had zero character, Ath, but you are really scraping the bottom of the barrel now. I told you. You simply aren't listening. I don't love you. I will never work for you. I never want to see you again. My life is here now. In Lost Creek. With my business. My family." She paused. "And a man who really does love me."

That got his attention. Ath's eyes widened in surprise. "You're seeing someone? Already?"

She shrugged casually. "Why wouldn't I? You moved on. I have, too. If that bruises your tender ego, so be it."

Harper saw the shift in him. The desperation in his eyes.

"Okay, Harper. You're over me. I get that. You don't want to come to work on my campaign. I suppose I can understand that, too. But I need you to be sunny and supportive when those journalists come knocking." He glared at her. "How much?"

"That's the bottom line then? You came here, thinking I would crumple. That I was still in love with you and would go along with whatever you wanted. Work for you. Sleep with you. And now you realize neither of those will ever happen, you want to bribe me."

He frowned deeply. "Bribe is such an ugly word, Harper."

"I'm not taking any money from you, Ath."

"You did before," he said quickly.

Harper regretted now that she had done so, but that was water under the bridge. "It was money in our joint account," she said dismissively. "It was money you left there to assuage your guilt over how you treated me."

"That's probably what you've used to start your new little business," he said harshly.

"What I do now is none of your concern, Ath. I want you to leave, and I don't expect to ever see you again."

He studied her a moment, and she actually saw sadness fill his eyes.

"I did you wrong, Harper. For that, I am truly sorry. You always were a better person than I was. Mom says you weren't good enough for me, but the truth is that I was never good enough for you."

He squared his shoulders. "I'll have to live with what I did to you. To us."

His words did not move her in the slightest. Instead, she began slowly clapping.

"You'll be fine on the political stage, Ath. That little speech sounded very sincere. Voters will gobble it up. You'll spin it about how you weren't the man you wanted to be. How you've learned from your mistakes. How you're a stronger, better man now. Most voters will actually buy into that. Everybody loves a second chance story. One of redemption."

Harper looked at him with steely determination running through her. "But a handful of us will know that it's all an act. I don't have an ax to grind, Ath. I have no skin in this game. You've pivoted through all the scripts you brought with you today. Job offer. Mistress offer. Bribery offer. And redeemed man. You and I both know exactly what kind of snake in the grass you are.

"Get out. Don't come back to Lost Creek."

He changed in the blink of an eye, his eyes growing hard, anger sparking in them. "You better keep your mouth shut, Harper. Or my family will ruin you and your little business."

Wheeling, Ath strode from the office, slamming the door behind him like a petulant teenager.

Harper collapsed in the nearest chair, taking slow, deep breaths, trying to get her emotions under control. She didn't know how he might affect her business. Only that he could. The reach of the Armistead family stretched throughout Texas.

The question was, would they deliberately try to destroy what she was creating here in Lost Creek out of spite?

19

Harper returned home, still shaken, but determined not to mention Ath's visit to anyone.

Especially Braden.

She was surprised to see his truck already at home and then recalled it was their night to host Finley and Emerson for their weekly dinner. She found Braden in the kitchen, singing along to the soundtrack from *Grease*. He was at the stove, stirring something, and she went and wrapped her arms around his waist, resting her cheek against his broad back.

"What are you making?" she asked.

"Paella. I've never tried it before, but Finley mentioned something about it not too long ago. She sent me her recipe, and I am doing my spin on it."

He turned and enveloped her in his arms, making Harper feel safe from the world. It was amazing how his touch calmed her and at the same time caused desire to stir within her.

Dropping a kiss on top of her head, he said, "Pull out your calendar. Let's find a date to get married."

Reluctantly, she pulled away from him and went to her tote, which held her work calendar, and brought it back to the kitchen. They sat at the table and reviewed possible dates, settling on one a little more than three weeks away.

"You'll have to work fast to pull everything together," he told her.

She grinned. "Fast is my middle name. Along with efficient. I'm *Mission Impossible* all the way. The catering is the biggest piece of it. Let me call Shy Blackwood. If he can't cater, then we'll need to work around when he can."

Grabbing her cell, Harper dialed Blackwood BBQ, telling Shy the event center was now complete.

"Would you like to come check it out tomorrow?" she asked. "I hope you're going to be catering a ton of events for me."

"Can we do it early, Harper? Maybe eight?" Shy asked.

"Early is always good for me. I'll meet you there. Also, I want to have a grand opening party to show off the place. Would you be able to cater something three weeks from this coming Saturday?"

"I don't see why not. We can talk specifics regarding the menu tomorrow. See you then."

Harper set down her phone. "Looks like that date is a go. Now, we need to see if Finley can photograph things and if Emerson can bake the cakes."

He frowned. "I thought this was going to be more of a

surprise. Just spring it on those attending and have a spontaneous ceremony."

"Neither one of us have been married before, Braden. I may be willing to skip over a lot of the usual steps, but I do want a wedding cake and a groom's cake. We can swear Finley and Emerson to secrecy."

"Won't people figure it out when they see the cakes?"

"For the most part, the facility will be for weddings. I don't think people will question seeing a wedding and groom's cake on display. And I'm not going to be wearing a traditional bridal gown anyway."

She thought of the elaborate gown with a long train she had been slated to wear at her wedding to Ath. She had returned the dress to the bridal shop and told them she wouldn't be needing the gown after all, asking them to donate it to a bride who might appreciate it. Harper wanted no reminders of that wedding gown or the elaborate reception that had been planned by Bethany Armistead. Instead, she would go into San Antonio and find something appropriate for the grand opening. Or she might even wear something she already had.

Braden must have been reading her mind because he asked, "What will you and I wear then?"

"I haven't decided. I'll go through my closet and if I can't find what I want, I'll pick up something."

"I'll need a suit," he said. "I should have one anyway. In case Bill ever needs me to meet with clients."

Harper placed her hand over his. "Or to wear when we go to a wine competition. I know you're going to have plenty of wines nominated."

"We also need to get our license and pick up wedding bands, Harper. Maybe we could do a day together in San Antonio and run through our to-do list."

"I'm meeting with Shy tomorrow at eight. That shouldn't take more than an hour. Could you be ready to leave by nine? That would put us in San Antonio no later than ten. We could knock out everything in a day. Then I need to get busy hiring staff. Shy will bring people to plate things, but I'll need to have people to serve. Strike chairs for the dance floor. Serve as a clean-up crew. That kind of thing."

"You've got a lot on your plate. Are you sure you want to add a wedding to it?"

She beamed at him. "I'm ready to start my life with you, Braden. Planning is in my blood. It's what I do best. I'll be ready for this party—and our wedding."

He went back to nursing the paella, while Harper pulled up the online wedding application for the State of Texas. She filled out all she could, asking him a few questions, and then submitted it.

"Okay. The bulk is done, but we have to show up in person to finish up the process. We can apply for the license first. It's the most important piece of the puzzle. I'll make a list of everything else we need to do while we're there."

Ivy arrived home, bringing Finley and Emerson inside with her.

Emerson had a cake stand in hand and said, "I come bearing cinnamon roll layer cake for dessert."

"It looks delicious," Harper said. "I'm a sucker for cinnamon."

Finley had a pitcher in each hand. "And I've got us covered with sangria. Braden said he was making paella. I hope this will be okay."

She laughed. "I've never turned down your sangria. Ever."

They gathered around the kitchen table. Once everyone had bowls of paella in front of them, Braden nodded at her.

"Since the event center is completed, I've talked with Shy Blackwood about catering a big grand opening. Finley, I was hoping you might photograph everything. Three weeks from this coming Saturday."

"I'd be happy to do that, Harper. We also need a time for us to go through all the pictures I took today. I really got some good ones. You can choose which ones you want Ivy to put up on the website. I'm sure you'll also want to have some brochures on hand to give to clients. We can make sure those photographs are different from the ones on the website."

Turning to Emerson, Harper said, "I would like to have a wedding and groom's cake on display in the area designated for the cutting of the cakes. Just to give people an idea of the setup. Would you be able to bake both for me?"

"Absolutely," Emerson said. "Do you have any ideas about what you might like?"

"Not really. Can I look at some samples after dinner and go from there?"

"Of course," Emerson said. "How many guests will be invited?"

"It's close to two hundred. I'm inviting family and friends. Also, some locals. Friends of Mom and Dad's. I'll include winery workers and the local vendors I'll be using. I want those vendors to see everything on display."

"That gives me a better idea for how many tiers for the wedding cake," Emerson said. "With a groom's cake, I can be more creative."

"I think you should put something about the winery on the groom's cake," Braden suggested, smiling at her. He would probably be wondering why she had changed her mind at the last minute and not told her friends about the wedding itself taking place. It would be a delicate process, planning for their own wedding and groom's cakes without giving away the surprise. But she knew how much the winery meant to him, and it would be nice to feature something about it on the groom's cake.

"After all, the facility is at a winery," she agreed. "Incorporating the grapes into the cake's design is an excellent idea."

They finished the paella, everyone complimenting Braden on his first attempt at making it. Emerson sliced the cake, giving everyone a piece. The beautiful dessert, with its brown sugar glaze and creamy frosting, let Harper know she needed to firm up if Emerson would serve as her cake vendor.

With dessert finished, Braden said, "Let me get this cleaned up."

"No," Ivy interjected. "Finley and I can handle the

dishes. That will allow Emerson to show you and Harper different cakes. You can provide the male perspective, Braden," she teased.

"I'll need my tablet," Emerson said. "I have pictures of wedding cakes I've baked, as well as examples of other ones I like."

"We can walk over to your place," Harper said.

They spent an hour with Emerson, looking at dozens of cakes, talking about flavors and different kinds of icing. Harper was familiar with this end of the process, having gone to dozens of cake tastings with brides.

They decided on the wedding cake, which would be five tiers, and moved on to groom's cakes. Braden insisted the cake be chocolate on chocolate, and Harper knew it was because he was a chocoholic himself. Emerson sketched a few ideas, and they decided on a design.

"The groom's cake can be rectangular, based upon the elements you want," Emerson said. "I'll bake several small ones of each kind, with varying icings, in the next day or so and let you do a tasting. If you like what I've done, I can run with it. If not, I can adjust batter and frostings, and we can try again."

"I'm eager to see how things come out," Harper said. "Have you thought anymore about whether or not you'd like to leave your part-time job with Ethel and become the Weddings with Hart exclusive cake vendor?"

"Now that we're closer to the event center opening, I'm ready to give Ethel my two-week notice. I can do that this week."

She hugged Emerson. "You won't regret it. You're so

creative, and I think you'll make a lot more than you did working Saturdays at The Bake House. I thought of you when I had the kitchen designed. I had them put in double, industrial-sized ovens, and there's plenty of space to store your equipment and decorate the cakes. There's even a walk-in fridge if they need to be stored inside it."

"I can't wait to see it," Emerson exclaimed. "I will need to bake several cakes of varying sizes in the ovens, though. Ovens can be pretty temperamental," she explained. "You bake one cake at 350 degrees for forty-five minutes—and it's underdone. In another oven, it might turn out over-done. It'll be some trial and error on my part to build a relationship with these new ovens."

Emerson laughed. "You may be sampling several cakes before I get my timing down."

Braden grinned. "I'm happy to take on the position of chief cake sampler."

"We're set then," Emerson said. "I'll bake the cakes we discussed after school tomorrow. You can come over tomorrow night or the next to do your tasting. Waiting any longer, and the cakes will be stale. And if I can come by the event center Friday after school, I'd like to spend Friday night playing with the ovens if you don't mind."

"I'll make certain you have a key to the facility so you can come and go as you like," she promised. "Also, let me know what pans and baking supplies I need to order for you to get you started."

"No, Harper. That should be on my dime. If it's going to be my business, then I need to fully take ownership of it." Emerson grinned. "But I'm really excited about the opportunity you're giving me. I'm ready to be pushed out of my comfort zone. Thank you for making me the baker for Weddings with Hart."

They told Emerson goodnight and went back to their house, finding Ivy and Finley sipping the last of the sangria.

Finley stood. "It's a school night. I need to get going. I've got some papers to grade. Thanks again for dinner, Braden. Don't forget to text me your recipe."

She and Braden sat on the sofa, talking with Ivy about all they had seen today, and Ivy mentioned a few new pieces of merchandise she wanted to stock at the gift shop.

"Music!" Harper said out of the blue. "We need entertainment for the grand opening." She thought a moment. "I don't really want to hire a band. Maybe a DJ. He could play something soft in the background while people mingle and during dinner. Then he could crank it up when the dancing starts. I'll need to find one."

"No, you won't," Ivy said. "I've got one. Dax."

"I know you've mentioned Dax plays guitar and sings." Harper treaded carefully, knowing Ivy had been seeing Dax for a while. Her sister was gone a lot and while Harper knew a good portion of that time was being spent painting in the studio Ivy had rented in town, she suspected that Ivy and Dax were also spending a good deal of time together.

"Dax DJ'd through college and for a few years after. He would be perfect. He still has his turntable and speakers."

She pulled her phone from her pocket and typed a note to contact Dax.

"I'm going into San Antonio tomorrow, so I'll try to stop by the coffeehouse the day after and see if Dax might be interested in DJ-ing the event."

"I'll mention it to him if you don't mind," Ivy said, blushing slightly.

She wondered exactly what was going on between Ivy and Dax. While Braden had spent some time with the coffeehouse owner, Harper didn't know much about Dax. It was time to learn more about the man who was making Ivy turn pink. She hoped Dax Tennyson was good enough for her sister.

"Go ahead and share with him the date and that it's the grand opening. If he's any good at this DJ-ing, maybe he'd be willing to provide that service for Weddings with Hart. Or if he gets his band together and I like their sound, I can hire them to play if a bride wants live music instead."

"Dax is really talented," Ivy said confidently. "He can sing and play just about any kind of music. He also writes his own songs. He's started performing some at Java Junction."

Harper yawned. "It's been a long day. I think I'm going to hit the sack."

"I'll do the same," Braden said.

Ivy's eyes twinkled at them as they left the den, hand-in-hand. Harper went to her own bedroom and changed into pajamas, then washed her face and brushed her teeth before heading to Braden's bedroom. He was waiting for her in bed, bare-chested, the sheet pulled to his waist. He held up the sheet, and she slipped under it, anchoring herself against him, her arm across his waist.

"I see you changed your mind and decided not to let anyone know it's going to be our wedding."

"I liked the idea of surprising everyone."

"Should we give your mom and dad a heads-up?"

"No," she said, laughing. "Mom couldn't keep a secret to save her soul, and Dad would be so proud that he would be bragging all around town. Let's keep this between you and me."

She gazed up at him, and Braden lowered his lips to hers.

20

Shy Blackwood was early, but then again, so was Harper. Bill Hart had instilled in his three children that if you weren't early, you were late. She lived by that creed and had always been early to classes. Doctors' appointments. Client meetings. It gave her time to calm herself. Look over her notes. Focus on what was ahead.

"Hello?" Shy called, entering the hall and whistling.

Harper came to meet him. "You like it?"

Grinning, he said, "I thought it was a pretty place from the outside, but this inside knocks the stuffing out of me. That glass wall? Seeing the grapevines stretch as far as the eye can see and the hills behind them? It's a really unique setting, Harper. You aren't going to have any trouble booking weddings—or other events—at this place. I might as well tell Shelly she won't be seeing me on weekends because I'll be at Lost Creek Winery catering another wedding."

She chuckled. "I did also talk to your wife. If a couple doesn't want to go the barbeque route, Shelly said she's more than happy to provide down-home cooking. Chicken-fried steak. Chicken-fried chicken. And whatever side dishes are needed. I think between the two of you, I'll satisfy most of my clients. I have talked to the owner of Lone Star Chophouse, as well."

"Trying to line him up for your fancy clients who want steak?" Shy teased.

"Yes, but I'm going to push for Blackwood to cater most weddings. I think people will be more comfortable with simple, delicious country food. After all, Texas is the king of barbeque, no matter what Kansas City and Memphis say."

"Well, show me around. Kitchen first."

Harper led Shy to the kitchen area, letting him inspect everything. He took a few pictures on his cell, saying he'd share them with Shelly so she could also familiarize herself with the arrangements.

"How many are we talking for your big party?" he asked.

"I'm figuring one-eighty to two hundred," she replied. "You know Dad will be happy to claim any leftovers."

"Will you serve your wines? What about beer? Beer and barbeque just go together."

"I've been in contact with Lost Creek Craft Brewery. They're happy to supply the beer kegs for me."

"If you'd like, I can make up a list for you. The beers they make that go the best with brisket, sausage, and ribs."

"That would be terrific, Shy. Being a wine drinker, I've never been much into beers. I could use your expertise."

He belly-laughed. "That's a good one, Harper. Next time I'm chugging a beer, I'll tell Shelly I'm doing research for Weddings with Hart."

Shy examined the walk-in fridge and asked a few questions, including where trash was to be disposed. She took him out the back door, showing him where he could park his catering trucks.

"I like having direct access like this," he told her. "Parking so close to the kitchen saves a ton of time. Would I be able to get keys to the place?"

"Yes, I'm having some made up and will make sure you and Shelly get copies."

She took him to a miniscule office off the kitchen. It contained a desk, filing cabinet, and several whiteboards.

Pointing to the whiteboards, she said, "These will be used for whatever you need. I'll reserve one for that month's events so we can easily see them at a glance. The desk calendar is a sixteen-months one. You can reference it for events beyond thirty days."

"A lot of thought went into planning this place. You done good, Harper," Shy praised. "I'm hoping I'll only be doing this for six months or so."

"What?" she said, startled by his statement.

Grinning, he said, "It looks like Ry will be coming home sometime next year. I'll probably turn over the event catering to him."

"It will be good to have him back in Lost Creek again," she said, a lump in her throat as she thought of Todd's best friend.

"I know Ry thinks of you and Ivy as his little sisters," Shy said. "I doubt he's been in touch with you over the years, but he always asks about the two of you whenever he calls." He paused. "I did tell him about that asshole you dodged a bullet with. He told me he'll kick Armistead's ass when he gets home."

Harper laughed. "Tell Ry not to worry. The asshole isn't worth it. I'm over him. *Really* over him."

Shy studied her a moment. "Hmm. Sounds like you might have a new man in your life, Harper Hart."

"Maybe," she said mysteriously. "Let's go take a look at the hall."

The tables were still arranged from yesterday's photo shoot, and Harper pulled up a few different seating arrangements on her tablet, based upon the number of guests in attendance. They talked about the most efficient way to get food to the guests, and he asked about a serving line.

"I know a buffet would be easier on you and your workers, but I don't want the bride to feel as if her guests are going through a cafeteria line at the reception. I want everything plated in the kitchen and brought out. I'll be hiring servers to do that very thing, as well as clean-up."

"My staff will take all our trays and containers with us then. Since you plan to hire people to serve and clean up, I figure once everyone is served their meal, they'll be out the door. No need for us to hang around for the cake cutting."

"That's exactly what I had in mind. Anything else you want to see?"

"Nah. I'm good. The layout really works well, Harper. You can easily take out or move in extra tables. Same with the side where the weddings will take place. You've got yourself a winner."

"Thanks, Shy. I hope once the food is out for the grand opening, you and Shelly will come join the party."

"Hell, Harper. Shelly and I *invented* partying. We'll be ready to hit the dance floor and celebrate with you."

She hugged him. "Thanks for agreeing to be my go-to for barbeque. I also look forward to working with Ry on it."

Shy held up both hands, with fingers crossed on each. "Let's just hope that's what Ry wants. We really haven't talked about his plans after he finishes up his tour. We've always assumed he'd come home to work in the family business. He's got a nose for barbeque, that boy. Did from the time he was six or seven."

"I hope he will step up and be the next generation smoking meat."

They went to their vehicles, and Harper drove straight to the building where the wines were housed and Braden's office was located. She found him sampling a red.

"Hey, come try this blend. See what you think," he said, handing her the glass.

She swirled the liquid a few times and stuck her nose deep into the wineglass, inhaling the bouquet, her eyes closed so she depended more upon her sense of smell than sight. Then she held it up, checking it for color. It was a nice ruby red.

Finally, she sipped it, moving it across her tongue before swallowing. Harper paused and took a second sip, which was the one that really counted in wine tasting.

"This is excellent, Braden," she praised. "Is this the blend you've been excited about?"

"Yes," he said, nodding eagerly. "I think it will become the signature blend of Lost Creek Vineyards for this year."

"I'm going to have couples go to the tasting room for a complimentary tasting when they book their wedding here. This definitely has to be something they sample. I know Shy was just telling me how beer and barbeque go together, but this red would hold up really well with brisket."

"I think so, too."

He took the glass she offered and tried another taste before spitting it into the nearby bucket. While some winemakers drank every sip, many simply tasted their creations and rarely swallowed.

"I'm pleased with it. I guess you're ready to go?"

"Yes. Do you mind if I drive? My SUV is a smoother ride than your truck."

"Fine with me. You know San Antonio anyway. This way, I won't have to worry about traffic and what street to take. I can sit back and enjoy the sights."

They were quiet on the drive in, and Harper marveled at how much she was beginning to enjoy silence. Braden had definitely rubbed off on her in that regard. She believed with him, she savored those quiet moments more, either ones with him or separately. She felt she was growing more as a person, too. She had confidence in her abilities and knew she would make a success of Weddings with Hart.

All because she had the right man standing beside her.

That made her decide to speak up about Ath's visit.

While they still had about a quarter-hour before they reached the San Antonio city limits, she said, "I had a visitor stop by my office yesterday." She paused a beat. "It was Ath."

Immediately, Braden went from relaxed to firing on all pistons. "What the hell? What did he want? Why didn't you come and get me?"

She shot him a look. "I didn't need rescuing, Sir Galahad. I handled it. I just wanted you to know."

He wasn't letting it drop. "Why did he show up, Harper?" he demanded. "Did he want you back?"

She glanced at him and saw the fury in his eyes fade, doubt replacing it. Reaching for his hand, she squeezed it.

"I love you," she said firmly, glancing back at the road. "I plan to have a life with you. One so long, that we'll be rocking on our porch in our nineties, sipping wine, and looking back on the amazing decades we've shared together."

She sensed the tension easing from him. "It actually was pretty comical. He did want me back. As his mistress."

Braden's expletive caused her to laugh.

"He actually *asked* that?"

"Oh, he was on a fishing expedition," she explained. "It

seems Ath is going to run for Texas Land Commissioner next year. That office predates even the Governor of Texas. It's a powerful position because it handles everything from managing state lands to conservation and veterans' issues. A lot of candidates use it as a stepping stone to higher office."

"I guess that makes sense," Braden said begrudgingly. "His family's in politics. Hell, I've even read how his dad wants to move up the ladder to governor. But how would having an extramarital affair with you make any sense? Journalists are everywhere. Seems like they would expose an affair and give him a black eye with the voters."

"Well, sleeping him wasn't the first thing he offered. He started out offering me a job. Ath wanted me to be his event planner for various fundraisers he'd hold. Basically, he knew that the story of our wedding being called off and him marrying my best friend was already out there. He thought if others saw I'd gone to work for him and his campaign, that everyone would believe all was forgiven and we were simply the best of friends."

"That takes some nerve," he said.

"When I told him no—especially because I have a life here and my own business—he pretended that he still loved me. That we could continue seeing one another." Harper laughed. "I shot that down even faster than the job offer. After that, he pretty much wanted to bribe me to keep quiet and not say anything about our broken engagement and his marriage to Cynthia. While I won't seek out reporters, I'm certainly not going to sugarcoat anything I say to them if they ask me what happened."

"How did he react to that?"

"He played his final card. Gave quite a performance. Got all teary. Talked about how he'd done me wrong, but he'd learned from his mistakes. That he was a better man now, blah-blah-blah. That might play well with some of the voters, but I think women will turn on him if the ugliness of the situation gets any press. Right now, it's merely insider gossip around Austin."

"Armistead deserves to fall flat on his face," Braden said harshly. "He did something despicable. He shouldn't be rewarded with public office for being a jerk."

Harper shrugged. "We'll see. The Armistead name is pretty solid in Texas politics. It goes back several generations. I hate to say it, but a lot of voters don't really care about issues or even bother to learn where a candidate stands. They go on party affiliation, name, and looks." She paused. "I just wanted to let you know he'd stopped by. That I'd chased him off and told him not to come back."

"Thank you for letting me know," Braden said. "I still think he's a sewer rat. Let's hope it's the last you've seen of him."

They entered San Antonio just before ten o'clock, and Harper told him instead of the Bexar County Courthouse, she had seen on line they needed to apply for their marriage license a few blocks away in the Paul Elizondo Tower. Fortunately, she found street parking nearby. No one was waiting in line, and she told the clerk they had already submitted their online application. It only took a few minutes to issue the marriage license.

The clerk told them, "This is good for ninety days, but

you have to wait seventy-two hours before you can use it, with a few exceptions."

"Our date is in three weeks, so we're good," Braden told the woman, handing over his new credit card to pay the fee.

Back at the car, she pulled up the list on her phone and asked, "What would you like to do next?" She turned the cell toward him so he could read the items to be accomplished today.

"Rings," he said. "And I want you to pick an engagement ring, too, Harper. No buts. You deserve one, a nice one, and I don't care how long it takes me to pay it off. I've got steady employment now."

Her gaze met his. "I really don't want anything fancy, Braden. I had that before—and it wasn't my choice. The ring Ath gave me was... just... gaudy. The stone was far too large, as if he were trying to make a statement with it about how rich and important he was. I didn't have a choice, though. He had already picked it out. Or I'm assuming Bethany did. His mom."

She cupped his cheek. "I really want something simple. A small solitaire would be nice. A thin band to go along with it."

"I have no idea how much something like that costs," he admitted. "I'm afraid my credit card's limit might not cover it."

"Mine will," she told him. "I can charge the rings today."

"I will pay you back, Harper," he said earnestly. "It's rough, being in a financial hole."

"Hey, everything I have is tied up in the event center. I get it. Things will be tight for a while, but we'll get on our feet soon." Harper smiled. "We have each other. That's all that matters to me."

Their lips met in a sweet, lingering kiss, and she knew that happiness wasn't a four-carat diamond. It was being with this incredible man and building a life with him over the years to come.

They left the city six hours later. Harper wore an engagement ring with a tasteful, one-carat solitaire. Their matching wedding rings had also been purchased, as had a dark suit and dress shoes for Braden and an A-line midi dress in soft rose with fluttering sleeves and a belted waist for her. She already had the perfect pair of Jimmy Choos with a crystal ankle strap that would look perfect with the dress. And unlike her original wedding gown, she would get a lot of use out of this dress, as well as remembering her own wedding when she wore it to future events.

On the drive back to Lost Creek, they sang along to songs from Stevie Wonder, Elton John, Fleetwood Mac, and KC & the Sunshine Band.

As they pulled into their driveway, Harper thought this had been one of the best days of her life.

21

Harper drove into town to meet with Dax Tennyson the next afternoon at his coffeehouse on the Lost Creek Town Square. She entered Java Junction, her first time in the place, and immediately spotted Dax. Going to the order bar he stood behind, she introduced herself and asked, "What's good?"

"If you're a coffee lover, everything," he replied with a smile. "But I've also got a great variety of teas and sparkling waters."

She could see why Ivy would be attracted to Dax. He was long and lean, with dark brown hair and warm brown eyes, and his smile drew a person in.

"It's warm today. I think I'll go with something cold," she told him. "What coffees would you recommend?"

"I've got iced lattes and mochas. Some nice nitro cold brews."

"That sounds interesting. Anything with cinnamon or vanilla in it?"

"Cinnamon caramel," he said. "Coming right up. Take a seat. I'll join you when it's ready."

She strolled around the coffeehouse first, looking at the wall décor and groupings of furniture. The dark, wooden floor gave the place a comfortable feel. She chose a table and pulled out the chair, taking a seat. Glancing to Dax, she saw he was preparing her coffee himself instead of passing it off to the other barista behind the bar. She liked that. Most owners would've shared her order and had their employee make the coffee and bring it out.

Dax joined her, setting the cold brew in front of her. "I don't think you'll need to add anything to it. The caramel sweetens it just enough, but I know some people need the pop of sugar."

Harper took a sip. "This is delicious just how it came. Thank you."

He seated himself across from her. Only two other patrons were in the shop, one engrossed in his laptop and the other reading on a Kindle.

"I hope you're making money."

Glancing about, he said, "It's a slow time of day. Mornings are really busy as people stop by for their morning jolt before they go to work. Then I get a mom crowd in, after they've dropped kids off at school, as well as the old-timers who congregate for a couple of hours. Things pick up around lunch and then slow down again until four o'clock. The teenage crowd comes in then."

"How are weekends?"

"Pretty busy. I can't complain. So, I hear you might need a DJ."

"Yes, for a big party I'm holding to celebrate the opening of the event center I'll be managing at my family's winery," she explained.

Briefly, Harper told him what she had in mind. "More background music as people chat when they get there. Same through dinner. I don't want guests having to raise their voices to be heard over the music. After dinner, though? I'm ready to raise the roof off the place. Tell me a little about your experience."

"I started in high school. Some birthday and graduation parties. Pretty small stuff, to be honest, but I really liked how what I played could change the vibe in a room. I mowed lawns summers and put that money into buying some decent equipment. That helped my DJ business take off in college. I went to SMU, so I did a lot of parties for the fraternities and sororities there. Thanks to word-of-mouth from students attending those parties, I started booking events for their families. Weddings. Bar mitzvahs. Even some corporate events for things such as the Cotton Bowl Association, when they have their week of parties leading up to the football game."

"I'm glad you've done weddings. I'm assuming you have set playlists for events such as that."

"I knew you'd be interested in that." Dax pulled his cell from his pocket. "What's your cell number?"

Harper gave it to him, and he said, "I'm texting you example playlists from different events I've worked. I'll also include a couple of videos that show me in action. I can provide some references for you, people I DJ'd for in the past."

"No, that won't be necessary," she assured him. "Ivy says you're good. I trust my sister. But seeing the playlists would help."

She took out her phone and brought up the email he'd just sent to her, looking through the wedding playlists first, nodding to herself.

"You've got some great variety. You go back and pull in some golden oldies, but you have the Ed Sheerans and Taylor Swifts, too."

"Since I haven't DJ'd in several years, I want to bring in some new acts from the past few years. Still, there are classics that everyone wants to hear at parties, particularly weddings. Certain ballads that couples like to have their first dance to, or dad-and-daughter songs. And then I have to play some cheesy numbers like *Macarena*. That even gets the grannies on the dance floor, doing the motions."

Placing her phone on the table, Harper said, "I'll study the playlists more carefully later and let you know what I'd like played at my grand opening. That is, if you're interested in working it."

"Absolutely," Dax assured her. "Ivy said you'll be booking lots of weddings. If you like my DJ style, I hope we can work together in the future." He hesitated. "I'm also putting a band together. We need some practice time, but if your brides are interested in live music at their reception, maybe we can fill that need, as well. Not for another couple of months, though. We need to find our groove."

"I would like to hear you play once you're ready to perform."

"We'll start here at the coffeehouse and then see if we can book any other dates."

"What kind of music will you play?"

"Pretty eclectic," Dax told her. "Covers of popular rock and pop songs. Since we're in the Hill Country, a good smattering of country songs, as well."

"Yes, *The Cotton-Eyed Joe* will definitely get a ton of people on the dance floor if you play it. In fact, you should add that to your playlist."

"I'm not as well versed in country music," he said. "I grew up in Dallas. Though they do have stations which play country music, for me, I was strictly a rock and pop guy. Being here in the Hill Country, though, it's a different pace of life. I've started listening to more country. In fact, Ivy has introduced me to some great artists. She's even taken me dancing and taught me the two-step."

Harper filed that bit of information away. Ivy had kept very quiet about her relationship with Dax. She regretted not asking her sister more about Dax and thought to remedy that now.

"Well, if you want Hill Country people to dance, play *Friends in Low Places. Boot Scootin' Boogie. I Like It, I Love It.* And I'll tell you now, Tim McGraw's *My Best Friend* will probably be your most requested song for a couple's first dance. It's a timeless love ballad."

"Thanks for the tips, Harper." He typed a few notes into his phone. "I'll have the band learn some of these if we can. I'll do most of the singing, but our drummer's also got a nice voice. We'll see if any of these songs you mentioned fit our range."

"If you'd like to come see the facility and where you'll be able to set up, I'm sure Ivy would be happy to bring you out," she said. "You two seem to be spending time together lately."

"Ivy and I have grown really close," Dax confided. "Your opinion means a great deal to her, so I hope I've impressed you today."

"Braden and I would like to get to know you better, Dax. Especially since you're seeing a lot of Ivy."

"Let us know. Maybe we can do dinner together soon."

Harper stood. "I don't want to take any more of your time. Would you like me to draw up a contract for the grand opening? We haven't talked specifics."

"A handshake is good enough for me," Dax said. "I'll let you set the fee since I've been out of the game for a while. In fact, let me do this first time on the house. Just to give you a chance to see what I can do."

"I can't ask you to work for free, Dax," she protested.

He came to his feet. "Ivy would've asked me to the party anyway. I'll just be helping out. I insist. If you like what I do at your grand opening, then we can talk about my rates. I guess I'll need Ivy to help create a website for me with stuff like that."

"She's done mine for me. I'm really happy with her work. And you'll need a website for my couples to look at, anyway. Ivy can do brochures for you, as well. I want to have those on hand when I meet with clients and be able to pass them along."

Dax smiled. "I'll get Ivy on it." He offered her his hand. "Thanks for stopping by and giving me a go."

They shook. "I'm eager to hear what you do. Look at the center with Ivy and then give me a call if you have any questions."

"Will do."

Harper drove back to Lost Creek Vineyards and decided to stop at the tasting room, knowing Ivy was working today. She liked how so much more parking was available at the new tasting room, as well as the addition of the outdoor space. She still needed to work on finding some talented local bands so she could start up a Friday or Saturday night concert series. It might have to be put on hold until she began booking weddings, though. They had listed on the winery's website that a picnic area was now open, with pre-made baskets available, or people could bring in their own food. They had installed a speaker system, so she would need to make certain music was playing in case some people decided to take advantage and come to the winery for a picnic. Bartenders had already been hired for this and would start this weekend.

A few cars were outside the tasting room, and when Harper got inside, she saw two couples sitting in an area, drinking wine. A platter of cheeses, crackers, and fruit sat on the table near them, along with an open bottle of wine. She didn't know if they had done a tasting or had merely stopped by to enjoy a glass of wine.

Ivy was in the middle of a tasting at the tasting bar.

Harper nodded to her and sat nearby, enjoying hearing her sister walk the couple through various wines. While Harper enjoyed wine and could tell a good one from a great one by tasting it, she didn't have Ivy's nose or knowledge. She listened in, seeing how Ivy answered questions and seamlessly moved on to the next wine to be sampled.

When it concluded, Ivy reached under the counter, bringing out two boxes, saying, "Here are your complimentary wineglasses for attending a tasting at Lost Creek Vineyards. You'll find our logo on the glasses."

"Oh, thank you," the woman said. "We weren't expecting this."

While they had raised their tasting price by a dollar to cover the cost of the glass, they deliberately had decided not to advertise that the tasting including a free wineglass. Ivy said she liked surprising tasters when the tasting concluded, and she thought word of mouth would help this little perk spread.

Harper continued to eavesdrop, noting how Ivy didn't push the couple into buying wines, but she subtly nudged them—and they did.

"You might also like to browse our gift shop and pick up some barware," Ivy told the tasters. "And if you need a restroom, they're located at the back of the gift shop."

"Thank you so much," the man said. "We've done several wine tastings, but we really learned a lot from you today."

Ivy smiled brightly. "My pleasure. I hope you'll come again."

The couple headed to the gift shop after Ivy rang up the three bottles they purchased. Harper went to sit on one of the stools.

"No one's here. Want to enjoy a glass of wine together?" her sister asked.

"I'd love that. Pick something fun."

She returned to where she had been sitting before, and Ivy brought a small cheese platter with crackers on it. Setting it down, she said, "These platters are really put together well." She indicated the two couples nearby. "They wanted to know where the cheese came from. I told them The Cheese Connoisseur on the square in Lost Creek, but I think I could have sold some cheese to them if we'd had them on hand, beyond the plate they purchased. We've got space in the fridge. It would be smart to have some on hand."

"Good idea. Want me to talk to them?" she offered.

"No. I have an idea what I'd like to carry. I can do it. Be right back."

Ivy soon returned with two glasses of a crisp Sauvignon Blanc. Harper savored her first sip.

"I met with Dax this afternoon," she said, watching the blush fill Ivy's cheeks. "I really like him. I think he'll do a great job DJ-ing the grand opening." She paused. "How are the two of you getting along?"

"Really well." Ivy took a sip of wine. "I'm just so comfortable with him, Harper. It's... easy."

"I get that. It's the same way with Braden. We can talk. We can sit quietly. It never feels awkward. Ath didn't appreciate silence like Braden does. He always had to be talking. Or on his phone. The TV was rarely off. Not that he watched it. It was merely background noise."

"I don't think I'd ever run out of things to talk to Dax about," Ivy revealed. "Nothing is forced. He's… nice. And he's really interested in my art. And me."

I'm glad to hear it. You haven't dated anyone in a long time."

"No, I haven't. The gallery kept me too busy to do so. And I don't think any man in Houston would have interested me the way Dax does."

Harper made a decision, one which she thought Braden would approve of.

"Braden and I are getting married. We picked up our license in San Antonio yesterday."

Ivy's eyes lit up. "Really? Oh, that's wonderful, Harper."

They hugged one another, and Ivy picked up her wine glass. "To a marriage that will last, just like Mom and Dad's."

She snagged her own glass, clinking it against her sister's. "I'll drink to that."

"Have you set a date yet?"

"Yes. But you can't tell a soul. You're the only one who will know."

Curiosity filled Ivy's face, and then she said, "You're using the grand opening as the date, aren't you? Emerson is actually baking wedding and groom's cakes for you and Braden."

"Yes. How did you know?"

Her sister smiled. "I know you, Harper. And it makes perfect sense. You'll already have family and friends there to celebrate the facility opening. Why not turn a big party into a spontaneous wedding and reception?" She laughed. "And your wedding will be the dress rehearsal for others to come."

"Yes, if there are any kinks, they'll pop up that night. I'm hoping that won't be the case, but at least I would know how to fix them in the future."

"Mom is going to kill you."

"Mom would tell the first stranger she saw about it. You know she can't keep a secret."

"Dad won't mind," Ivy continued. "I think he'll like it. It really is romantic, your wedding being the one to kick things off."

Harper asked, "You don't think it's too soon, do you? I mean, I was supposed to marry Ath not that long ago."

"I think when it's right, you should go for it. After all, Mom and Dad got married six weeks after they met, and they're still going strong."

"True. It's just that I love Braden so much, Ivy. I don't want to miss a minute with him. I'm ready to start the rest of our lives together, as man and wife."

"Guess I'll need to find a new place to live."

"No," Harper said. "You can stay as long as you like. We would enjoy having you around."

"I don't know. Living with newlyweds might be a little awkward," Ivy told her. "I'll have to think about it." She paused. "I'm glad you told me, though."

"You'll be my only attendant."

"I better see if I have something to wear."

"Oh, you have lots of things because of working at the

gallery and all the openings you managed. Besides, you can't look too wedding-y and give away what's going to happen."

They talked for another half-hour, sipping their wine. Harper thought the cheese really added to things and was glad it was an extra being offered at the tasting room. She told Ivy about the rings they had picked out and the dress she had bought to wear.

"We really didn't have time to see much of San Antonio, though," she said. "I'd like to take Braden back for a long weekend. Show him the restaurants along the river and eat at a couple. Go to the market. Even the Alamo."

"That can be your honeymoon," Ivy declared. "Go midweek when the crowds aren't as large. Besides, your weekends are going to be booked up soon with weddings."

"Good idea." She drained her wineglass. "I'm glad you had time to talk."

Ivy grinned. "I'm glad we had something so fun to talk about." She hugged Harper. "Congratulations. You're getting a really great guy. He's got the Ivy seal of approval."

"I'll see you at home."

Harper went to her SUV and decided to head home. On the way to Lost Creek, her cell rang. Glancing at the screen, she saw it was an unknown number, which she didn't like to answer. With the new business starting up, though, she didn't want to miss an important call, so she answered.

"Hello?"

"Don't hang up, Harper. I need to talk to you."

Bile immediately rose in her throat.

It was Cynthia.

Obviously, her former friend had discovered Harper had blocked her number and was calling from another one.

"We will never have anything to talk about," she said brusquely, hanging up.

Her phone rang again quickly, and Harper blocked the number. Cynthia was persistent, which made her a successful realtor, but she had no desire to hear anything Ath's wife had to say. From now on, Harper would let all unknowns go to voicemail.

It had been bad enough having Ath show up in Lost Creek. Harper couldn't let Cynthia back in her life.

22

Braden had the house to himself. Harper and Ivy had left hours ago, Ivy to check on the wines to be delivered to the event center, with Harper checking on everything else. The party—and surprise wedding—would start in two hours. Not wanting to be rushed, he took a long, hot shower and shaved, dressing in the suit he had purchased at Rivercenter, the large complex of shops and restaurants along San Antonio's famed River Walk. He and Harper had a reservation at a small, boutique hotel in San Antonio for next Tuesday and Wednesday nights. It would be the only honeymoon they had time for. She told him she wanted to introduce him to some of the historical and cultural sites of the city, as well as stroll along the River Walk and sip margaritas as they did a little people-watching.

As he shaved, he found it hard to believe that he and Harper would be married by the end of the night. His life had changed—for the better—ever since he began work at Lost Creek Vineyards. He had hit rock bottom and plunged even lower, losing everything and everyone he loved. Yet he could now see that Freya hadn't been the one for him. While he might have been happy with her, Harper was his soulmate. The connection between them was powerful. The sex was off the charts. They both had jobs they were passionate about. He looked forward to one day starting a family with her, raising their kids in a small town, and introducing them to the wine business.

The creation of this year's Lost Creek wines was continuing to run smoothly. He had developed several flavor profiles that he knew would be popular with the public. Using Texas grapes and his California smarts, Braden believed he was creating a strong line of wines, especially blends. Since Lost Creek Vineyards had an excellent track record in the industry, including their blends, he felt he was off to a strong start. He was still keeping his eye on the Texas weather, knowing it could be unpredictable. He liked the viticulturist he'd hired from Fredericksburg and thought they would continue to have a solid working relationship.

Dressing in a new, white dress shirt and the suit, he went to the mirror, pleased at his reflection. Though he'd purchased two different ties, one to complement the dark suit and one which brought a pop of color, Harper had said not to wear either. She wanted their wedding to be relaxed and fun, a true celebration of their marriage and the start of her business.

Braden combed his hair and retrieved his cell from the

charger and set it to silent, slipping it into his pocket just as a text buzzed. Pulling it out again, he was shocked to read the name on the screen.

Stan Clark...

It had been close to two years since he'd heard from his older brother. With reservations, he read the text.

> If you want to talk, call me.

He stared at the message, not knowing if he should call now, so close to leaving for the winery. Then again, if he didn't take advantage of the window Stan had opened, his brother might never contact him again.

> Calling now.

"Hello?" Stan said, and Braden could hear the hesitation in his voice.

Though he had a thousand questions, he decided he would let Stan steer this conversation. "Hey. It's me. I'm glad you wanted to talk."

"I didn't know if you'd want to hear from me or not. Especially after I took off without a word."

"Stan, I'm just glad you reached out. Are you okay?"

"I am now." A long pause. "I went to rehab, Braden. I was spiraling down fast. I'd been drinking too much. Then I dabbled in drugs. The dabbling picked up once the whole situation with Dad exploded. I know I avoided you and Beau. You probably had no clue how bad off I was. But I knew if I didn't remove myself from the whole mess

—Dad, Mom and the actor, the FBI swooping in and freezing all the business assets—then I wasn't going to make it. I already wanted to kill myself."

Stan fell silent, and Braden asked, "Why? You weren't the one who'd done anything wrong."

"But I knew Dad was up to something. I overheard a few phone conversations he had. Took a few glances at the books and smelled something funny going on. I should have confronted him, Braden."

"I doubt that would've done anything, Stan. Dad could talk his way out of anything. He oozed charm. He would promise anyone anything he thought they wanted to hear. If you'd said anything to him, he would've given you lip service—and then gone right on doing what he was doing."

"But I could've threatened him. Said I'd go to authorities. He might've backed off."

"No," he said sadly. "He wouldn't have. Dad was living beyond his means and would've refused to tighten his belt. I hate to say it, but he really didn't care enough about you—or any of us—to change."

"We come from a really messed up family, don't we Braden?" Stan asked, and they both laughed.

"At least you did something about it. I hope rehab took."

"It did. I knew I didn't have anything to go back to, and so I stayed at the facility. Said I'd do anything. Janitorial work. Help with the website. Be a counselor. Actually, I've done all of those things, though the counseling is more mentoring patients and not actual therapy as a licensed professional. I live on the grounds. It's about twenty miles south of Santa Clara. My world is pretty small now, Braden. I'm no longer the big shot, making deals. But I'm helping people. I like what I'm doing. I think I'm going to go back to school and earn my counseling degree."

"That's fantastic, Stan. I'm glad to hear that."

"I've also joined AA and NA. That's why I'm calling you now, Braden. I'm going through the Twelve Steps. I'm making amends to those I harmed. You were at the top of my list. I thought after I reached out to you, I'd do the same with Beau, even though we were never that close. Mom? I have no desire to contact her. She's living her own life and doesn't miss any of us."

Braden steeled himself. "I have something to tell you, Stan. Beau's gone. He took his life not too soon after you left."

Stan cursed softly.

"It wasn't your fault," he reassured his brother. "It wasn't anyone's fault. Well, Dad's. If he hadn't broken a dozen laws, the FBI would never have showed up at Clark Vineyards. Their seizure of the winery and the business being gone in the blink of an eye really rocked Beau's world. You know he was pretty fragile."

"I'm still sorry I left you to deal with Beau. And his death. I'm sorry, Braden," Stan apologized.

"I was pretty low after it happened," he admitted. "Thought I should've seen it coming. I realize now that it wasn't me. It was Beau who was in charge. It's a choice he made."

"What are you doing now?" his brother asked.

"Believe it or not, I'm in the Texas Hill Country, working for Lost Creek Vineyards as their enologist. I was out of the wine business for over two years. You know how we were treated. Like pariahs in the wine community. My last shot at being a part of anything having to do with wine was here in Texas. I served as viticulturist first, and now I'm the head winemaker."

"That's fantastic, Braden," Stan said.

"It gets even better. I'm getting married today."

"What? Well, congratulations, little brother. Who's the lucky lady?"

"Her name is Harper Hart. She's actually the daughter of the winery's owner. She runs her own event planning business and has just overseen the construction of a new facility here at the winery. The grand opening party is in an hour, and we're going to spring it on everyone and hold our wedding."

"Good for you, Braden," Stan said, his voice breaking. "You deserve every bit of happiness you can grab. I better let you go so you aren't late for your own wedding."

"Stan, thank you for calling. For letting me know you're okay. Could we stay in touch?"

"I'd like that. Yes. Text me some wedding pictures, okay?"

"I will," he promised.

They said goodbye, and relief washed over him, knowing Stan was alive and well and had found a purpose in life. Braden didn't have anyone from his family present today, but he believed Stan would be with him in spirit.

Harper looked around, pride filling her as she saw how nice everything looked. On one side, chairs had been set up for a mock wedding, which would turn out to be a real one very soon. On the other side, the reception tables were set to perfection, the centerpieces varied, using the three different levels of decorations she would offer. The table settings had been a good choice. She'd splurged a bit on them and was now glad she had done so. Of course, knowing breakage occurred, she had ordered extras of the dinner, salad, and dessert plates, as well as glasses.

She looked to the cake corner, where Emerson was setting up the wedding and groom's cakes. They had turned out perfectly. Finley was already making the rounds, taking photographs from varying angles. Dax had his DJ equipment set up and was helping Ivy check the two bars which had been set up.

Her staff was now complete, from bartenders to servers to the security guard she knew was rarely needed. His presence alone would keep trouble to a minimum and on the rare occasions it was needed, she would be glad he was on site.

Returning to the kitchen area, she saw Shy and Shelly were in full swing, barking orders as chafing dishes were set up to keep food items warm.

"Looking good," she told the pair. "We'll be serving in about eighty minutes."

"We'll be ready," promised Shy.

Harper wandered back to the main room, nerves flitting through her. By now, Dax had soft music playing. She decided to give him a heads up about the ceremony because she had a few things she wanted played during it. Bethany Armistead had commandeered all music selections for Harper's wedding to Ath.

This time, things would be her choice.

Ivy had joined Dax and smiled as Harper approached. She told Harper, "Wines are ready. Shy brought plenty of tea and lemonade for those who will pass on alcohol. And we also have sparkling water on hand if it's needed. Also, the beer kegs are set up for those wanting beer with their barbeque."

"That sounds great." Looking over her shoulder, Harper turned back to the couple. "Dax, try not to react, but I need you to know there'll be a wedding taking place tonight."

He didn't look surprised in the least and she turned to Ivy. "You told him."

Her sister nodded. "I knew he wouldn't tell anyone, Harper. Are you upset?"

It spoke volumes that Ivy had confided in Dax.

"No, I'm not. But I do have a few requests."

"Name it, Harper. I've got a lot at my fingertips to choose from," Dax told her.

"Once I let everyone know they need to be seated, I'd like you to play a song from *Love, Actually*. The *Portuguese Love Theme*."

"I've got it," Dax told her, picking up his tablet.

"I don't want to make my way to the altar with the

traditional *Here Comes the Bride*. I'd prefer *Canon in D.* Pachelbel instead."

"Pulling it now," he said, clicking on his tablet. "I've used it a lot before. Anything during the ceremony?"

"No. For the recessional, though, it's back to *Love, Actually*."

"*The Prime Minister's Love Theme*?" he asked.

"Yes. You know it?"

Dax nodded. It'll be perfect." He tapped again at the keys. "We're all set."

"Thank you," she said. "I had Braden watch the movie with me not long ago. I don't know if he'll recognize the music, but I think it really fits us. And Ivy told me that you can put the dinner music on a loop and join us."

"I can. If that's what you want."

She didn't have to see the look in her sister's eyes. "I do. It's a special occasion. Ivy will save a seat for you. The other times you're working? I'll be sure someone brings you a plate of food. Can't have our DJ go hungry," she teased.

"Harper, looks like someone wants to speak to you," Ivy told her.

She looked toward the door and saw a reporter she'd spoken to from the *San Antonio Express-News*.

"It's Peggy Lyon. She's from the newspaper. Works their Lifestyle and Food sections and agreed to do a possible feature on the event center and vineyard. Excuse me."

Going to greet her, she said, "Hi, Peggy. Thanks for coming tonight."

The journalist's eyes roamed the room. "Looks really nice, Harper. My editor liked your idea of featuring wedding venues this fall. I've started gathering some other places, but I promise Lost Creek Vineyards and Weddings with Hart will be the first spot featured."

"Go ahead and walk around the place." She motioned to Finley, who joined them. After introducing them, Harper said, "Finley Farrow is the event center's photographer. She can provide pictures for your article."

"Did you take the ones on the website?" Peggy asked.

"I did."

"Nice work," Peggy praised. "Good lighting and use of shadows." The reporter passed Finley a card. "Here's my contact info. Let's keep in touch. I think my feature will run two Sundays from now."

"I can email you several pictures by tomorrow. We can go from there," Finley said.

Peggy excused herself, and Finley said, "This will be great publicity, Harper. It will really help get the word out. I can see the calendar fill up quickly. Hey, what about Christmas?'

"What about it?"

"I think you should have different table arrangements or greenery available. Or at least order poinsettias from the local florist."

"Good idea, Finley."

Braden appeared at her arm, kissing her cheek. "Everything looks terrific, babe. And a lot of cars were pulling up behind me and parking. Get ready for the deluge to hit."

He was right. Suddenly, guests were pouring in.

Friends and family. Workers from the vineyard. Residents of Lost Creek. Vendors. She moved smoothly about the room, chatting briefly before continuing on.

Harper turned—and stopped in her tracks.

Cynthia Armistead stood in front of her.

23

"I am not going to let you ruin this for me," Harper said succinctly. "You can leave on your own, or I can call my security guard over and have you escorted off the premises."

"Give me sixty seconds, Harper," pleaded Cynthia. "After that, I'll go. I promise."

Harper glared at Cynthia. This woman—next to Ivy— was the closest friend she had ever made. They had gone through classes together, studying late into the night. Attended parties. Double dated. Beyond college, they had been roommates and vacationed together. She had let Cynthia in, sharing her deepest fears and biggest dreams. And yet Cynthia had betrayed her in the worst way possible.

Before she could say anything, Cynthia said, "I know I let you down."

"Let me down?" she hissed. "You hurt me as much as—

no, even more than—Ath did. I probably loved you as much as I did him. Our history together made me feel as if we were family. No, Cynthia, you didn't let me down. You crushed the life out of me."

Despite what Harper had said, Cynthia linked her arm through Harper's and eased her away from the crowd, moving her to a corner. She didn't protest because she wasn't about to make a scene at her own grand opening. Once they were isolated from others, though, she deliberately extricated her arm from her former friend.

"Why are you here?" she demanded quietly. "Tonight means the world to me. I won't let you ruin it."

"I wanted you to know that I've filed for divorce," Cynthia said bluntly. "I thought I had grounds for an annulment, based upon fraud, but my attorney says I would have needed to file with the court no more than thirty days after the marriage occurred."

Cynthia's eyes swam with tears. "I know how much we hurt you, Harper. I still am not quite certain how I got caught up in it or why I went along with Ath. I suppose it's because he's so magnetic. So charming and persuasive. But it's a different Ath behind closed doors than the one he shows to the world. I've eavesdropped on a few phone calls and didn't like what I overheard on my end. That caused me to snoop. I found out some things, Harper. Terrible things. I've already spoken to a pair of Austin police detectives. They've contacted the FBI to investigate. Ath is going down for crimes he's committed."

Shock rippled through Harper. She had thought Ath

was a jerk, but she'd had no inkling of any criminal activity on his part.

"Do you know that he came to see me recently?"

Cynthia shook her head. "No. But it doesn't surprise me. I know he's running for office next year, and he's mentioned how he needed to get you onboard. That the optics needed to look better to the voting public regarding what went down between the two of you."

Cynthia took Harper's hand, squeezing it. "I know I can never regain your trust. Nor your friendship. I just wanted to warn you about the shit which will hit the fan soon. I'm sure reporters will be contacting you. I wanted you to be prepared and not blindsided."

Her throat swelled with emotion. Cynthia started to pull away, but Harper held fast to her hand.

"We can never be friends again," she said, "but I'm sorry you'll be caught up in this mess."

Cynthia blinked back tears. "Thank you." She glanced around the room. "It looks as if you've done quite well for yourself, Harper."

"I have my own event planning business now. I've started a new life, away from Austin, and I'm sinking roots into the Lost Creek community."

She deliberately left out mentioning her relationship with Braden. The days of sharing any and everything with Cynthia were long gone.

Cynthia nodded. "I wish you the best, Harper. I really do. I hate myself for what Ath and I did to you. I suppose what will break in the news will be my punishment."

"No," she said fiercely. "The only crime you committed

was betraying a friend. Hold your head high, Cynthia. And get as far away as you can from Atherton Armistead and his family."

She embraced her old friend, doubting she would ever see Cynthia again. "Goodbye," she whispered.

Cynthia's arms fell away, and she stepped away, turning and not looking back as she moved through the crowd. Out the door—and out of Harper's life.

Braden suddenly appeared, taking her hand. "Are you all right? Who was that?"

"It was Cynthia."

He looked startled. "The one who married Ath?"

Harper nodded. "She came here to tell me she was divorcing him. It seems that Ath has broken some laws, and it's about to catch up to him. Cynthia wanted to warn me of the reporters who might come calling once the scandal breaks." She swallowed. "And to tell me she was sorry."

He wrapped his arms around her, kissing the top of her head. Once again, Harper felt safe.

And loved.

Braden's gaze met hers. "Are you okay enough to go through with our plans this evening? We can wait if you need more time."

"Nothing is going to stop me from marrying you now." She surveyed the room. "It looks full to me. Let's clue everyone in."

Taking his hand, she led him toward Dax, telling him she would like the music to pause a moment so she could address the guests.

"You got it, Harper," Dax said. He lowered the volume until no music could be heard, just the chatter of voices throughout the room. In a smooth voice, he said into a microphone, "Thank you for coming tonight, everyone. Harper would like to say a few words."

He handed her the microphone, and she accepted it, gazing out at all the smiling faces looking at her. Sandra Bellows, her former boss. The Alamillas and others from the shelter she supported. A few sorority sisters and their husbands.

"I've always been a practical person, but I did have a dream to open my own business someday. Thanks to my parents, Bill and Cecily Hart, that dream has become a reality tonight. I built this facility at Lost Creek Vineyards because I believe couples who are married should do it in a serene, lovely setting. There's nowhere more beautiful to me than the Texas Hill Country, which is home. I can't think of a better place for a wedding—and other events of celebration to take place."

Harper paused, looking at the crowd. "Tonight, I am surrounded by family and friends. Residents of Lost Creek, some whom I've built business relationships with, and they will help me to turn brides' dreams of the perfect wedding into reality. Thank you for coming this evening to celebrate the beginning of this dream with me."

Thunderous applause erupted, and she could see how happy everyone in the room was for her. She let the applause die down and continued.

"You can see what an incredible setting this will make for a wedding, and I want you to know not only have you been invited to the grand opening, but you are about to be a witness to the first Weddings with Hart."

She smiled up at Braden and then looked back at the guests gathered. "If you'll go and find a seat, you'll get to watch Braden and me begin our lives together as husband and wife."

Those gathered broke out in smiles, some cheering. Finley, who was nearby, snapping pictures of Harper as she spoke, beamed at her. Her eyes swept across the room and stopped at her parents. She motioned for them to join her and Braden.

Her mother reached her first, throwing her arms about Harper. "Oh, honey, this is perfect. Braden is such a good man. He's going to make a wonderful husband."

"I think so, too," she said, smiling warmly at her mother. "I hope you don't mind us springing this on you and Dad."

"It's perfect," Mom said, and turned to hug Braden, who was shaking hands with her dad.

Braden said, "May I escort you to your seat, Cecily? We've got a place of honor in the first row saved for you."

Mom slipped her arm through the groom's. "Lead the way, Braden."

Dad embraced her, saying, "I'm glad you're following your heart, Harper. I believe you and Braden have a beautiful lifetime ahead." He paused, wiping a tear from his cheek. "He asked me to stand up with him. But first, I need to walk you down the aisle."

"I would like that so much, Dad."

She looked to the ceremony side of the center, seeing

all the guests had taken their seats. She could hear the music softly in the background as she saw Braden seating her mother. Finley was busy with her camera, capturing everything.

Suddenly, Ivy appeared at her elbow, handing Harper a bouquet of asters and white roses.

"I know we didn't talk about it, but I thought you needed flowers. Before you ask, yes, I have Braden's ring."

Her dad patted his pocket. "Braden gave me yours. Are we ready to do this, girls?"

"Let me go get situated," Ivy said, leaving them and moving along the wall until she took her place at the front of the room.

Harper slipped her hand through the crook of her father's arm. "I'm ready."

She noticed the seamless change of music as Dak switched to the Pachelbel, and she and her father moved down the aisle to a blurry sea of faces. Harper's heart beat rapidly as she turned her gaze to her groom. He stood with Judge Grady, a retired judge whom Harper had hired to perform ceremonies at the facility, one of two judges who would alternate performing weddings at the winery.

They reached the front, and she handed her bridal bouquet to her sister, who beamed at her. Dad shook hands with Braden and then went to the groom's side, allowing the groom to join hands with his bride.

"This seems so surreal," she whispered up at him.

"I love you, Harper. I'm going to treasure every day with you."

They turned and faced Judge Grady, who led them

through the ceremony with ease, throwing in a bit of folksy humor, which had the guests chuckling. They exchanged vows and rings, and Harper gazed up at the man who was now her entire world, a man who loved her and allowed her to be the best version of herself.

Judge Grady told Braden to kiss his bride, and that first married kiss was full of sweet promises of the years to come. They turned, Ivy handing Harper her bridal bouquet again.

"I present to you Mr. and Mrs. Braden Clark," called out the judge.

She could feel the love in the room, and it washed over her. She looked up at her husband, who kissed her to more cheers, and they started down the aisle to the joyful sound of the love theme which she had first fallen in love with when she heard it in the background as Hugh Grant gave a stirring speech.

Her new husband said, "I recognize this song."

"I thought you might. It's not a seventies love ballad, but we're going to dance to one of those tonight."

"I will dance with you every night of our lives, Harper. You will always be the one that I want." He paused and teasingly added, "Ooh, ooh, ooh, honey," causing her to burst into laughter as he imitated John Travolta's Danny Zuko in *Grease*.

Dax asked the guests to move to the tables for dinner, and she and Braden circulated throughout the room as servers delivered plates of barbeque, along with sides of potato salad and baked beans, to their guests. They went to the table for two, designated for the bride and groom, and she assessed the speed with which the servers were getting the plates out to the guests. By now, two of the workers she had hired had already moved the chairs used during the ceremony, placing them on rolling flatbeds and moving them from sight. Where the guests had witnessed the wedding was now open as a dance floor.

Braden took a bite of brisket and declared, "This is incredible. I hope every bride who books her wedding here is smart enough to ask for Blackwood BBQ to cater their reception." He glanced toward the cakes. "And I'm more than ready to try a piece of each cake Emerson baked."

She realized how much she was enjoying her own reception. The food. The music. The people. The dancing would merely be icing on the cake, a true celebration. For a first wedding held at the event center, everything was turning out as well as she could have expected. She was not only celebrating the opening of her own business but her marriage to the only man who completed her.

Emerson got her attention, and Harper told Braden, "I think it's time for us to cut the cakes. That way, people can enjoy eating it as the dancing begins."

They made their way to Emerson, who hugged them both. "What a wonderful surprise!" she said. "Now I know why Braden was so invested in the groom's cake."

"If it's chocolate, I'll always be interested," he said, grinning.

Harper signaled Dax, and he lowered the music, informing the guests the cake was ready to be cut. Everyone gathered around them, and they sliced into it together, feeding each other a bite of both wedding cake and groom's cake.

"Grab a piece of cake—and then let's get ready to party," Dax told the crowd. "Right after our bride and groom's first dance to Billy Joel's *Just the Way You Are*."

Braden led her onto the dance floor, and their guests watched as they danced to their first song together as husband and wife.

"I'm glad you've introduced me to Billy Joel. Carly Simon. Kiss. Toto. Hall & Oates. The Doobies. You've opened the world of music to me, Harper."

She sighed. "And you've opened yourself to me, Braden. You've already taught me so much about life. Myself. How to be happy. You support what I do, and that means the world to me."

He kissed her softly. "You do the same for me. We're good together, Harper. I told you—we're the perfect blend. And I love you just the way you are."

The song ended as everyone applauded, but Harper had already shut out the world as she kissed the man she would walk beside for decades to come.

EPILOGUE

PARIS

Harper closed her eyes, leaning her head back until her neck rested on the edge of the tub, savoring the warm water and silence. She had given up long, leisurely baths when Beau had arrived a month after their first wedding anniversary. Their little boy was two-and-a-half now, always throwing a ball or swinging a golf club. He did love to snuggle, though, and he was wild about reading. She had probably read *If You Give a Mouse a Cookie* over a thousand times—and loved every word of it and the sweet smell of Beau.

As she'd suspected, Braden was a terrific dad, doing his fair share of reading and playing with Beau every day, no matter how busy the wine season was. Her husband had also been a true partner, doing his fair share of changing diapers, cleaning puke, and working with their son on his potty training, which was going better than she had expected.

She brought her hands to her belly, feeling the slight bulge, knowing in her gut it would be a girl this time.

Braden came in and sat on the edge of the tub, cupping her cheek. "Hey. What's it like being in the bathroom by yourself without hearing someone calling for Mommy?"

Harper giggled. "Actually, it feels pretty good, but I miss our little guy."

"Enough to cancel the babymoon?" he asked.

"No," she said quickly. "This is the first time I've had you to myself in ages. Besides, we're going to FaceTime with Beau. And Ivy promised she'd text me pictures of him every day. I've already gotten twelve so far."

"Send them to me." He leaned in and gave her a soft kiss. "And I'm glad you want to stay. Coming to Paris—and seeing different regions of France—has always been a dream of mine."

They would spend three days in the city before visiting the Loire Valley and Alsace for their whites, the Rhone Valley for its blends, and Bordeaux for its reds. Harper hated that she would only be able to taste and spit the wines because of her pregnancy, but she planned to make up for it by eating all the wonderful French foods, especially the croissants which would be calling her name. It would be hard to spend two weeks away from Beau, but Harper had learned as much as she loved her son, she needed to carve out special time to spend alone with her husband. This trip would be one to build many memories for them.

"Help me out so we can go see another dream realized."

She was referring to the wine competition awards they would attend tonight. In the past four years, Braden's wines for Lost Creek Winery had won numerous awards, beating U.S. wines from Santa Barbara, the Willamette Valley, and the Texas Plains. He'd also bested winemakers in countries such as Portugal, Australia, Chile, and Greece.

Tonight's awards boasted the largest number of entries from around the world. Braden had high hopes for two wines he'd created, in particular.

Harper gave him her hand, and he pulled her to her feet, getting a large towel and wrapping it around her before drying her off. He even paused at her belly, kissing it.

"Hello, baby inside there," he said. "Your mom and I can't wait to meet you. We already have your ultrasound appointment."

She ran her fingers through his hair. He lifted his face to her. "I love you."

"I love you more," she told him.

Braden swept Harper off her feet, carrying her to the obscenely large bed, making slow, sweet love to her. They lay together, limbs entwined, talking about some of the places they would see during the next few days. Sainte-Chapelle. The Eiffel Tower. Notre-Dame Cathedral. The Arc de Triomphe. They had a scheduled a dinner cruise along the Seine tomorrow night, and she was eager see what the city looked like when lit up.

"We should get dressed," she told him.

Harper dressed in a black, tiered, ruffled midi dress. The wrap dress was comfortable and one she'd worn throughout her last pregnancy to various events she'd held at the winery. It could be dressed up or down. Tonight, though she probably would regret it, she slipped into a pair of Michael Kors stiletto sandals. They made her legs look fantastic, and she could always take them off in the cab on the way home. She'd brought much more sensible shoes for touring the country, but tonight she wanted to look her best for Braden.

Her husband dressed in a charcoal gray suit. She had added one suit each year to his wardrobe, not wanting him to wear the same one to competitions and dinners with clients. She'd also bought several ties for each suit to give it a different look. While some men might be wearing a tux tonight, Braden's suit was impeccably cut, and he looked like a model in it.

They left their hotel room after a quick call to Ivy. She gave the phone to Beau, who told them about the pancakes he'd had for breakfast. Since it was a Saturday, he wasn't at nursery school, and Harper was glad they had been able to talk with him.

Arriving at the ballroom where the awards would be announced, she and Braden mingled, seeing friends and acquaintances from previous wine shows. Everyone was complimentary to one another. She knew from tasting many of these wines that it had been an exceptional year in the wine industry.

The evening began and they took their seats. Her parents joined them. They had taken the Chunnel yesterday since they had been in London for a week. It was the first time her mother had traveled abroad, and she had wanted to see a bit of England before they made their way to Paris. They would stay in France another two days before flying home.

"Are you missing Beau?" her mother asked.

"Yes—and no. I actually took a long bath, not a three-minute shower," she joked. "No one came looking for me, bringing me a Gerald and Piggie book to read. I don't remember the last time I was in a bathroom that long, uninterrupted. But I do miss Beau's sweet smile. We Facetimed with him before coming here tonight."

The catered meal was delicious, and Harper watched everything around her with her professional planner's eye, always wanting to add new tricks to her bag.

The awards began, and they were pleasantly surprised to learn that one of their Sauvignon Blancs won a Platinum award.

"I was hoping for Silver. Maybe Gold," Braden said. "Platinum is huge honor for this wine."

"I told you it was an excellent profile," her dad reminded Braden. "Let's see how the blend came out."

Braden took her hand as the winners in Best of Show were announced. When they heard the Lost Creek Vineyards name called, he wrapped his arms around her, kissing her hard.

"I knew it," she told him enthusiastically. "It's the best blend you've ever created."

His gaze met hers. "No, the best blend—the perfect blend—is when we came together."

Harper couldn't argue with that.

PREVIEW: PAINTED MELODIES

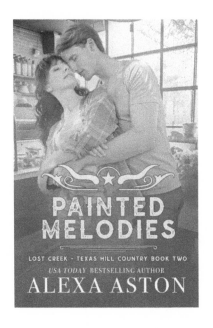

Read on for a preview of Painted Melodies, book 2 in the
Lost Creek, Texas Hill Country series.

DALLAS—OCTOBER

Dax Tennyson left his office a little before six and drove home, hoping to find his wife there. Shailene was a realtor and worked odd hours, sometimes showing homes in the evening and oftentimes on weekends. Sometimes he felt they were becoming more like roommates who shared a few things in passing as one went in the door and the other went out it. He hoped tonight would be different.

Because he really was ready for them to have a baby.

They had been married six years, and he was eager to start a family now. Actually, Dax had been ready to have children from the moment they got married, but Shailene had said she wanted to become more established in her career. He had agreed to put it off and kept quiet for five years. Last year, he'd brought up the subject for the first time, and Shailene had seemed surprised. She had agreed, though, to go off her birth control pills and see what happened.

Nothing had. At least, not yet.

With both their careers in full swing, though, finding time to be together—much less be intimate—was getting in the way of accomplishing that goal. Dax hoped not only would his wife become pregnant soon but that it might spark a deeper closeness between them. He longed for the early years when they discussed their plans for the future.

He had given up a lot of his dreams when he married. Before he'd tied the knot, he'd had steady employment with his accounting job and played the market on the side, making quite a bundle. Weekends, he'd served as a DJ for weddings and other events, which generated a terrific income. He'd been dabbling in songwriting for years and had thought about chucking the day job in order to pursue a career in music— until Shailene came along. She was very conservative in her outlook, and the thought of her fiancé giving up his lucrative career in business to try and earn a living as a musician had horrified her. She'd threatened to break off their engagement if he pursued those dreams.

Instead, he'd put them on hold. At least, that's what he told himself. That someday, he would make enough money to break out of the eight-to-five rut and follow his heart back to music. Dax had put his DJ-ing equipment into storage and shelved his songwriting. He couldn't even remember the last time he'd picked up his guitar. He focused on work and had moved up the corporate ladder swiftly, now managing an accounting group of over thirty employees.

His instincts for the market had also paid off, and he was at a point where he could actually quit work if he wanted and pick up music again. Dax had even thought about being the stay-at-home dad to allow Shailene to keep working since she loved what she did so much. It would be a blessing to be able to remain home and raise their kids, writing music on the side, and hopefully performing some on weekends.

But first, they needed to get pregnant. Once that happened, he'd talk things over with Shailene and make new plans for their future, ones that included their growing family and his desire to follow his passion.

He arrived home, parking in the driveway of their Park Cities house, an exclusive area in the heart of Dallas and close to where he'd attended college at SMU. Dax had DJ'd many fraternity and sorority parties during his college years, as well as events throughout the Park Cities. They'd purchased this home three years ago, a pocket listing Shailene had, and he knew today, after the work he'd put into it, that they could sell it for double what they'd paid for it.

Selling their home was something he wanted to broach with his wife. While he liked the house, he wanted more room for their family, even if that meant leaving the Park Cities. His gut told him Shailene wouldn't go for that, though. She liked the fancy address, plus most of her showings were in this area, which made it easy for her to come home in-between clients.

Dax entered the house, calling, "I'm home," but he sensed it was empty. He'd wanted to get a dog, but Shailene was allergic to pet dander. Maybe he could look into dogs that were hypoallergenic. He'd always wanted a pet growing up, but his mom said they were too poor to have one. Since she worked three jobs and they still barely had food to put on the table, he'd known not to press the issue. But he wanted his kids to have a pet and bond with it.

Checking his phone, he saw he had no texts from his wife, which disappointed him. It was his birthday, and a part of him had wanted her to make a fuss over him because of it. Presents for birthdays or Christmas had been unheard of in his household, but now that he had money, he wanted to celebrate some, be it with a gift or an evening at a nice restaurant. He decided to text her and see if she wanted to meet him somewhere.

> Just got home. Can you meet me for dinner?

Dax waited, knowing if she were with a client that she wouldn't reply immediately. After a few minutes, he grabbed a beer from the fridge and went upstairs, getting out of his work clothes and throwing on a T-shirt and faded jeans. He returned to the den, flipping on the TV, holding his beer up to the screen.

"Happy birthday to me," he toasted, unhappiness rolling through him.

He was thirty-two and hoped he would've done more with his life by now. Yes, he made a terrific salary and had a beautiful wife and nice house, but he felt so empty inside. Maybe this would be the year of change for him. He would quit his job. They could buy a bigger house with some land. It was time to start writing music again. And hopefully, Shailene would finally become pregnant. After a year of trying with no results, he'd insisted they both get checked out two weeks ago. Their physicians gave them each a clean bill of health. Her OB/Gyn had even told Shailene not to stress about it. That the more they relaxed, the easier it would be to become pregnant.

Of course, they'd actually have to make love for that to happen.

Standing up, he went to take his empty can into the kitchen and make himself a sandwich since he hadn't heard back from his wife. He tripped over one of her shoes and stumbled, falling on his hands and knees. A fingernail caught against a wood plank and tore, and Dax cursed loudly. Pushing to his feet, he had sore knees, aching palms, and a bleeding finger. He rinsed the beer can in the kitchen and placed it in the recycling bin and headed up to their bathroom to doctor his finger.

Under the strong light, he saw how jagged the wound was. Dax washed it thoroughly with soap and needed an emery board to smooth out the nail since clippers wouldn't do the job. He knew Shailene had to have one, so he went to her side of the bathroom and opened a drawer, digging through lipsticks and other assorted makeup, not finding one. He opened a second drawer and struck out and moved to the third one.

"Bingo!" he said, finding the emery board and sanding down his nail, which hurt like hell.

As he started to place the emery board back in the drawer, he paused. His gut tightened as he dropped the nail file.

And picked up a familiar-looking, plastic package.

Surely, this was an old birth control pack, one Shailene hadn't bothered to throw away. Yet his senses were on high alert as he popped open the pack. Today was the twelfth.

The pill pack was missing twelve pills.

It felt as if a heavyweight boxer had slammed a fist into Dax's gut.

Why had Shailene lied?

Digging around the drawer, he found two more pill packs, both full. She'd always gotten them in groups of three from their mail order insurance company. Which meant she'd recently started this pill pack. All the while, she was bemoaning how they couldn't get pregnant. Everything that came out of her mouth was a lie.

Dax took all three packs with him, closing the drawer, not knowing if or when he was going to confront her. If the pills were missing and she went to take one tomorrow morning, that would clue her in that he had discovered her secret. Should he wait until then to say something? Or should he confront her and accuse her of holding out on him the moment she got home?

His finger was throbbing madly now, as was his head, where he knew a monster headache was building. He put a little antibiotic ointment on the nail and then wrapped a bandage around it, still not quite being able to come to grips with the situation.

Going back downstairs, he placed the three pill packs on the center of the kitchen table and sat, disbelief pouring through him. Then he heard the garage door going up and knew Shailene was home. He steeled himself for the fight that would play out in mere seconds.

She entered the kitchen, looking chic in her smart, designer suit and sky-high stilettos. She spent a small fortune on her wardrobe, telling Dax she had to dress as well as her clients in order to be successful and gain their trust.

"I got your text," Shailene said, setting down her tote on the kitchen counter, along with a large brown sack.. "I thought I'd just pick up something for dinner. It's Chinese."

She turned and started to say something else to him, their gazes meeting. He stared hard at her, anger building inside him.

"What's wrong with…" Her voice trailed off—because her eyes had caught sight of what sat on the table in front of him. Then anger sparked in her eyes. "You had no right going through my things," she spat out.

Dax crossed his arms. "You had no right to lie to me, Shailene. Yet you have. Over and over again. You said you wanted a baby as much as I did. We even had our doctors run a mess of tests, trying to see if either of us had something wrong with us. And all along, you're calmly ordering and taking a birth control pill each morning, preventing the very thing you know we want. Or should I, what *I* want? Because apparently, we are on a different page from one another. Maybe even a different book. I want a family. You obviously don't. And you were coward enough to take these behind my back."

"I'm not a coward," she said quickly, crossing her own arms defensively. "I just wasn't ready to be a mom." She huffed. "Frankly, I don't know if I ever want to be one, Dax."

He shot to his feet. "Why didn't you tell me? We could have talked about this."

"Because you wouldn't have listened to what I wanted," she snapped. "We always have to do whatever you want."

"What?" he said. "Are you kidding me? I'm the one who gave up DJ-ing for you. You told me I'd never make a decent living in music, so I put away my dreams of writing and performing. I've toed the line these last six years of marriage, trying to fit into the corporate world and dying a little more each day when I went to work. And you're never home, Shailene. We don't do anything together anymore. You're always out showing houses and attending open houses and corporate parties. I can't remember the last time we went to a movie or concert together. Couples need to do things together. Spend time together."

He paused. "Make love together. Or else their marriage won't survive."

"This marriage is already dead," she said succinctly, another blow to him.

"No," he protested. "No. We can keep trying. See a marriage counselor. We can—"

"I don't want to see anyone, Dax. I got tired of you a long time ago," Shailene admitted. "I don't want to have your baby. I don't want to stay married to you. I've... I've found someone else."

All the air seemed to go out of the room. He grew dizzy and collapsed into the chair again.

"You don't love me anymore?" he asked dully, suddenly realizing he felt so empty because the love he'd had for her had withered and died a long time ago. That he'd been holding on to her out of habit.

"I don't know if I ever did," she said, biting her lip. "I've been seeing someone else. For a while now."

He shook his head. Just when he thought this day couldn't get any worse, it did.

"Who?" he demanded, but a part of him felt as if he didn't really care enough to know.

Her face flamed. "Alex," she spit out.

Dax went cold inside. "Alex. *My* best friend Alex? The one you always complain about."

She shrugged. "It just... happened."

No wonder Alex had seemed so distant lately. Because he was banging his best friend's wife.

Scooping up the birth control pill packs, he shoved them at Shailene. "Then I guess you'll need to keep taking these. Alex has said repeatedly that he never wants kids."

He turned to go. Where, he didn't know. Just that he had to escape.

"So, that's it?" she demanded.

"What do you want me to say, Shailene? You've lied to me repeatedly. You're sleeping with my closest friend. This bomb has gone nuclear. There's no coming back from it. I certainly don't want to stay married to you. I'll file for divorce online. A guy at work did it last year, so I'm familiar with the steps he took because he talked about it so much. If you don't contest it, it's pretty smooth sailing. We file. Wait sixty days. Get a court date for a hearing and then appear before a judge."

Stubbornness filled her face. "I want my half of things," she said. "You owe me, Dax."

It appalled him that she was thinking about money at a moment like this. "I'll give you this house outright, plus half of what's in our savings and checking accounts."

Shailene had no idea how much money Dax had accumulated through his stock trades. He had several accounts solely in his name. She knew he played the market, but he never really talked about his losses or profits. Giving her the house was more than fair. He supposed in his gut he had known Shailene wasn't in the marriage for the long-haul, and that was why he'd set up a few accounts she didn't know about. Dax felt no guilt at this moment about doing so.

"I'll take it," she said abruptly. "You can leave now."

Dax shook his head. "No," he said firmly. "I'll stay in the guestroom, but I won't leave this house until the day the divorce decree is issued. Then I'll move out. You can keep all the furnishings. I'll want to start over."

She pursed her lips in thought. Lips he used to want to kiss. Once, he'd thought her so beautiful. He realized now her outward shell held beauty, but her heart was dark inside.

"Then I'll come and go as I please," she told him. "Don't

ask where I am and don't expect me to be home every night."

She grabbed the Chinese takeout and her purse and left without a word.

He placed his elbows on the table, dropping his head into his hands. He felt totally wrung out, physically and emotionally, though no tears came. Inside, he felt dead.

Raking his fingers through his hair, he sighed loudly. He had a chance to have a new life, pursuing the things he wanted to do. He definitely would never get married again because his trust had been so badly damaged, he couldn't imagine ever letting any woman get close again.

Dax went to the fridge and removed another beer. He made himself a PB&J and sat at the table.

"Happy Birthday to me," he said, knowing he'd never celebrate another birthday again.

Get your copy of Painted Melodies!

ALSO BY ALEXA ASTON

Hollywood Flirt

Hollywood Player

Hollywood Double

Hollywood Enigma

LAWMEN OF THE WEST

Runaway Hearts

Blind Faith

Love and the Lawman

Ballad Beauty

SAGEBRUSH BRIDES

A Game of Chance

Written in the Cards

Outlaw Muse

KNIGHTS OF REDEMPTION

A Bit of Heaven on Earth

A Knight for Kallen

SUDDENLY A DUKE

Portrait of the Duke

Music for the Duke

Polishing the Duke

Designs on the Duke

Fashioning the Duke

Love Blooms with the Duke

Training the Duke

Investigating the Duke

SECOND SONS OF LONDON

Educated by the Earl

Debating with the Duke

Empowered by the Earl

Made for the Marquess

Dubious about the Duke

Valued by the Viscount

Meant for the Marquess

DUKES DONE WRONG

Discouraging the Duke

Deflecting the Duke

Disrupting the Duke

Delighting the Duke

Destiny with a Duke

DUKES OF DISTINCTION

Duke of Renown

Duke of Charm

Duke of Disrepute

Duke of Arrogance

Duke of Honor

SOLDIERS AND SOULMATES

To Heal an Earl

To Tame a Rogue

To Trust a Duke

To Save a Love

To Win a Widow

THE ST. CLAIRS

Devoted to the Duke

Midnight with the Marquess

Embracing the Earl

Defending the Duke

Suddenly a St. Clair

STANDALONE ROMANTIC THRILLERS

Leave Yesterday Behind

Illusions of Death

ABOUT THE AUTHOR

USA Today and Amazon Top 100 bestselling author Alexa Aston lives with her husband in a Dallas suburb, where she eats her fair share of dark chocolate and plots out stories while she walks every morning. She enjoys travel, sports, and binge-watching—and never misses an episode of *Survivor*.

Alexa brings her characters to life in steamy historicals, contemporary romances, and romantic suspense novels that resonate with passion, intensity, and heart.

KEEP UP WITH ALEXA
Visit her website
Newsletter Sign-Up

MORE WAYS TO CONNECT WITH ALEXA